WHERE THE SNOW BLEEDS

An utterly gripping crime thriller

WENDY DRANFIELD

Dean Matheson Book 2

Choc Lit

A JOFFE BOOKS COMPANY

Revised edition 2023
Published in Great Britain by
Choc Lit
A Joffe Books company
www.choc-lit.com

First published in Great Britain in 2019

This paperback edition was first published
in Great Britain in 2023

Cover art by Nick Castle

ISBN: 978-1-78189-629-7

This book is dedicated to my brothers and sisters.

PROLOGUE

Lone Creek, Colorado

Trixie — the pure white Pomeranian who, on any other day, would vanish against the thick blanket of snow but for her small black nose and fake Chanel collar — is doing something very unladylike. But boy, is she enjoying it.

As she licks away, relishing the salty flavor and thick, greasy texture of the red liquid she's never tasted anywhere before, she can hear her mother shouting for her. This is followed by crunching and panting sounds as her mother treads closer into the dense, snow-covered woods.

"Trixie? Trixie, baby! Where did you go?"

Trixie yaps in excitement as her mother approaches, happy to share with her this new culinary delight. But she doesn't turn around just yet because she wants some more for herself.

A shadow suddenly blocks out the daylight.

"Here you are, baby! It was very naughty to run away like that! Mommy's trying to eat warm cookies after a long day on the slopes."

Trixie's mother, a wannabe socialite from New York State, sounds relieved to have found her. She doesn't notice or care what's caught Trixie's interest, probably assuming it's the scent of yet another pine squirrel. Instead, in her relief, she reaches down, scoops her up, and rubs her face all over Trixie's without looking, which is their usual way of greeting.

"Here's Mommy! Yes, here I am!" she coos.

Suddenly, she stops.

She holds Trixie out, to look at her properly for the first time since she ran off.

Trixie blinks at her, then wags her tail. She's eager to please but even more eager to get back to the good stuff.

The scream, as her mother notices the bright red blood that covers Trixie's soft white face, echoes through the Rocky Mountains and almost pierces poor Trixie's delicate ears. Trixie suddenly finds herself discarded on the ground, confused.

As her mother dives away in disgust, hurrying back to the resort and its nearest restroom, Trixie trots back to the discarded hiking boot which her mother never even noticed.

"Trixie!" her mother yells over her shoulder. "You come away from whatever dead animal you've found right now, you naughty girl!"

Trixie looks longingly at the jagged ankle bone that's sticking out from the snow-covered boot. Eventually, she leaves it behind to obediently run after her mother.

CHAPTER ONE

Las Vegas, Nevada

"Stop! Turn around or I'll shoot! I won't ask you again."

Terry Andrews finally stops running. He's cornered at the end of the alley. He slowly turns around and grins. "Come on! Are you seriously going to shoot me over a damn poodle?"

Dean Matheson smiles back at him. "Try me."

Rocky must smell defeat because he runs away from Dean's side and up to the poodle thief. Terry immediately tries backing away from the huge Rottweiler as Rocky barks menacingly, just as Dean taught him.

"Alright, alright! Take the stupid dog!" Terry throws the tiny poodle at Rocky in an attempt to block an attack and then runs away, fast.

They let him run. The fuzzy, prize-winning poodle seeks solace under Rocky's thick black-and-tan chest, as he licks her head. His tongue is so huge he almost pushes her over with each lick.

Dean holsters his gun and sighs. "Is this what our life has come to, Rocky? Catching dog thieves?"

Rocky wags his tail in response. *He's* having fun at least.

"Come on, you two," says Dean, as he picks up the flowery-smelling poodle.

He notices her toenails are painted pink. She's so nervous she trembles against his chest so he slips her inside his jacket as he walks the short distance to her owner's place. It's December, and if Dean were back home in New Hampshire right now, he'd be wearing something a lot warmer than a thin jacket. "Let's get you home to your adoring mother."

The poodle's mother is so grateful to get her back in one piece that she slips Dean a hundred-dollar tip. He tries to refuse it, but she won't have it, dismissing him out of her tiny apartment so she can concentrate on her dog.

By the time Dean arrives back at his small office behind the Vegas strip, it's empty apart from Marilyn Rose, his boss and fellow private investigator.

"How's your day been?" asks Marilyn. She doesn't look up from her computer screen. She's a petite woman who likes showing off her curves in skin-tight leopard-print dresses. The biggest thing about her is her Dolly Parton-style wig.

"Pretty slow," he says. "All I've done is rescue dogs again today."

Marilyn laughs. Which makes her cough violently. She's in her sixties and, having been a chain smoker all her life, Dean knows she's reluctant to give up now.

"What are you watching?" he asks.

She turns her screen to face him. "David Hunter getting arrested for killing his wife."

Dean sits down. David Hunter is someone Marilyn clashed with a few months back. Running this business puts her in dangerous situations, but nothing will ever compare in danger to her own life.

Not long after she took him on, Marilyn confided in Dean how she had suffered years of domestic violence at the hands of a husband she never wanted. She ended up killing him. She was able to claim self-defense because he was holding a gun to her head at the time, in a busy grocery store.

She'd told Dean that she had always known that day would come eventually, so she carried a knife on her.

When her husband, Bob, found her in the bread aisle of the grocery store that day, after she'd told him she was leaving his lousy ass for good, he pulled his gun on her. Luckily for Marilyn, he was high on meth, which slowed his reactions. When a customer distracted him by screaming, Marilyn reacted by pulling her knife and stabbing him straight through his heart without any hesitation.

"It went in like a knife through butter," she'd said. "Probably because he didn't have a heart there in the first place."

Once she was cleared of any criminal offenses ("Lucky for me, the store had CCTV, otherwise I'd be in the pen right now!") she decided to live her life how she'd always wanted to. She moved away from her small town in North Dakota to come here to Vegas, hoping she could make enough money to support herself. She changed her name from Susan to Marilyn, after her favorite actress — Marilyn Monroe — and found love with a woman, Martha. She took shooting lessons and started this small PI business.

Dean's her only employee and she treats him as her partner. She always says he's more trustworthy than her previous employees.

Dean reads through the messages Marilyn's left on his desk. Three clients want updates on their missing pets and two want photographic evidence of their partners' cheating. He throws the slips of paper back on his desk and runs his hand through his thick black hair.

"How do you do it, Marilyn? How do you deal with crap like this—" He gestures to his messages "—every day when there's so much real crime going on all around us? We're in *Sin City*! My life should be much more exciting than this."

This isn't the first time they've had this conversation. Dean's been sharing this Las Vegas office with her for a year now, ever since he left New Hampshire after the year-long trial of his wife's killer. He asks Marilyn the same question at least once a month.

"Listen to me, Dean," she says. "You're meant to be a cop, not a private eye. Get yourself back on the government payroll and go catch the bad guys. Leave it to me to find the stolen dogs, cheating husbands, and the prostitutes who've rolled their clients. That's enough drama for me, but you? You're too good for this racket."

He leans back in his chair. The problem is, he doesn't know whether he *is* too good for this racket. Not after everything that happened back home two years ago.

"You're handy to me for the legal stuff," she continues. "I mean, thanks to your law enforcement background, I don't have to Google every damn law and regulation anymore. But just remember, kiddo — no one's irreplaceable. Go and do what you need to do. Sure, I'd miss gazing into your deep blue eyes and staring at your rapidly increasing biceps, but don't tell Martha that." She winks at him.

He smiles. "You'd never get with a man now, would you?"

"Hey, if you were a few years younger you'd be fighting me off."

Dean's thirty-six, at least twenty-five years younger than Marilyn. "You mean older, right?"

"Nope."

He laughs, assuming she's joking. He knows she's not a fan of men, and with good reason. Many angry wife-beaters out there would love to catch her off guard and take revenge for her daring to help their spouses escape.

A shadow crosses the large front window of the office. It looks out onto the street. A man with an unkempt appearance stares in through the grimy glass. He bangs on the window, clearly angry about something.

"You better watch yourself, lady!" he shouts. "I haven't forgotten about you!"

Dean looks at Marilyn who rolls her eyes.

"Not him again." She stands up, pulls a gun out of her top drawer, and waves it at him. "Come get me, moron!"

6

When the man sees her walking toward him with her gun out, he runs.

Dean used to be shocked by this kind of behavior, but not anymore. Not in Vegas.

"Another fan?" he asks as she returns to her desk.

She picks up a cigarette. "He's annoyed he doesn't have a wife to beat anymore. She's in Sacramento now, living with a hunk half his age."

Rocky looks up as Dean gets out of his chair to grab an iced tea from the small refrigerator they keep beneath the messy, unattended reception desk. "Want a Coke?"

"Always," she says.

"You need to switch to the diet version. This stuff will rot your teeth."

"No, it won't," she says. "They're all fake. Which means they're stronger than real ones and they don't stain. I treated myself one Christmas."

He laughs. "I should've known."

As he closes the fridge, the bell over the front door jingles and they both immediately look up. A short white woman with disheveled brown curly hair and bright red cheeks walks in, sweating. She leans heavily on the front door while she tries to catch her breath.

Dean's heart sinks. He knows exactly what she's going to say before she says it.

"It's my Tinkerbell!" she pants. "She's been stolen! And the police don't even care!" She starts wailing so dramatically that Rocky barks, as if he's telling her to shut up.

Dean leads her to a seat and asks hopefully, "Is Tinkerbell your daughter?"

"Yes! Yes, she is! She's *like* my daughter! She's my precious purebred Bichon Frisé. I can't live without her and she definitely can't survive without me! We spend twenty-four hours a day together."

Dean looks at Marilyn who's struggling to contain her laughter. Not at poor stolen Tinkerbell or her mother, but at Dean's bad run of cases.

"You finish up for the day," she says to him. "It's my turn to take on the dog thieves."

He doesn't need to be told twice. Feeling like he's dodged a bullet, he grabs his keys and heads for the door.

"Don't forget Rocky's appointment."

He looks at his watch. They were meant to be there five minutes ago.

"Thanks for reminding me."

Dean's noticed that Rocky has slowed down lately, compared to what he was like when he first rescued him. That was two years ago now, before Lizzie Glover's murder trial and their new life in Vegas. Back then Rocky was bouncy and fast, but Marilyn thought she saw him dragging his leg recently, so she suggested Dean take him for a checkup.

"Come on, boy."

Rocky appears to be suspicious, as he hesitates to get up, even though they were careful not to use the V word. Eventually, he accepts the chicken treat Dean holds in front of him and he stands.

With the leash clipped to his collar they leave to walk to the nearby veterinarian surgery. Rocky picks up the scent of disinfectant as soon as they enter the sparse reception area. He immediately tries to back out the door but Dean's fast. He manages to close it behind him before Rocky can escape. The cute brunette receptionist smiles sympathetically as they're called into a small examination room.

Inside, the veterinarian, a tall man named Greg, tries to lift Rocky onto his examination table.

Dean can't believe it when he succeeds. "That dog weighs more than me," he marvels.

Greg has a deep, hearty laugh. "I bet I could get you on here too then. So what's wrong with this magnificent beast?" He starts stroking and prodding Rocky.

Before Dean can explain, Greg hits a sensitive spot when he examines the dog's shoulder. Rocky whines. Then he licks the guy's hand to let him know it's not Greg's fault.

"That area's a little tender," says Dean. "A bullet skimmed his shoulder two years ago. It seemed to heal well but he doesn't like anyone to touch it."

Shocked, Greg says, "You were shot at! Who would do such a thing to you?" He turns to Dean. "What are you, some kind of drug dealer? How could you let this happen to your dog?"

Dean's surprised. "What? No! Of course not. I was a police officer at the time. Rocky was trying to save me."

Greg smiles broadly and pats Rocky's large head. "So you're Rocky the Rockstar! What a good boy." He retrieves a treat from the pocket of his white coat and gives it to the dog. "He probably has some nerve damage there."

Dean wonders how Rocky isn't obese with all the treats he gets, although he has put on a bit of weight recently.

"Is that why you're here?" asks Greg. "Is it acting up?"

"I don't think so, but he's slowed down recently. And we think he may be dragging his left leg occasionally. He just doesn't seem as fast as he was."

Greg examines his hips while Rocky slobbers at the treat. "Well, he's an old dog. What do you expect? We all slow down as we age."

Dean's confused. "Old? What do you mean? He's still young. I got him when he was five or six and that was only two years ago."

"Do you know he was definitely five or six, or is that a guess?"

"It's a guess but he was so healthy and fast. I knew him as a puppy, and I'm pretty sure he couldn't have been older than six when he came to live with me."

Greg looks at Rocky's teeth and shines a light in his eyes and ears. "I'd say he's eight, maybe eight and a half years old. Which would fit with what you're saying if you've had him for two years."

"So that's still young then?" says Dean.

Shaking his head, Greg explains, "No. Rotties have a lifespan of about nine to ten years, maybe up to eleven years at a push, and only if they've led a sedentary life."

Dean looks at Rocky. He's shocked. He's never owned a dog before so he had no idea they lived such short lives. His childhood cat lived to twenty-two. He'd just assumed Rocky would be with him for a long time yet.

"Don't look so devastated," says Greg. "If Rocky's nearer eight than nine, you still have a good two years left with him. If you stop getting him shot at, that is."

Dean has to swallow his shock. This isn't what he expected to hear today.

"I'd say he has some ailments though. Maybe arthritis. I'll take some blood to rule out a few other things first. He'll probably need to come back for an x-ray, depending on the results."

Rocky doesn't flinch while the blood is drawn. He finishes a second treat and sits up, wagging his tail and ready for action. Greg picks him up like it's no effort at all and gently places him back on the floor while Rocky licks his ear.

"He's got a great temperament. And I'm glad to see you kept his tail."

Dean's too stunned to say much. He thanks Greg, settles the bill with the receptionist, and walks Rocky back to the office.

Marilyn's still busy with Tinkerbell's mother so she doesn't pay him any attention. Once Rocky's settled on his large blanket, Dean heads back out, alone this time.

He needs a drink.

CHAPTER TWO

McArthur, Colorado

Detective Eva Valdez is sick to death of her co-workers. She drops her heavy leather briefcase onto her desk, almost knocking the aging computer monitor onto the floor. She sets to work loudly clearing away the filthy coffee mugs that have accumulated next to her computer while she's been off work grieving for her husband.

Any paperwork left lying around that isn't hers goes straight into the shredder. She's not in the mood to deal with other people's mess today. This is her first day back at work after losing Frank and not one person has even acknowledged her presence, never mind asked how she's coping.

They attended his funeral happily enough, in full uniform, of course, pretending to be the concerned professional team they never were. It was purely to look good in the papers. In reality, she had to fight with Chief Carson just to take a week's bereavement leave.

It's clear to her now she's back that they all resented her taking the time off. It's as if they believe she's been sunning herself on an expensive cruise or something. Either that or they still hate her for snitching on Detective Alan Garner.

While she was grieving for her husband, she didn't keep up to date with any of the department's cases in the press. She couldn't bear to watch the news in case she saw Frank's uniformed photo staring back at her. The murder of a cop is always big news so she avoided the papers and news sites. Now she's back at work, she wants to update herself on the case with the two missing girls from Vegas. It wasn't her case but she felt it had been mishandled by Detective Garner.

She logs into the database to see where he's at with it. Which is apparently nowhere.

"You've got to be kidding me?"

No one has added any updates to the case in her absence. These girls have been missing for three and a half weeks now and, although they're from Nevada, they were working the winter season at a ski lodge in Lone Creek when they vanished. It's not really McArthur PD's jurisdiction but Garner is friends with the local sheriff up there, who's due to retire at the end of the year. Eva knows Sheriff Bowerman is too lazy to investigate it this close to his retirement, which is why he asked for Garner's involvement. But to Eva, it looks as though Garner's done absolutely nothing.

She feels the blood rising in her face. She's quick to anger lately — one of the stages of grief, according to her foster dad — and this might just make her explode. Pulling up the website for the local paper, she searches for one of the girls. She can't believe this is how she has to get information about cases her department is meant to be investigating. Scrolling through the results, she finds very few articles, fewer than she would expect about the unexplained disappearance and possible abduction of two white girls.

Most of the articles aren't even that recent.

Rocky Mountain Telegraph
November 16, 2018
  Two eighteen-year-old females have been reported missing from the Winter Pines Ski Resort in Lone Creek. Jodie Lawrence and Hannah Walker — friends from the North

Las Vegas suburb of Willington, Nevada — were here for the winter season, earning money as live-in employees at the lodge.

All was well until they went missing three days ago. Since then, no one has heard from them and they've missed several shifts. An employee at the lodge, who wishes to remain anonymous, has told us that nearly all of the girls' belongings were left in their shared room. Hannah's mother, Jackie Walker, had this to say: "Hannah was being so good about Skyping me almost every evening to let me know how her job was going, which was putting my mind at rest. I know they're eighteen years old but I was worried about them traveling out there alone and working so far away. And now this has happened."

When asked what she thinks has happened to the girls, Ms. Walker replied, "All I know is they were enjoying their jobs, happy to be making money for college while exploring Colorado. But Hannah hasn't contacted me or her father in three days, which just isn't like her."

Ms. Walker is concerned the case has been handled poorly by the detective in charge. "Detective Garner tells me he and his team are out searching for them but I haven't heard from anyone for over twenty-four hours now. The police won't return my calls. I just hope that means they're busy doing a proper search."

We approached Detective Garner for an update. "When we were made aware of the girls' disappearance, I immediately attended their last known location and interviewed employees at the lodge. At this stage, it would be inappropriate to comment further. We'll obviously keep the relevant people fully updated with our investigation, but we don't suspect any foul play as there are no signs at all to suggest the young ladies were abducted. As we all know, teenage girls don't always keep their parents informed of their whereabouts. That certainly doesn't mean any harm has come to them."

It's believed Jodie is estranged from her family and we have yet to track down a relative for comment.

Jodie Lawrence is described as five feet nine inches tall with an athletic build, long dyed red hair, and green eyes.

Hannah Walker is described as five feet six inches tall, of medium build with brown hair and brown eyes. She is originally from England and speaks with a British accent. If anyone knows of the girls' whereabouts, please contact the McArthur Police Department immediately.

Eva moves on to the next article, which is just a filler explaining there's nothing new to report in the investigation. The final article, dated just seven days ago — two weeks after their disappearance — is more alarming.

Rocky Mountains Telegraph
December 1, 2018

There have been no new developments in the investigation into the disappearance of Hannah Walker and Jodie Lawrence, the two females from Willington, Las Vegas. However, Hannah Walker's mother has contacted us out of frustration as she feels no progress is being made. "I'm not being kept informed so I have no idea what stage the investigation is at. The detective from the McArthur Police Department hasn't helped matters at all. I'm beginning to believe Detective Garner is incompetent and, unfortunately for us and the girls, that might mean we have no chance of seeing them alive again. If communication from the police doesn't improve, Hannah's father and I will consider hiring a private investigator because we're at our wits' end."

We approached Detective Garner for a statement but he declined to comment, stating it would be inappropriate as the case is an ongoing investigation. If anyone knows anything about the whereabouts of Hannah Walker or Jodie Lawrence, you are urged to contact Detective Alan Garner at the McArthur Police Department immediately.

"They might as well have given Mickey Mouse's contact details," mutters Eva.

She leans back in her chair, embarrassed for the department. They look like a bunch of fools with Garner leading

14

this case. If the family really does hire a PI and he does better than Garner, they'll all be ridiculed.

She stands up, planning to make herself a strong white coffee.

"Everyone in room two for a briefing. Now," announces Chief Carson. He stares briefly when he spots Eva, then turns away and walks off.

She rolls her eyes as she mumbles, "I'm fine, thanks for asking."

As everyone files into the small, airless conference room, Eva notices her co-workers are all giving her a wide berth, as if grief is catching. Only Sergeant Nick Roberts, the last person to arrive, takes a minute to come over to her.

"It's good to have you back, Valdez. If you need anything, ask."

"Thanks, Sarge. I appreciate it."

She looks around the room and is met with lowered eyes. She's not after a pity party, just a supportive work environment. She knows the women in this department aren't allowed to express emotion — it makes the men feel uncomfortable — but she expected them to at least welcome her back. She should've known better. After she reported Detective Garner for sexual harassment a few months ago they all had to take sides, and it made their lives easier to pick Garner's. She's glad Roberts stayed neutral though.

There was already friction between her husband and Detective Garner by the time Garner decided to feel her up, so Eva didn't tell Frank about it for months, worried he'd punch Garner and lose his job. When she did finally tell him, things got worse. He and Garner could barely hide their mutual contempt at work and she'd heard from Sergeant Roberts that Frank had been bad-mouthing Garner during a drunken night out. Eva's convinced his reaction made things worse for her around here.

Chief Carson slams his paperwork down on the table at the front of the room to attract everyone's full attention.

"Does everyone know what they should be working on? Or do I have to babysit you all?"

He gets a ripple of mumbled affirmatives in response.

"Good," he replies. "So, let's share. Who wants to go first?"

Everyone hates it when he does this and none of the team ever volunteer to give their updates first.

Eva speaks up. "I see no one's followed up on the two missing girls up in Lone Creek while I was off. Don't you think we should be out looking for those girls? There must be some leads to follow, and the press is ruining our reputation."

Chief Carson looks at her like she's a troublemaker which he must believe, thanks to the things his buddy Garner probably tells him. She defiantly stares back, unwavering. It's a reasonable question to ask.

"Detective Valdez. Glad you could join us. Detective Garner told me the girls most likely moved on to a different town without telling anyone. Isn't that right, Alan?" His eyes stay on Eva.

Garner clears his throat. "That's correct, Sir. Valdez obviously hasn't checked the system for updates since her week off. Otherwise, she'd know that." He looks at her with that arrogant stare of his, as if he's won an argument.

Her blood boils. "Since my *week off*? You mean since I took just *seven* days to get over the loss of my husband, who was stabbed to death working for this department? Stabbed to death being a great cop. Unlike you, you arrogant piece of shit!"

"Whoa! Valdez? Follow me." Sergeant Roberts heads for the door, motioning for her to follow him.

But she's not finished. "And you never updated the system actually, dipshit, because I've been here less than ten minutes and I've already checked. There's nothing on there. So that's yet one more thing you're incapable of doing right. I bet if I asked your wife, she'd have a long list of things you're incapable of. Most of them involving your—"

"Out! Now." Sergeant Roberts leads her out of the room by her arm before she can finish. He obviously doesn't trust her to come of her own free will.

Garner slams the door to the briefing room closed behind them and Eva imagines they're all laughing at her, taking his side as usual. She knows flying off the handle only makes her look unhinged and Garner look justified for ridiculing her, but she can't help it. While Frank is killed in the line of duty these assholes get to sit around, drink coffee and pretend nothing's wrong with how this department is run.

She feels like she could kill someone right now, and not just metaphorically. She was never this way before Frank died but doesn't know how to rein it in.

Roberts makes her sit at her desk as he perches on the corner. She slips her hands under her thighs to stop them from shaking and barely holds back the hot tears that threaten to fall. It wouldn't be a good idea to give in to them. Not here.

Roberts sighs as he rubs his face. "You're not fit to be back at work yet."

"Really? Where am I supposed to be?"

"In therapy." He looks at her with what appears to be sympathy in his eyes. "Come on, Eva. Your emotions are all over the place. You shouldn't come back just because you can't afford any more unpaid leave. You need time to grieve properly. Otherwise, I'm scared you're actually going to kill us all."

She laughs, despite her anger. She knows he's right but she can't bear the thought of sitting at home alone any longer. She's not sleeping, and her mind has been buzzing for days. She had hoped being back at work would give her something different to focus on. Plus, it's warmer at work. She can't afford to burn the heat all day at home. It's cold in Colorado right now and it's only going to get colder.

"I will get therapy," she says. "But I need to be at work. Seriously. Who cares if I punch a few assholes in the meantime?" She grins. "I promise I'll be selective. You'll be spared . . . Probably."

Roberts shakes his head in exasperation. "You're going to get us both fired . . ." He smiles. "Fine. What do you intend to work on? Please say something that gets you out of the station and away from Garner."

She doesn't hesitate. "The missing girls. I don't believe Garner investigated it properly and the chief probably doesn't even care, and he won't care until we're reported to internal affairs for screwing this up. You know as well as I do they're both too busy with their little side projects to do their jobs properly."

"Careful, Eva," says Roberts as he looks around to make sure no one heard her. "You've got to stop accusing them of being involved in side projects. If anyone hears you and repeats it to the wrong people you'll be fired."

"They can't fire me for exposing crooked cops."

"But you have no evidence. It's just rumors. You know they're too clever to get caught."

"Too clever?" she exclaims. "Don't make me laugh. The only reason they get away with doing whatever they want is because they're buddies with Mayor Reynolds and they all grew up together in this shitty town. It's like the Wild West all over again, the way they run things around here. Even Sheriff Bowerman's in their little club, which is the only reason Garner got to investigate up there in Lone Creek in the first place. Everyone knows the Sheriff's already mentally checked out, ready for retirement."

"Exactly," says Roberts. "It's like the Wild West. So you need to keep quiet and get your head down if you want to stay here."

"Who says I do?" she says. Since Frank was killed, she's been considering going home to San Diego, where she grew up. "Let me at least take the missing girls' case on for a few weeks and see what I can find out. I can stay at the same lodge they worked at, undercover, and be out of your hair. Plus, it'll look good to the families. Ms. Walker needs someone better than Garner to communicate with her. She's talking about hiring a private dick! How would that make us look?"

She waits while Roberts thinks about it. He doesn't usually say no to her, not because he's in love with her or anything, but because he's the only fair cop here. He did ask her out once but on the day they were meant to have their first date, about four years ago, Officer Frank Morgan joined their department. That changed everything.

The immediate sexual tension between her and Frank was so obvious that everyone assumed they were a couple before they actually were. Roberts stepped aside because Frank was a friend from his neighborhood when they were growing up. It's never been awkward between them since, as Roberts has never been anything but professional. But she sometimes wonders if he thought less of her when she immediately hooked up with Frank instead of him.

"Okay, fine," he says. "But you've got to work fast. If you don't find these girls or any credible information about what happened to them, I'm putting it on the back burner until we get a new lead."

She smiles at him. "Thanks, Sarge. You won't regret this."

He sighs. "I better not, Valdez."

CHAPTER THREE

Las Vegas, Nevada

After a long day dealing with dog thieves and learning the unexpected news about Rocky's life expectancy, Dean's on the Vegas strip looking for somewhere to buy a drink. It's early evening but already the strip is starting to get busy and loud with ticket touts, honking cabs, and drunk gamblers having fun, and the casinos are looking festive for the holiday season.

When Dean had told his friends back home that he was leaving Maple Valley for Vegas, one of them — Marty Swan — had warned him it was a convention of lowlifes and thieves. "That's why it's my favorite vacation destination," Marty joked. "I love the place, but you're definitely not Vegas material, my friend."

Dean has to agree now he's lived here a while. And there *are* days when that's the only side of Vegas he sees. But he also sees the side where tourists walk around with their winnings in their pockets, enjoying themselves without causing trouble. There's a buzz about Vegas that's contagious, but a year is probably long enough for Dean.

The flashing lights and loud music never seem to stop and when he first arrived, he was totally overwhelmed and had to fight the urge to drive home within a month. He doesn't even know what made him choose Vegas other than the obvious reason of wanting to disappear and not think about everything that had happened back home. It's so different from the small, quiet town he grew up in. There are hundreds more people everywhere, and most of them are drunk or high on something.

Rocky, on the other hand, loved it immediately. He finally has the audience he craves, with scantily clad women stopping to pet him all the time and drunk people willing to feed him their fast food. He's been in his element since they arrived. The only thing he can't take is the dry heat in the summer. Every time they left an air-conditioned building, the heat enveloped them immediately and traveled around them, like a bubble, to their next destination. As soon as Dean showered and dressed, he'd already be sweating again. There's no East Coast breeze here.

Things have cooled down now it's early December, but Dean doesn't think he wants to spend another summer here. Even though he has the apartment over Marilyn's office, living here still doesn't feel permanent. He still can't sleep well through the sirens and constant street noise, and now it's the holiday tunes playing on repeat that's driving him crazy.

Truth be told, he'd love to see some snow right about now. He scoffs, realizing he's missing his thick Maple Valley PD coat, something he never thought possible.

As he enters a small casino, he ignores the many slot machines he has to walk past to find the bar. It's not too loud or crowded yet as it's not in the center of the strip, so he sits and orders a beer from the bartender, who looks like he'd rather be on Dean's side of the bar.

Dean hasn't had a proper drink since he arrived in Vegas, not willing to revisit where his wife's death took him, but every now and then he feels the need for a beer. After the first sip, he sits back and thinks about his earlier visit to the veterinarian. He wonders if Greg's advice means Rocky shouldn't be out on assignments with him anymore. But the thought of not having the big dog as a partner is depressing.

A woman sits down near him at the bar and looks over. "First drink of the day?" she asks, with a smile.

He turns to look at her, trying not to think of the last woman he met in similar circumstances. "It is."

"Question is, will it be the first of many?"

"Not really," he says. "I'm not a big drinker. Not anymore anyway."

"You're not from around here, I take it?"

"No, I'm from the East Coast. And truth be told, I don't know how many more Vegas summers I can take. They're too hot for me."

"It would be a shame if you left," she says. "You're pretty hot yourself."

Dean smiles. He's avoided dating while he's been here, despite Marilyn's best efforts to hook him up with some women she knows. His last relationship was deadly and he doesn't want to make that mistake again.

She leans over. "I'm Maria. I don't mean to embarrass you; you just seem different to the tourists and it's refreshing."

"Dean. Pleasure to meet you."

She rests a hand on his and whispers, "Let me take you to a club. We'll have some fun tonight."

Dean can't say he isn't tempted. She's an attractive red-head with a model's body, but she just approached a stranger and offered to show him a good time. Although he comes from a small town, he's not completely naïve. This woman doesn't come for free. He finishes his drink, smiles at her, and briefly places his free hand on top of hers.

"Maria, I'd love to. But I've got to be somewhere." Not wanting to embarrass her, he adds, "Perhaps some other time?" He stands and drops some money on the bar for his beer. "Have a good evening."

* * *

Dean heads back to the office to fetch Rocky. Thankfully, Tinkerbell's mother is gone and he doesn't ask about her.

Marilyn's busy filing papers, sipping vodka, and tidying up for the night. She has two cigarettes on the go: one hanging out the corner of her mouth and the other sits forgotten in her ashtray.

"Are you going home anytime soon?" he asks.

"I'm putting it off. Martha's mad at me."

"What for?"

She starts coughing. Really hard. Dean's learned not to worry about her hacking cough as Marilyn doesn't seem fazed by it and she's refused to see a doctor. He waits for her to finish. She stops and takes a sip of vodka to clear her throat. Just as she's about to speak she starts coughing again. Dean walks over to her and tries rubbing her back but she's struggling to breathe.

"Marilyn? Are you okay?"

She nods. Then she shakes her head. Her lips turn blue as she alternates between gasping for air and coughing.

"Marilyn?"

She dramatically jumps out of her seat, clutching her throat, and then drops to the floor.

"Shit!" Dean grabs his cell phone and dials 911.

A woman answers almost immediately. "911. What is your emergency?"

"I need an ambulance, right away. I have a female in her sixties who appears to be having a stroke or a heart attack." He gives her their address.

"An ambulance is on its way. Is the patient still breathing?"

"Hold on."

Rocky stands next to Marilyn, prodding her with his paw. Presumably trying to wake her.

Dean puts his phone on her desk and crouches on the floor next to her. "Marilyn? Can you hear me?"

It's no good. She's not breathing.

Dean shouts to be heard by the dispatcher. "She's stopped breathing. I'm going to commence CPR."

Rocky moves out of his way as Dean leans down to begin. He can taste vodka on her lips as he tries to breathe air into her lungs. He doesn't need to give any chest compressions as it doesn't take long for Marilyn to revive. Dean suspects whatever made her collapse isn't heart-related. She takes in a big, gasping breath of her own.

"Marilyn, honey? It's Dean. Don't panic. Just stay where you are."

She makes a gurgling noise, which is better than silence. Her right eye is opening and closing but the left side of her face has dropped. He's pretty certain she's suffered a stroke.

"You're going to be fine," he says. "The ambulance is on its way, Marilyn." He puts the cushion from her chair under her head and Rocky's blanket over her torso to try to keep her warm.

Rocky, who is whining now, sits next to her.

It takes just minutes for the ambulance crew to arrive and they work fast. Within ten minutes Marilyn is strapped to a gurney and pushed into their vehicle.

"Are you coming with us?" asks the male EMT.

"Yeah, I just need to lock up."

He has no choice but to leave Rocky in the office as he locks up and gets into the back of the ambulance with Marilyn.

CHAPTER FOUR

McArthur, Colorado

Eva Valdez is at home in her small, two-bedroomed rental apartment, researching the missing girls online. She's eating a bad frozen pizza — spicy meat feast — when her cell phone rings. It's her foster dad. She answers it immediately, glad of the distraction.

"Hey, George. Everything okay?"

"I'm ringing to ask you the same," he says.

She smiles. She's so glad she has him. He's really the only person she has left. He and his wife Mary were the fourteenth and final couple to foster her. She moved in with them when she was fourteen and they were the only couple who stuck with her. Mary lived long enough to see her marry Frank but died from cancer just a year later. After her death, George coped better than Eva or Mary could ever have hoped. He not only finally learned how to cook for himself but he started volunteering at a kitchen for the homeless. Now he runs the place. He told Eva he wanted to do something to make Mary proud and shocked at the same time.

"I'm fine," she says.

He scoffs. "That's all you ever say; *I'm fine.* How about telling me how you're really feeling, Eva? You recently lost your husband, who was a wonderful man and the only man in your life you ever introduced us to. Don't you want to tear people's heads off? Don't you want to scream at couples who walk down the street holding hands? Don't you want the pain to end?"

She can't help but smile. George likes to keep things real, but he's very dramatic. Trust him to know what she's feeling.

"All of the above," she says. "But I can't do any of them so instead I'm sitting at home, working."

"Well, at least that's productive, I guess. How did your first day back go? Did you kick some ass?"

"Not really, but I almost got fired."

"That's my girl!" he laughs. "Was it for punching Detective Garner?"

"Of course not! That really would get me fired. My sergeant wants me to attend therapy."

"What on earth for? Like that's going to make any difference. It won't bring Frank back, will it? Besides, you have me to talk to. I'm your therapist."

She sighs. "But you don't give me the best advice, George. You tell me to punch my fellow officers and scream at people in the street."

"Exactly! Think how much better you'd feel after doing that. I'm sick of everyone having to pretend they're fine all the time. I'm not fine about seventy percent of the time and I damn well want people to know about it. It's not feeling sorry for yourself, it's being real. People need to have real conversations again. I'm sick of all the fakeness. And you know who I blame?"

Here he goes again.

"Social media. That's who. Specifically, that Tuckerberg fella who started it all."

"Zuckerberg," she says, not bothering to remind him that her favorite social media site back in the day — Myspace

26

— was well ahead of Zuckerberg's Facebook. More fun too. "But other people don't care what I'm going through so why should they listen to me?"

"You're right," he says. "I blame the invention of selfies or whatever you call them. I almost ran a boy over yesterday who was taking a selfie in the middle of the damn highway. Even when I spotted him in time I still wanted to run him down, to teach the asshole a lesson."

"Please don't do that. I'd be the laughing stock of the station if someone from my department had to arrest you."

"Why should I be arrested? He's the one standing in the middle of the highway, obstructing traffic!"

She knows he has a point, but still.

"Anyway," he says, "are you managing any sleep yet?"

Eva's always suffered with insomnia during stressful times. "Not yet. Well, maybe an hour or two a day but not always at night. Although, last night I went sleepwalking for the first time since I was a kid."

George laughs. "Really? I remember the first time you did that after you came to live with us. You scared Mary so bad! We were having some alone time, if you catch my drift, and you just walked right into our bedroom and sat next to us on the bed! You babbled something incoherent and then Mary led you back to your room. She was buck naked!" He laughs hard. "You didn't remember a thing the next morning."

Eva's heard this story a million times but it still makes her blush and smile at the same time. "I remember you telling me, George. Anyway, before you get carried away, I need to tell you my apartment's going to be empty for a while. I have an assignment that means I get to stay at a ski lodge up in Lone Creek. You may not hear from me for a week or two because I really need to concentrate on this case."

"Did you choose that case or did they pick you for yet another crappy assignment?"

"I chose it. I need to get away from Garner and there are two missing girls who need finding. One of them is like me when I was younger, a runaway with no family."

"That's sad," he says. "You go find her and bring her to our next family dinner."

Eva snorts. "Are we really still classed as a family when there's only two of us left and we're not technically related?"

"Listen," says George. "You and I were family as soon as we met, and we will be until I die. Frank and Mary were part of our family too. Family doesn't mean blood relation; it means a bunch of people who voluntarily care about each other."

Eva smiles, but his words make her tearful. She's never known any of her blood relatives as she was given away as a baby. Child Protective Services lost her file when she was young so she knows nothing about her birth parents or their heritage. She was bullied in high school for her looks as she's obviously biracial, but because she doesn't know where her birth parents are from, she's never really felt like she belonged anywhere. Some people have thought she was part Hawaiian, some part Mexican, but no one really knows. Her last name — Valdez — is the only thing the CPS kept when she was handed over to them. She knows that could be her mother's married name so it may not be a clue to her mother's heritage, but she made sure she kept it when she married Frank. And she liked it better than his last name.

"You're not crying on me, are you?" he asks, softening his tone. "I can be with you in an hour if you need me tonight."

She sniffs and wipes her eyes. "No, don't be stupid. I'm fine."

George laughs. "There you go with the *I'm fine* again! Sheesh . . ."

"I'll visit you as soon as I've found the girls, okay?"

"You'd better. I have a new recipe I want to try on you. It's extra spicy so no one else is willing to be a guinea pig. Everyone's scared of everything these days. Even spending an extra hour on the commode. Look after yourself, honey."

"You too, old man."

She ends the call, glad to have spoken to him. It's lonely in the apartment without Frank. And she's never told George, but she suspects something doesn't add up about

28

the way Frank was killed. She doesn't have any evidence to back up her suspicions and if she tells George, she just knows he'd come and live with her until they found out what really happened. He followed her to Colorado after Mary died and lives just an hour away now, near Denver.

He has a strong sense of justice so he loved it when she became a cop. He lives vicariously through her when she catches the bad guys. But she doesn't have any proof that Frank's death was suspicious, just a horrible gut feeling and the experience of working with assholes. Some of the department had it in for Frank but he never told her why. She assumed it was because he married her, because she's been known as a troublemaker for a while. All because she stands up for herself.

She picks up their framed wedding photo, which has been face-down on the sideboard ever since his funeral.

"What were you up to, Frank? Did you get too close to the truth and they had to shut you up?"

He stares back at her in the navy-colored suit he wore for their quickie wedding. They married in the snow at the bottom of a mountain, with just her foster parents as witnesses. Frank's family wasn't invited because of a big falling-out a few years back. They haven't even reached out to her after his death. His parents flew in from Virginia for the funeral and then flew out the next day, all without saying a word to her.

Mary was horrified that they opted for a small wedding, as she wanted the full wedding experience at home in San Diego with extended family and friends, but Eva and Frank weren't show-offs. They just wanted to be tied together forever. Eva regrets nothing about that day or their marriage. And, even though she hoped she would grow old with him, she always had a nagging sense of doubt about their future. Their life together had been too happy and easy and, when you're used to hardship growing up, you constantly expect something to go wrong.

She just hadn't expected it to go *this* wrong, and so soon into their marriage.

"This sucks, Frank. I hate being without you."

He smiles up at her and she strokes his freshly cut brown hair before putting the photo back in its place, face-up this time.

It's time to start packing for her trip to Lone Creek.

CHAPTER FIVE

Location unknown

After trying every other option she can think of, Jodie Lawrence knows it's better to cut off her own foot than to stay in this hell hole any longer. She knows in her heart that they'll never be freed or found after this long.

A chain is padlocked unbearably tight around her left ankle, secured to one of the rusting metal posts that stops the floor above them from collapsing into the basement. She's unable to stand because the chain is so short, leaving little room between her leg and the post and forcing her ankle to remain close to the ground.

Her body protests at having so little room to change position. Both she and Hannah are experiencing terrible muscle cramps that grow worse with each day they're trapped here. Their pathetic rations of food and water aren't helping.

Hannah keeps a tally of the number of days they've been held here. She uses a rusty nail to etch into the wooden floorboards. Today is day fifteen.

Jodie never expected her time in Colorado to end like this, but then she never expected her life to end like this either. She only knows that if she doesn't cut her foot off with the only sharp object within her reach, she can't get out of this chain. And if she doesn't get herself out of this, she's dead anyway. So is her best friend.

They discovered the chainsaw by accident when Jodie reached for the dirty tarpaulin on a shelf over their heads. Only Jodie could reach it, but that took everything in her to stretch against the resistance of her ankle. They wanted to use the tarpaulin as a blanket, to keep warm, but as Jodie pulled, it dragged the previously hidden chainsaw down with it, almost knocking her out with its weight.

At first, Jodie naively thought it might be possible to use the chainsaw to cut the chain in half and free herself, but it's a large tree-felling chainsaw and there isn't enough room between the post she's secured to and her leg for it to fit. If she tried using it within that space it would take off half of her leg. So Hannah suggested sawing off the chain that's wrapped around the metal post, and that's when they quickly discovered a chainsaw won't cut through metal. The sparks and the noise were almost as scary as the way the heavy chainsaw jumped and kicked back in protest, swinging for Jodie's face before it stalled.

So she's left with just two options: wait here to be killed by their captor in possibly the worst way imaginable, or try using their only means of escape, perhaps dying as a result but knowing that she at least made a bid for freedom.

She hesitates for one last time knowing that, if she does this and bleeds out, she's failed them both. But she's watched documentaries about people who've miraculously survived after sawing off a limb in desperate situations. It's all about stopping the blood loss as fast as possible, and she has a belt ready for that. She just needs enough time to get outside, figure out her location, and find a tree branch big enough to lean on as she hops to safety.

Jodie thinks about it for less time than she would have expected. She pulls up the left leg of her jeans, exposing her ankle, which is raw where the tight chain has worn away her skin every time she moved just an inch. As a makeshift tourniquet, she pulls her leather belt around the flesh just above her ankle, as tight as she can, which makes her wince. When it's secured, she holds the chainsaw facing away from her now that she knows how unpredictable it is and says a quick prayer that it still has some gas in it, while simultaneously hoping it hasn't.

She places the sharp, rusty teeth against her skin, bizarrely marveling at how much her leg hair has grown in the two weeks she's been trapped here.

Jodie ignores her shaking hands and mentally blocks out Hannah's cries. Her friend doesn't want her to do this. She thinks they should stay together. Die together.

Jodie's determined not to let that happen.

She screams to motivate herself and then pulls the cord, quickly forcing the saw into her skin. The chainsaw matches her screams as it roars to life and the teeth start tearing their way through her flesh. Then, as quickly as it started, it stops. She drops the chainsaw when she passes out from the pain.

When she comes around, the room is filled with stunned silence.

She forces herself to look at the damage and is disappointed to see she hasn't even hit bone yet. She has to go again.

The pain is delayed until she's fully conscious. Then it hits her. She immediately starts sweating and seeing stars. Blood covers her gray hiking boot but the warmth of the liquid spreading down her foot feels comforting in this freezing cold, hopeless pit.

Trembling heavily from a fresh rush of adrenaline, Jodie starts again before she has time to change her mind.

CHAPTER SIX

Las Vegas, Nevada

The day after Marilyn's stroke, Dean's at the office with Rocky when Martha stops by to see him.

"How's she doing?" he asks.

"She'll be fine if she gives up the booze and cigarettes. And the doctors have told her she seriously needs to slow down and take it easy now. She's going to be a pain in the ass, I can tell. She'll be in the hospital for at least a few days."

"Do you think she can do any of those things?" he asks.

"Of course not, she'll probably be dead within the year." Martha smiles sadly, trying to make light of the situation. She's younger and fitter than Marilyn and she has a dark sense of humor.

She strokes Rocky, who's asleep on the floor, before taking a seat at Marilyn's desk. "Listen, I've got some bad news."

Dean knows what's coming and he isn't sure how he feels about it.

Martha sighs. "I've told Marilyn she needs to close the business and retire. This place is killing her. She thinks she's some spring chicken who can get away with working twelve-hour days and getting all riled up about other people's problems. But I've told her it has to end. She should've retired years ago. I'm just sorry for what that means for you."

He sits back in his chair and nods. "It's not your fault. And you're right, she needs to take it easy."

"You can still lease the apartment upstairs," she says. "We're going to let this office out but Marilyn owns the building so you won't get kicked out anytime soon. The money will come in handy for us."

Dean thinks things over. "Do you think she'd consider selling the business to me?" He doesn't really want it, but he also doesn't want to be unemployed.

Martha smiles. "She said you'd ask that and told me I'm to say no. Marilyn thinks you're too good to be working as a PI and you should consider joining the Las Vegas Met PD. She has a contact there. If you want her to put in a good word for you, she will."

Dean grimaces. The thought of dealing with drunk tourists all day doesn't appeal to him, although he does want to be a police officer again one day.

"She's closing the business and all open cases as of today, but we won't see you out of pocket."

The door swings open and a tall middle-aged woman hesitantly pokes her head inside. To Dean, she looks out of place here immediately. Too middle-class.

Rocky looks up at her but he doesn't move.

"Hi. Can I help you?" asks Dean.

The woman reluctantly steps inside but keeps hold of the door. She obviously doesn't want to commit, as if she's in denial about why she's here. She's dressed smartly, and conservatively for Vegas. "I need help."

Dean looks back at Martha who says, "Husband beating you?"

The woman looks shocked by the suggestion. "What? No. Nothing like that. I'm just not sure what to do."

Dean gets her a bottle of water from their small fridge and leads her from the reception area to their desks, just behind. He points to one of the two spare seats. "Here, sit down. Tell us what the problem is."

He knows Martha just said the business is closed as of now, but this woman really looks like she needs some help. He can at least listen and then maybe refer her to someone else.

She tries to pick up the bottle of water but drops it on the floor. "I'm sorry! My hands are shaking. I can't even think straight at the moment."

Martha picks it up and puts a hand on the woman's shoulder. "How about you start with your name? Then we'll take it from there."

Dean has his notepad ready. He noticed her British accent straight away. He can't help but remember his last encounter with a British woman. That didn't end so well.

"My name's Jackie Walker. I'm here because my daughter is missing. The police haven't been very effective. In the eyes of the law she's not a child, but she's still a missing person. Can you help me find her?"

"What's her name and how long has she been missing?" asks Dean. He feels bad for her but this is the most interesting case to fall into his lap since he moved here.

"Her name's Hannah Walker. She's been working in Colorado with Jodie Lawrence, her friend, for almost a couple of months now. She was Skyping me almost every night but I haven't heard from her in over three weeks. She last phoned me on the thirteenth of November and then she and Jodie went missing the next day."

She breaks down in a quiet, dignified way. Martha hands her a tissue from Marilyn's desk. It's well stocked for situations like this.

Dean thinks about the time frame. It's been twenty-four days since they went missing. That's a long time for Jackie not to have heard from her daughter. He wonders why the police haven't been more helpful. "How old are they?"

"They're both eighteen. They went there to earn some money for college. The local police department didn't take their disappearance seriously from the very beginning. The

36

detective they assigned has been nothing but patronizing and rude to me. So I flew out to Colorado and basically sat in their office until he agreed to update me. But apart from speaking to the locals and the employees, I felt like he quickly gave up on the case and now he's working on some ridiculous theory that the girls moved on to another town without telling anyone."

"Did the girls take their belongings with them?" he asks.

"No. Most of their belongings were still in their room at the lodge. They'd left the laptop they were sharing, their phones, bags, and all of their clothes. The only thing missing was Hannah's camera, but she's always losing cameras and phones so that might not mean anything." She looks at Dean. "How could they have moved on to another town without any of their belongings? It's so obvious something has happened to them and yet no one is willing to help us."

Dean and Martha share a look. It doesn't sound good for the girls.

"When you say *us*, do you mean Jodie's parents?" asks Martha.

"No, I mean my ex-husband, Hannah's dad. Jodie doesn't have any close family. She told Hannah she ran away from home years ago and has been taking care of herself ever since. I don't even have an address for her. She said her parents are drug addicts who wouldn't care if they never saw her again. I'll have to try to track them down if the girls don't come home soon." She looks at Dean. "Maybe you can help me with that? If it comes to it. I've been to Colorado twice already but I have a job to keep. I work for a bank and they've already given me lots of time off. If I lose my job, I'll have to leave the country."

"You're British, I take it?" says Dean.

"Yes. Hannah and I moved here two years ago to have a fresh start with my sister. She's lived over here for years, so we moved in with her. Jodie has spent some time at our house but not much, so I really don't know her all that well. Hannah seems to like her though."

"Does your daughter have a good relationship with her father?" Dean asks.

"They keep in touch but he hasn't heard from her either. He still lives in England, you see. He flew out here as soon as they went missing, to support me, but he's got his own family back home to think about so he left after ten days. It's such a long way for him and so expensive to fly. I'm keeping him updated, not that there's anything to tell him."

Dean writes everything down. The first twenty-four hours may be crucial in missing person cases but that doesn't mean they can't still be found alive at this stage. He wants to help this woman find them and feels a renewed enthusiasm about his job at last. He just wishes he was investigating the case as a cop so he would have access to all the police resources. Once again, he wonders why he left policing to go it alone.

"Ms. Walker, my name's Dean Matheson. I'm an ex-police officer and I'd like to help you."

Jackie exhales and relief shows on her face.

Dean can feel Martha looking at him, wondering what he's doing, but he can take this case on alone.

He continues, "I don't want to sound insensitive but I have to mention there will be fees involved."

"Of course," she says. "I don't expect you to work for free. Gary — that's Hannah's father — will help me with the fees. We just need to find the girls."

She doesn't seem alarmed at the prospect of paying for his services, which is a good sign. It means she's genuinely trying to find her daughter and isn't involved in her disappearance. Family members can be excellent at playing the part of a grieving parent or sibling when they're actually the killer or the mastermind behind the disappearance. He doesn't think that's the case here, which means he's finally got a real investigation to work on.

"I just want Hannah back," she says with tears in her eyes. "She's been through so much in her life already."

That last statement rings alarm bells for Dean. He glances at Martha and he can tell she wants to ask for more information about what Hannah's been through, but she must think better of it as she closes her mouth. Dean knows there will be time for that later.

"How soon can you be there?" asks Jackie. "They were working at the Winter Pines Ski Resort in a small town called Lone Creek."

"Why did the girls pick that area?" asks Martha.

"Jodie heard they could make good money working at a mountain resort as they could more or less work whatever hours they wanted and the tips were supposed to be good. I don't think that turned out to be true at their resort though. Hannah assured me they'd done lots of research on the town and that it got mostly good reviews on the travel blogs. But to be honest, after having visited it myself, it's not exactly a luxury resort and it's so far out from any city or large town. I guess that's what people want from a holiday, I mean vacation, but I'd hate to be so isolated. I didn't want her to work so far away from me but she's just turned eighteen so I couldn't really stop her. Jodie seems to be a strong influence on her."

"I take it you're not that keen on Jodie?" says Martha.

Jackie lowers her eyes. "She's okay. But from the sound of it, she has some questionable friends and I worry about Hannah being involved in the same social circle. She doesn't need any more drama in her life."

Dean considers how long he can stay in Colorado. He has no ties here at all now, other than Rocky. He leases the apartment over the office from Marilyn so he knows it'll be secure while he's gone. He's not sure whether to take Rocky with him after what Greg said, but he's pretty sure Rocky would be happier by his side.

"I can set off tomorrow. I'll need to drive because I wouldn't want to put my dog through a flight." He pulls his phone out to check the distance and driving time. "Apparently it takes about eleven hours, plus gas and restroom stops. I can set off early and be there by the evening."

Jackie looks relieved. "Thank you. I feel like someone's taking me seriously at last."

"I'll do the best I can," says Dean. "But you need to be prepared for bad news if I find out the worst has happened. I don't want to seem negative, but when people have been missing for this length of time, it's unlikely they left of their own free will."

Martha puts her arm around Jackie. "Let's try to think positive though."

The woman nods. "I just need to know, one way or the other. I can't live with the not knowing. My life is on hold."

As she holds back tears, Rocky approaches her and drops his massive head in her lap.

"Go home and email me any details you think might be relevant." Dean hands her his business card which lists his cell number, email address, and the agency's contact details for when he can't be reached. He draws a line through that last number, knowing there will be no one here to answer the phone.

"I need access to their social media accounts if you have any passwords, or their usernames. If you put it all in emails, I can read it on the go. Even if you don't think something is relevant, include it anyway. I need to build a picture of what they've been up to on their travels and who they've met."

She nods as she gets up. "I can do all that, but passwords will be a problem. I have the contact details for the detective we've been dealing with: Alan Garner from McArthur PD. Will he speak to you, do you think?"

Dean doubts it. "I hope so," he says. "Do you have their belongings or did the police keep them?"

"They've kept them. But I do have Hannah's diary. The front desk manager, a lovely lady called Olivia, said she found it in the women's restroom. It was missed by the police. I was so grateful because she didn't want to give it to them. I could tell she doesn't like the detective either. The thought of handing Hannah's personal thoughts over for that man to read makes me feel sick. But I realize now it might help find them."

"Did you bring it with you?" asks Dean.

She opens her bag and pulls out a battered yellow notepad with an elastic placeholder. She seems reluctant to pass it over. "I read a few entries from the beginning of her trip, but I can't bear hearing her voice again, even if only in my head. It's just too upsetting while she's missing. Nothing stands out from the entries I read. She just sounded like she was having fun being somewhere new." She hands it over to Dean and then pats Rocky's head. "I've included my address and contact number in the front of the diary." She stops for a moment before looking up. "If she's dead, I don't know what I'll do."

"Let's not jump to any conclusions," says Martha. "Go home, make yourself a drink, and then update Hannah's dad on what's been agreed here today."

Dean adds, "I'll keep you updated but I'm guessing cell phone coverage isn't great out in the mountains."

Jackie nods as she heads to the front door. "Thanks so much. I feel better already. You're not what I expected a private investigator to be like. I was so anxious about coming here today, but I'm glad I did. Please do whatever it takes to find them, Mr. Matheson."

She reluctantly leaves the office and walks away.

Dean turns to Martha. "Something doesn't add up. The police should be helping her. It makes me wonder if something's going on that they haven't shared with her."

Martha nods. "Those small resort towns are pretty incestuous. They take care of their own over outsiders, any day."

Dean paces the office as he thinks. "There's so much to do."

"Well, you wanted a juicier case," says Martha. "Now you have one."

CHAPTER SEVEN

Dean pours a large amount of turkey kibble into Rocky's food bowl in their apartment upstairs. Then he checks the time. It's just after eight p.m. Detective Harry Jones, his former mentor and friend from Maple Valley, will be video-calling him in fifteen minutes. New Hampshire is three hours ahead of Vegas, so it must be eleven there.

He looks forward to their monthly video chats. It's like checking in with his parents, even though Jones and his wife Barbara aren't related to him. His parents have been dead for years, and his brother's suicide was just over two years ago, so he doesn't have any close family left. But Jones and Barbara have always looked out for him, ever since Dean joined the police force as a fresh-faced, naïve rookie.

Despite knowing each other for so long, Dean can't bring himself to call Jones by his first name and still thinks of him as Detective Jones. It would be like calling your high-school teacher by their first name when you bump into them later in life. It just feels wrong.

While he waits for their call, he switches his laptop on and opens the chicken salad he picked up after leaving the office. As he eats, he looks around his apartment, which has never felt like home. He's used to living in a three-bedroom house with a large backyard, a small cat, and a wife. Going from that to a small apartment, a huge dog and no wife is a big change.

While he's away from New Hampshire, he's leasing his house out to Maple Valley's medical examiner, Dr. Sheila Didcott. He knows she'll take care of it. It felt a bit weird at first, thinking of someone else in the house he shared with his wife, Linda, but he's not allowed himself to think about Linda since he left — not consciously, anyway. He has mornings where he wakes with a scream in his throat after dreaming about her car crash and the person who was responsible for it. He even dreams about their unborn baby, but in his dreams the child is always about five years old and calling him daddy. Sometimes it's a boy, sometimes a girl. Those dreams are worse than the dreams about Linda.

He didn't bring anything with him to Vegas apart from his clothes and Rocky, but Marilyn's spare apartment came fully furnished. When he told her he needed to shop for blankets and towels, she came over with Martha and every spare household item they owned. To say they've been good to him would be an understatement. He hopes Marilyn takes her doctor's advice and focuses on improving her health, but he can't imagine her without a cigarette hanging out of her mouth.

As he eats the last bite of salad, throwing a slice of the chicken toward Rocky, his laptop screen lights up with a Skype call. He accepts it. Jones and Barbara both appear on screen and he can't help but smile.

"Dean! How are ya?" asks Jones.

"We're still missing you!" says Barbara, leaning in behind her husband. "When are you going to visit? It's been so long since we last saw you!"

"Stop pressuring him, woman," says Jones. "He's a single man living it up in Vegas. I wouldn't come back if I were him."

Dean laughs. "Hey, Barbara. I'll visit soon, I promise. But I'm pretty busy at the moment."

"Oh yeah? How many dogs did you rescue this week?" Jones teases him.

Dean grimaces. "About ten. How are things there? Everyone okay?"

"To tell you the truth, I'm looking forward to my retirement again." Detective Jones came out of retirement to help Dean track down a killer, and he did a much better job of it than Dean did. "Oh, and Miller's had his stomach stapled. His doctor suggested it. He was at high risk of another heart attack. I told him they should've stapled his mouth shut at the same time. He could've gotten a two-for-one deal."

Dean laughs.

"Don't be so mean!" says Barbara.

"When's the new detective starting?" asks Dean.

"Apparently, they've hired a woman, some hot shot from New Jersey, so I should be able to retire again soon. I can't wait. It's been boring since Lizzie Glover got locked up and you left. All that drama you caused was exciting for a while."

Dean's stomach flips at the mention of her name. "You haven't heard anything about her then?" Although she's in a secure psychiatric unit, Dean can't help but worry about what she's up to.

"Don't worry," says Jones. "I'm still checking on her every now and then through one of the employees up there. She's still playing by the rules, probably hoping for early release for good behavior. But she won't get out without me knowing about it. She'll be in there for years and if they ever declare her sane, she'll go straight to prison to complete her sentence."

Wanting to change the subject, Dean says, "Well, I have an interesting case to work on for a change. Got it just today in fact."

Jones leans closer to his screen, making him appear bigger. "You don't say? Fill me in. Barbara, fetch me some coffee, would you?"

Barbara playfully slaps him across the head for dismissing her, but Dean sees her walk off in the direction of their kitchen, smiling. They both know she's in charge really.

"A case of two missing eighteen-year-old girls out in Colorado," says Dean. "They were working in one of the ski towns before vanishing."

Jones' eyes widen. "How long have they been missing?"

"Just over three weeks. Most of their belongings were found in their room. The mother of one of the girls has asked me to see what I can find out because the local PD doesn't appear to be cooperative. I'm heading there first thing tomorrow."

"You lucky son of a bitch. It sounds like a good case. I'll do some research online about it. What are their names?"

Dean smiles. Although Jones is nearing sixty-nine, he relishes the opportunity to research things online. He says it's easy to be a detective these days as the internet does everything for you.

Looking at his notepad Dean says, "Jodie Lawrence and Hannah Walker. And I don't want to make you biased in any way, but Hannah and her parents are British."

"Well, I'll be damned," says Jones. "We need to check whether they're related to Lizzie Glover."

"Come on. How likely is that?" Dean thinks about everything he went through with Lizzie. She's the only reason he ended up in Vegas. He'd still be living in Maple Valley and working at MVPD if it wasn't for what she did.

"I'm already on it," says Jones, typing away in the background.

"If I need any help, I'll let you know," says Dean.

"Where exactly will you be?"

Barbara comes into shot, bringing her husband of over forty years a mug of coffee. She stands behind him.

"Somewhere called Lone Creek," he says. "I don't know all the details yet and I've never been to Colorado before, but I'll keep you posted. Even though you should be thinking about retirement instead of armchair sleuthing."

Jones turns to Barbara. "Honey? Haven't you always wanted to go to Vegas?"

She looks at him incredulous. "No! I've never in my life said I wanted to go to Vegas!"

"Of course you have, you never stop going on about it! Come on; slot machines, Elvis impersonators, Barry Manilow, although he might've retired by now . . . You'll love it, I promise." He looks back at Dean. "Once this new detective starts after Christmas and I'm out of a job, I'll need a vacation. Perhaps, if you haven't found the girls by then, we could have ourselves a little reunion in Vegas. I could help you with the case?"

Dean hasn't seen them in person for a year now. He'd love that. "That sounds good to me. Retired Detective Jones to the rescue again, stealing my thunder. You know, I could have the case all wrapped up within a week. Have some faith in me."

Jones leans in and winks at the webcam. "Well, in that case, maybe we'll visit a few casinos instead."

Barbara rolls her eyes in exasperation.

After saying their goodbyes, Dean checks his email and notices he already has a message from Jackie. It's a brief one, confirming the name and location of the resort the girls were working at and the name of their manager, plus a promise to provide more information in a separate email later.

Dean pours himself a cup of coffee and then settles onto the couch, ready to dig deeper into the lives of the missing girls.

He opens Hannah's diary, feeling guilty as he does so. He's never read anyone's diary before and it feels wrong. But, as it's potential evidence, he starts by reading her last entry first. He notices it was written the day before she went missing.

13th November 2018

I've had a massive blood spot in my eye all day. Olivia said I must've burst some blood vessels because of all the crying. It took loads of makeup to try to look half decent. Today was so crap. My supposed 'best friend' and I were scheduled to be on shift together all day but Jodie didn't show up, so I've done enough work for both of us. She didn't even apologize when she finally appeared. She didn't tell me where she'd been either.

We'd already agreed to have dinner together and she did show up for that but she was far more interested in Bryan. She even asked him to join us! Then, she got stupidly drunk because he was buying wine for her and they only got away with it because Sandy wasn't around. Then, to top it off, she blew me off after dinner to go out with him somewhere. And she's still not back!

She's going to get us both fired if she doesn't start pulling her weight and stop sleeping with gross married guests. She truly believes one of them will whisk her away to a life of luxury, when the truth is, they can barely afford their bar tab at the end of their stay. I need to have it out with her tonight. If she's not careful she'll end up in the same position she found herself in with Leroy last week. How she didn't get raped, I don't know. He's crazy.

I'm so ready to quit this job and go home. I've had enough of this place. Enough of her.

Just this one entry alone provides Dean with potential leads. He needs to find out who Bryan is, as he could've been the last person to see Jodie. He also needs to find out who Leroy is, as well as question the employees and the guests who were staying at the resort that week. That's if he can persuade the manager to give him a list of the guest names and their contact numbers.

He notices the simmering tension between the two friends. Dean thinks it could just be travel fatigue. He imagines sharing a room with someone for weeks on end with no privacy will do that to you. The fact that Jodie got drunk and went off on her own with what sounds like one of the guests isn't great, but she's old enough to make her own decisions.

He wonders whether Detective Garner interviewed Bryan and Leroy and what came of that. After what Jackie Walker told them about how badly the case has been handled so far, he thinks it's possible their alibis might not have been checked.

Dean's mind buzzes with potential leads to follow. He needs to get to Lone Creek as soon as possible.

CHAPTER EIGHT

Lone Creek, Colorado

Detective Eva Valdez arrives in Lone Creek by midafternoon. She couldn't drive her own car because she can't afford to have the broken alternator repaired any time soon, so she called a cab. She'll claim the cost back through expenses. Once she gets in the cab though, she wishes she'd hired a rental instead.

After a treacherous journey in heavy snow and a bitter wind that felt like it was going to force the car off the narrow icy roads, she makes it to the Winter Pines Ski Resort just before it gets dark. She intends to stay for as long as necessary so she doesn't have to experience that drive again.

The cab driver drove like a maniac and almost rammed them into the compacted snow that's built up at the sides of the roads. Her fingers hurt from where she was holding onto her seat so hard, trying to stay upright. Then, against her wishes, the driver gave her his number written on the back of a cigarette packet. As if he had a chance with her after that drive! She tore it up in front of him.

With him gone, Eva looks up at the lodge. It's not huge but it has two floors of guest rooms above the first floor and the many lanterns and sparkly lights make it look festive. The parking lot is covered in snow and it looks like no attempts have been made to make a safe clearing to the entrance. The recent turn in the weather has obviously taken them by surprise. There aren't many cars in the guest parking lot. She expected it to be busier, but maybe the ski season isn't in full swing yet.

According to Detective Garner's brief police report, this was the last place the girls were seen. At least that's what the employees here told him but, at this point, she's suspicious of everyone. It doesn't help that Garner's report is severely lacking in any detail. Instead of recording which employees he spoke to and who claimed what, all he noted was; *Spoke to employees. No answers there.*

It's infuriating for her to read. She'd never get away with such brief reports.

She quickly realizes she's not dressed warmly enough for the mountains. A thick blue parka over a blue and red plaid shirt and skinny black jeans isn't keeping the cold out. She's glad she packed her sweaters and extras.

She treads carefully to the entrance. When she steps inside the building she spots the front desk ahead. Eva's already decided not to let on that she's with the police. She has a suspicion she might get more information that way. News travels fast in small towns like these and if anyone is keeping the girls against their will, they'll be alerted to the fact the police haven't given up on the case yet. She wants everyone to assume it's over so they can relax. That's how they'll make mistakes.

The lobby is impressive. It's filled with beautiful oak furniture and snug-looking seating areas. It's decorated for the holiday season with wreaths everywhere and a pine tree that looks like it's been dragged in straight from outside and decorated with lights. She was hoping she could skip Christmas this year but it doesn't look like she'll be able to forget about it during her stay. A log fire in a large stone fireplace quickly warms her.

49

An older male guest is enjoying the papers and a whiskey in one of the comfortable leather couches as he soaks up the heat from the fire.

Eva heads to the front desk where a middle-aged woman wearing too much makeup and a blue uniform greets her.

"Hi, my name's Olivia. Do you have a reservation?"

"I don't but I'd like a room, please." She stands her suitcase on the ground and removes her parka. The log fire is doing its job. "I'm not sure how long I'm staying yet, but probably at least a week."

"Not a problem," says Olivia. "We still have some rooms available at the moment, but not many."

Eva raises an eyebrow. That must be a line to make the lodge sound more popular than it is. Apart from the man seated next to the fire, she sees no guests walking around. She notices a glass display cabinet next to reception with some hunting guns. Some look like antiques.

"The minimum we can charge you for is a week. I'll just take your details and I'll need to see some ID."

Eva slides her driver's license across the desk and gives Olivia the details she needs, as well as her credit card. She's relieved when it isn't declined.

"Okay," says the woman. "You're in room twenty-eight which is on the second floor. The elevator is just to your right. We don't have a bellhop until January, I'm afraid, and you've probably figured we don't have valet parking either."

"That's fine," she says. "I didn't bring a car."

"Here's your key."

Eva's surprised to see an actual key and not a key card. This place must be older than it looks.

"A full welcome pack is in your room and I hope you'll consider using our ski concierge service while you're here." Olivia smiles.

"Thanks."

"My pleasure. Have a good afternoon."

Eva wonders how someone can be so cheerful when they're repeating the same lines every day.

She picks up her suitcase, heads to the elevator, and then takes the stairs instead. She's the kind of person who can't stand still on an escalator. She prefers to keep moving as she gets bored quickly. Her room is located near the end of a clean, dark hallway. Some of the bulbs have blown at this end as it's not as well-lit as elsewhere in the lodge.

Her first impressions are that Lone Creek is definitely no Aspen, and this resort, if you can call it that, couldn't compete with a more up-market version. But it's still a nice place if you want to get away from life for a while. It's remote and quiet, and she suspects it serves the lower price range clientele.

She glances at the ceiling for CCTV cameras but there are none. "Shame," she mutters. If they don't have cameras there's no way of finding footage of the girls before they went missing.

Before she enters her own room, she stands outside the room next door, which is the last room on this floor and the only one close to hers. She puts her ear to the door but doesn't hear anything. Assuming it's empty, she enters her room.

CHAPTER NINE

After hanging up a few items of clothing from her suitcase and checking out the bathroom facilities, Eva's keen to start looking around the lodge. It's almost dark out now so exploring downtown and the tourist stores will have to wait for tomorrow.

She checks the 9mm Glock pistol in its holster under her shirt. She doesn't expect to need it but she can't leave it unattended in her room. Apart from the gun, she only takes a small cross-body purse with her, which houses her cell phone, wallet, keys, and badge. She heads downstairs and wanders around the various guest spaces. None of them are busy with employees or guests. She wonders if news about the missing girls has put people off staying here.

Although Eva grew up in San Diego, she moved to the city of McArthur, Colorado almost eight years ago in her early twenties, so she knows the state fairly well. She's worked for the McArthur Police Department for five years and they've experienced so many budget cuts in that time that they run on what feels like a skeleton crew now. Everyone's under pressure and underpaid. The only cops who smile are the ones who are too dumb to care.

She's never visited Lone Creek before as she prefers large cities, like Denver, because it's got everything she needs.

Besides, she figures all these winter ski towns are the same as each other and, as she doesn't ski, they don't interest her. Detective Garner usually takes on any cases that come up around here if the Sheriff's Office requests help. Not that there's usually much serious crime in a place like this. Maybe just theft and domestics.

As she turns right at the front desk, she walks toward the large bar area at one end of the restaurant. It's dark and atmospheric with subtle, soft lighting. She thinks it would make a great filming location for a clichéd horror movie. As she's about to step toward the bar she passes two young men, both probably in their mid-twenties and wearing the same blue uniform as the front desk clerk. They stop to look at her.

The blond one says, "Well, hello there, ma'am. I don't remember seeing you around here before." He looks like he's taking a break from the slopes, probably after a day spent teaching bored housewives how to have affairs. His nose is sunburned and peeling and the skin around his eyes is white compared to his tanned face. He's obviously not bright enough to use sunscreen.

She forces a smile, which feels more like a grimace to her. Not stopping, she tries to brush past them but the second man, a redhead who's taller than his friend, puts his arm across the doorway, blocking her entrance. She can smell his sweaty pits.

"I definitely haven't seen you here before," he says. "I'd remember a woman like you."

"Excuse me." She pushes past him, forcing his arm painfully away from him. She enjoys the surprise in his expression. They've already underestimated her. She likes it when that happens.

The redhead is persistent. He leans in close to her face. "That wasn't very friendly. Tourists need to make sure they're friendly to the locals, otherwise they might find themselves in trouble. Especially a pretty lady like you."

There's nothing she'd like more than to pull her weapon on him and show this asshole who he's dealing with, but she's not blowing her cover for him. Instead, she forces her knee into his groin as she passes him, pretending it's an accident. "I'm so sorry! You really shouldn't have gotten in my way."

Her knee hurts, so she can only imagine the damage she's done to his balls. Hopefully, that'll stop him breeding.

"Hey! You can't do that!" exclaims his buddy.

"You . . . bitch!" pants the redhead, letting go of her as he sinks to his knees.

The bartender runs over to intervene.

"Are you okay, ma'am?" he asks her.

"I'm fine. I was accosted by these two, and then I accidentally hurt this one. It was just a tap, really."

The bartender's face lights up. "Well, well, well. You've finally met your match, Leroy! I never thought I'd see the day you couldn't charm a lady."

Leroy slowly gets up. He looks at Eva with menace in his eyes. "You touch me again and you'll regret it."

The bartender looks shocked, but Eva laughs, which again surprises the redhead. She's laughing because he has no idea how pathetic he sounds to her. "I'd have to be scared of you to find that threatening, but I'm not. Sorry, Red."

She walks into the bar, leaving the bartender to get rid of them. She's already failed at keeping a low profile but figures it couldn't be helped.

When the bartender returns, he offers her his hand to shake. "I'm Sandy, I own this lodge and I'd like to fix you a drink on the house, as an apology for those two. I can assure you I'll be having words with them later. What'll it be?"

She had come in for coffee but now she feels like something stronger. She takes a seat on a leather stool. "I'll have a glass of red wine."

Sandy's face lights up. He's obviously relieved she accepts his apology. "Excellent! A glass of red wine coming right up. What's your name?"

She unclenches her fists, feeling the adrenaline slowly leaving her body. "Eva."

He pours her drink and hands it over. "What are you doing in town, Eva? Apart from emasculating the likes of him."

She likes Sandy. He has a good sense of humor and a friendly face. She guesses he's in his mid-fifties because of his gray hair, but he's tall and strong-looking. He looks like he could be a rancher or someone who's worked on farms all his life, not the owner of a ski resort.

"I hear the skiing is good here."

"Really?" he says. "Skiing? You don't strike me as the type. No offense, but you're not like the others."

She bristles. "You mean I don't look like I can afford it?"

"No, not at all! I mean you don't look like you have a stick up your ass or that you're bothered about trying to keep up with the Joneses. I just assumed you were here with the other influx for tomorrow's historical talk."

"Historical talk?" She snorts. "No. I'm just trying to fill my time and a friend said I might enjoy snowboarding."

"Well, you may not be as interested when I tell you who our snowboarding instructors are."

She raises her eyebrows. "Surely not those two morons?"

"Afraid so." He laughs. "If that's put you off, we also offer paranormal investigation nights. Maybe that's something you'd enjoy?"

She thinks of the missing girls and wonders whether they went on a ghost tour near the time of their disappearance. It sounds like something young girls would enjoy. "Who runs those?"

"Oh, many different paranormal groups have come and gone over the years, so I don't know who's running the current one. Olivia, the front desk manager, is into that kind of thing so I leave her to organize them. All I know is they're good for business. I make more money in the bar and restaurant when there's a group of ghost hunters in town than two weeks put together otherwise."

"I'll bet." She sips her wine. It feels good to relax. She hasn't thought about Frank since she arrived.

Sandy leans against the bar. "I was even thinking of making up a paranormal history for the lodge and pretending one of the rooms up on the second floor is haunted. The one at the end of the corridor would work because it's dark up there; I can't get the light fitting to work. The darkness adds to the spookiness." He laughs. "The ghost could be a woman who tragically lost her husband down an old silver mine. Legend has it she's been spotted sitting at her bedroom window waiting for his return . . ."

Eva smiles. "I like the idea," she says. "But why can't it be a man waiting for his missing woman instead for a change? Perhaps she was the local sheriff and she was killed in a gunfight, protecting the town's residents against lawless bad guys?"

Sandy grins. "You're right, my idea is sexist! I just think people prefer the idea of seeing a female ghost than a male one. They might not want to spend the night in the same room as a male ghost. There's something more demonic about them, don't you think?"

"That's true. Do you actually believe in ghosts?" she asks.

"I do if it means I can afford a new Mustang!"

Eva finishes her drink. She hadn't meant to drink it so quickly, but she's enjoyed her little detour into the bar. "How come you're tending bar if you own this place? Shouldn't you be living it up on the slopes?"

His expression changes and she can tell he's not so happy himself with the arrangement.

"Well, I co-own it but some people don't exactly pull their weight around here. It's pretty much down to me to run the place. I have a good team to help but I pitch in wherever I'm needed. As you'll know, the economy isn't great, Eva. So if I can save money by doing some of the leg work and the repairs myself then I will."

Eva thinks that's a good attitude to have. She's enjoyed talking to him. It's the first time in weeks she hasn't wanted to kill the person she's talking to.

She stands. "I should get going. Thanks for the drink. I appreciate it."

"Sure thing. You want anything to eat?"

"Not yet, thanks. I'll be back down for dinner later."

As she retrieves her wallet, he refuses to take her money. "On the house." He smiles.

"Thanks. Do you think those two will be looking for revenge?" She nods to where the men were earlier.

"Probably, but they're pretty harmless. They're brothers; Leroy and Patrick. They think they're God's gift to women, but I don't think they've ever broken the law. Some of the younger female guests actually fall for their charms, if you can believe it. Are you here alone?"

"Yes, but I can take care of myself. I don't mean to sound flippant, but let's just say I've had some training."

Sandy smiles. "I like you, Eva. You've got secrets."

She laughs as she heads to the exit. "I like you too, Sandy. But don't tell anyone. I wouldn't want to ruin my new reputation as a badass."

Eva spends time walking around the grounds outside the lodge but she doesn't want to go far. She didn't dress warmly enough. The daylight has gone completely now and the lodge is even more lit up. It's snowing lightly and there's a gentle breeze. She can see her breath in the air as she slips her hands into her coat pockets.

The lodge is in a desolate location and the white peaks of the mountains in the distance are a little unsettling. At this time of night, it feels to Eva as if they loom out of a dark ocean like icebergs.

While the main building sits on the edge of a thick pine tree wood, there's a large opening used for skiing around the back, with some small cabins dotted around, presumably for people who want to pay for a more private stay. They sit in darkness, looking empty.

She spots a few guests out for a walk but they ignore her. Everyone's coupled up and in their own vacation bubbles. She can see the attraction of a place like this if you're after romance. But she still prefers cities.

As it's getting near dinner time and she's had enough of the cold, she walks back toward the entrance. No one's behind the front desk when she enters but, as she passes the restaurant, she hears voices and spots a group of about sixteen people huddled together. They're listening to a woman talk about the plan for tomorrow's tour of the lodge and town. This must be the historical group Sandy mentioned.

Feeling cold and tired, she climbs the stairs and enters her room near the end of the corridor. She wants to shower and change before dinner. She notices she has an inter-connecting door with the room next to hers so she tests it, to check it's locked. It is.

She undresses and enters the bathroom. Now she's beginning to relax, she takes her time under the steaming hot water and doesn't want to get out. After washing her hair, she wraps herself in a fluffy white towel that just about covers her modesty and walks toward her suitcase which is open on the bed. She stops before she reaches it.

"What's that?"

She hears noises from the room next door. She walks to the adjoining door and puts her ear against it. She hears a man's voice, but she can't tell what he's saying and she doesn't hear anyone respond to him.

He shouts out in pain, surprising her.

Without thinking, she leaves her room and rushes next door. She knocks twice and waits. The door is opened by a man slightly older than her, maybe mid-thirties, with black hair and blue eyes. She immediately blushes, which isn't like her at all, but she hadn't thought to put any clothes on.

He glances at her towel-covered body, but only for a second. He seems amused.

"Hi. I didn't order entertainment, thanks. Must be the next room." He smiles, which annoys her.

"What do you mean?" she asks.

"Sorry. It was a stupid joke that I couldn't resist. What can I do for you?"

Before she can speak, a huge Rottweiler appears from behind him and lunges at her. She reacts instinctively by moving out of its way, into the man's chest. He puts his arm around her and manages to pull her out of the way so that the dog jumps at his back instead of at her chest and the towel that covers it.

"Rocky! No! Get down."

The dog lies on the floor and rolls onto his back, exposing himself.

As he lets go of her, the man says, "I'm sorry, that's Rocky. He's completely harmless. He wasn't trying to remove your towel or anything. I haven't trained him how to do that yet."

She's annoyed and embarrassed about pressing herself against a stranger while practically naked.

"Let's start again," he says. "My name's Dean. And you are?"

"My name's not important," she says without smiling. "I just came to see who was shouting and who's staying in the room next to me, because it was empty earlier and we share an adjoining door. I didn't mean to come like this." She looks down at her towel.

"It's not a problem," he says. "Sorry for grabbing you. I was just trying to protect you from Rocky. He loves jumping at people but only so he can lick their faces. That's why I was shouting; he took me unawares and headbutted me."

Not sure what to say she blurts, "Why have they let a dog stay here anyway? Isn't that unhygienic?"

Dean looks down at Rocky. "He won them over with his charm, I guess."

She looks at the dog, still on his back. He might seem friendly now but he could flip in a second if it's in his nature. Eva's never been a dog person; she finds them too needy. She leaves without saying anything and slams her door shut behind her.

She wishes she hadn't come off as bad-tempered but decides it doesn't matter. She'll probably never see the guy again. She drops her towel and dresses for dinner.

CHAPTER TEN

Dean's amused. It's not every day a mysterious woman turns up at his door in nothing but a towel. Especially one with such an alluring attitude. But, once again, he's mortified by Rocky's behavior.

"How many times have I told you to keep your balls to yourself?" he asks, as he scratches Rocky's stomach. "You're going to give me a bad reputation."

He looks at his watch. It's six-thirty. He's hungry. He hasn't eaten since a gas station stop a couple of hours ago and that was just a reheated taco washed down with bad coffee. He gets up and finds the dog kibble in his bag. The turkey flavoring is quickly pungent in this small room.

As Rocky noisily wolfs it down, Dean checks himself in the mirror on the dresser. He wouldn't normally bother but his neighbor might be eating downstairs and he doesn't want to greet her with Rocky's saliva hanging from his face.

"Be good, Rocky. I'll be back soon."

Rocky doesn't even look up from his bowl. With the door closed behind him, Dean walks to the room next to his. He listens at the door but doesn't hear anything so he heads downstairs to the restaurant.

His attractive neighbor is sitting alone at a table for two by the window. She stands out from the other people in the room because she isn't wearing ski clothes. She doesn't look like a typical tourist to him. She looks pissed off.

Not wanting to annoy her any further by getting too close, he takes the last two-seater table, which is a small distance away from hers and away from the group of chatty Canadian tourists who arrived off a coach just before him. He had to wait thirty minutes to check in because they were all taking their time and asking stupid questions. The front desk clerk could've worked a bit faster. By the time she got to him, she wasn't so cheerful anymore.

As he takes a seat and picks up a laminated menu, he notices his neighbor look over at him. She doesn't smile. He does. "Don't worry," he says. "I won't talk to you. I'm just here for dinner."

She rolls her eyes. "Look, I'm sorry about earlier. I'm Eva."

As she leans over to shake his hand, Dean spots her holstered weapon under her shirt. He realizes she's either in law enforcement or she's worried about being attacked. He sees a lot of that in his line of work, women carrying firearms because they have a partner after them. Either would explain her attitude toward him earlier. Her hand is small in his but she has a firm grip. She doesn't wear any rings, just a silver watch. Her nails aren't painted but they are manicured.

"Don't worry about it." He thinks about asking her to join him at his table but he suspects Eva is someone who would rather eat alone. He glances at the menu and sees he has a choice of pork roast or pork roast. He looks over at her. "Why bother with a menu when there's only one choice?"

She sighs. "I know, right?"

A thin older woman with jet-black hair and severe gray roots comes over and sets their tables with cutlery and napkins.

"I'm Delilah. I'll be your server tonight." She says it resentfully, like she would rather be anywhere else but here.

A small man, quite possibly her husband, follows her out of the kitchen and places two huge plates of food in front of them. They're stacked high with pork, vegetables, and roast potatoes.

"Wow, this looks amazing," says Dean.

Delilah doesn't even smile at him; she just walks back to the kitchen behind her husband. As Dean digs in, Eva only picks at her food.

"So what brings you here?" she asks him. "Are you into skiing or something?"

He thinks that's an odd question considering they're at a ski lodge. He nods. "I've never tried so I thought it would be fun to learn."

She casts a critical eye over him, even checking out his wedding ring finger. He hasn't worn his since the end of the murder trial. "Are you here alone?"

Dean doesn't want to tell her he's a PI investigating the missing girls. If she's carrying a gun, she could be here to investigate them too, in which case she'll shut down immediately. He's never met a cop yet who was willing to work with him, but then he doubts he would've worked with a PI when he was a cop. He has to be careful what he says.

"I am, yeah. I was recently made redundant from my job as an accountant so I'm just taking some time out to, you know, find myself, I guess." He inwardly cringes. He can't believe he couldn't make up a better story than that. To change the subject, he asks, "What about you? Are you here for the historical talk?"

She looks like she's trying to figure out whether he's a liar or a loser.

"I don't need to tell you why I'm here. I'm certainly not going to make up some bullshit story like you just did."

Dean laughs and almost chokes on some pork, which makes her smile.

They finish eating in silence. Dean finishes everything on his plate despite having had the best intentions to save

Rocky some of the meat. Eva's plate is only half empty when she puts her cutlery down.

When Delilah comes over to clear their tables, Eva asks her for a bottle of tequila for her room and the Wi-Fi password. "I need to get some work done online tonight," she says. "How's the internet speed here?"

Delilah writes down the password on a napkin. "It's better than you're probably expecting but it takes time to upload videos and photos. It may be slower with that group here." She nods to the Canadian tourists who don't look particularly impressed with their huge plates of food. "I'll get your liquor and a glass before you leave."

"Thanks." Eva starts tapping away at her cell phone.

Delilah picks up Dean's plate. "Any dessert for you? We have key lime pie."

Since Dean moved to Vegas, he's taken advantage of the many gym facilities in the area by working out and taking care of himself. He doesn't want to ruin that now. "No, thanks. I'm full."

When Delilah goes to fetch the liquor for Eva, Dean gets up from his seat. "I'm going to take Rocky for a walk to try to burn off some of that meal. Want to join us?"

Eva doesn't even consider it. "No, I'm busy." She doesn't look up from her phone as Dean and Rocky leave the lodge.

Dean's glad to be outside and stretching his legs after the long and dangerous drive here. It took longer than he anticipated because of the weather conditions. He watches Rocky who's happy to be outside too. He got a glimpse of the snow when they first arrived, but now he gets to play in it.

In the parking lot, a small white Pomeranian runs up to Rocky at full speed. It's yapping non-stop and obviously wants to be chased. Rocky's about to oblige until the dog's owner shouts across the lot at them.

"Trixie! Come back here, you naughty girl! Don't make me put your leash on you!"

Dean nods at the woman and shouts, "Cute dog."

The woman shouts back, "Actually, she's a diva and a menace! Trixie, get over here right this minute! It's time to go home."

Dean watches Trixie and he can tell she's conflicted. She would rather play with Rocky. She yaps a few more times while running in circles, which winds Rocky up, then she runs over to her mom, who picks her up and bundles her into the car, next to her suitcases.

Dean continues his walk, rubbing his hands together to keep warm. Rocky picks up speed, the snow making him overly excited. He starts rolling in it and then gets up to run in circles with his tail between his legs, faster than Dean's ever seen him go. It's hard to believe he's getting older when you see him like this.

"Your dog's acting like Cujo right now."

Dean hadn't spotted the employee on the trail that leads into town. She's sitting on a wooden bench, smoking, and almost completely covered head-to-toe in warm clothes. Her hat and scarf don't leave much of her face visible but he thinks it's the woman who checked him into the lodge.

The snow falls slightly heavier than before and the trail is illuminated by a soft orange glow from the lanterns. It looks like a Christmas card.

"I don't know what's gotten into him," he says, as he approaches the woman. "He's meant to be an old dog."

"He's fine," she says. "He's just got a case of the zoomies, is all."

"The what-now?"

"The zoomies. That's what my mom used to call it whenever her dog turned wild. It would be completely random and usually followed by taking a crap."

Right on cue, Rocky crouches down to do his business. The steam rises off the snow.

The woman laughs. "Told you!"

Dean carries bags for moments like these. He cleans up and uses the trash can next to the bench.

The woman stands and stubs out her cigarette. "Are you a cop?" she asks.

He doesn't want to lie to the employees as they'll find out eventually why he's here, and he needs them on his side. "No, but I *am* investigating the disappearance of the two girls. My name's Dean Matheson. I'm a PI."

"Thought so. Do you know much yet?"

"I know Hannah's mother is frantic with worry and the police don't seem bothered about finding them."

She looks down at her hands. "Hannah's a good girl. I hope she's alright. I liked her mom too, when she came to find out what was going on."

"Are you the girls' manager?"

She nods. "Olivia Carlton. Hannah's a good worker; she's fast and she doesn't complain. I like her a lot. Felt she was being used by Jodie."

"In what way?"

"Well, Jodie would always skip work, leaving Hannah to cover for her. I think Jodie was sleeping with one or two of the guests, which is a big no-no in hospitality work. We leave the drama to the guests, otherwise we get negative reviews online and that's bad for all of us. If people stop coming, the lodge will close down and we'll all be out of work. I just wish the kids understood that."

"What do you think has happened to them?" he asks.

She looks him in the eye for the first time. "It's not going to be good, Mr. Matheson." She shakes her head. "Nothing good ever happens in Lone Creek."

"What do you mean by that? Are there others who have gone missing?"

She scoffs. "Oh, sure. I'm still waiting for my Aaron to return. Eight years isn't too long to find someone still alive, is it? He'll be fourteen now."

Dean can't believe what he's hearing.

Tears form in her eyes and run down her face as she suddenly shuts down. "I've got to get back to work," she says, wiping her eyes. "I've got other mouths to feed at home. Just not Aaron's anymore."

"Can we talk about this more tomorrow?" he asks.

"No. I'm not allowed to talk about it. But, here."

She pulls out a small digital camera from her pocket and pushes it into his hands like she wants rid of it as soon as possible. "This is Hannah's. She likes photography. I found it out here." She stuffs her hands into her pockets. "The police didn't investigate properly. Not for the first time. They never found Aaron and I highly doubt they'll find Hannah and Jodie. Maybe you will."

Dean takes it from her and watches her walk away, back up the trail to the lodge. He's starting to realize this place has some dark secrets. He doesn't want to turn the camera on out here. His hands are frozen and it may need charging.

"Rocky!"

Rocky comes bounding over from behind one of the large pine trees. His muzzle is covered in snow. Dean puts his leash on and leads him back to the lodge.

Back in his room, Dean opens his mini-fridge and is relieved to find a pack of Budweiser. After what he just heard, he needs a drink. He's hoping there's nothing in what Olivia told him, but why would she lie about her son going missing?

He hears a cough next door and wonders how much of the tequila Eva's had so far. He looks at their adjoining door. He never tested it to check it was locked but he wouldn't dare risk doing that while she's in her room. She'd probably shoot him.

He opens the first Bud and takes a long sip as he surveys the room. It's definitely not the luxurious hotel he'd been hoping for. But it's comfortable enough. His cell phone tells him it's only nine o'clock, but after a long day of driving from Vegas it feels much later and he already wants to sleep.

Rocky jumps onto the bed next to him and lets out a loud, deep sigh as he flops into his favorite sleeping position, immediately taking up most of Dean's side of the bed. Dean's ready to call it a night too but he needs to check Hannah's camera. He takes the memory card out and inserts it into his laptop's card reader. He has no idea what to expect.

As he clicks through the photos, he becomes alarmed.

What starts with random touristy photos of the town covered in snow, soon turns into photos of Hannah and Jodie together. Obviously, someone took these for them, and they appear happy enough with their arms linked around each other in some photos and smiling while eating at various restaurants in others.

Some of the most recent photos don't make any sense. Outdoor night-time shots of frozen water and large random stones. Nothing Dean would expect someone would want to capture a memory of. They're not artistic either, so he can't imagine why they were taken.

The next photo shows the back of what looks like a female's head with a deep laceration. Dark congealed blood is visible in the woman's bright red hair.

"What the hell is this?" he mutters.

The remaining photos are just snapshots of darkness, one after the other. There must be fifteen like that. No one is in them and Dean can just about make out a pine tree here and there, and then what looks like a small animal, its eyes lit up by the camera's flash.

The final photo isn't like any of the others. It's of the pitch-black sky. Dean can make out some stars, but nothing else. It's almost like the camera accidentally took the photo as it fell to the ground.

He's stunned. "What the hell happened to these girls?"

CHAPTER ELEVEN

McArthur, Colorado

Chief Carson feels the floorboards around his office vibrate and he smells Detective Garner's approach before he sees him. Garner's always been a heavy smoker. Cigars, cigarettes, weed, and who knows what else. He smokes it all and he stinks. Within seconds, he's bounding into Carson's office.

"Why is Valdez investigating my case?" shouts Garner as he slams the door shut behind him. "I've only just been told and apparently she's up there already!"

"Check your attitude at the door, Detective, and sit down," says Carson, unimpressed.

"No! What right has Roberts got to assign her to my case when I've already told him it's ready to be closed. He's like her damn puppet! I wouldn't be surprised if they're screwing each other now Frank's out of the way."

"Listen," says Carson. "Enough of your temper tantrums, Alan. You're just going to make things worse between you two if you keep bitching and moaning about her. So what if she's looking into it? She's probably just using it as an excuse to get some time away on full pay. I bet she's just getting wasted every night, crying over Frank. It's nothing to worry about. You should've closed it properly when you said you were going to."

Garner appears to relax a little. "I know she won't find anything wrong with my investigation, but that woman pisses me off. She's a pain in the ass to work with. She's stubborn and she's always riding my ass about every little thing. Roberts is a complete pushover when it comes to her. I'm not the only one around here to notice that."

Carson gets up and opens his door. He looks around the busy office and spots Sergeant Roberts. All he needs to do is point at him and Roberts walks over, joining them in his office.

"What can I do for you, Chief?"

"Sit down, Roberts."

"Thanks, but I'm pretty busy so I only have a few minutes." He remains standing.

Carson looks at him, trying to figure out whether he's one of them or one of the new breed of cops who believe the human rights of the criminal are more important than doing whatever it takes to get the job done. Nick's only in his early thirties after all. He doesn't look like your average cop. He's skinny, tall, and healthy-looking. He doesn't drink or smoke and he doesn't have a woman, that they know of. Carson thinks he's an odd one.

"Sergeant Roberts, I'm wondering why you let Detective Valdez re-open the Lone Creek case. Detective Garner has already thoroughly investigated the disappearance of those girls and concluded they voluntarily left town. That's why we haven't notified the FBI. Do you know something we don't?" He sits back in his chair, ready to listen.

Roberts looks confused. "Well, it's an open investigation according to the system, and Valdez requested it. No disrespect to you, Detective Garner, but she didn't feel comfortable with your conclusion, and I agree with her. It's unlikely two girls would voluntarily leave all their belongings behind and break all contact with their family and friends. I guess Valdez will investigate it from a female perspective."

"Bullshit!" spits Garner, turning red. "Next you'll be telling me only women can investigate cases of missing women, because they have a *female perspective*."

Roberts ignores his outburst and looks at Carson as he speaks. "Sir, I understand why he's unhappy, but look at it this way; Valdez is fresh back off bereavement leave after losing her husband *in the line of duty*. She's grieving and being back at the station will just remind her of his death and make it difficult to concentrate on work. She already has a strained working relationship with some of the male employees here because of what happened, so what harm is there in letting her work away from the station for a couple of weeks? If we aren't sympathetic to her needs during this challenging time, she could sue the department. She could even name individual employees for sexual harassment." He looks at Garner. "Just an example."

Garner explodes this time and jumps out of his seat. "Sexual harassment? *Sexual* harassment? She wouldn't have a leg to stand on! None of the other women around here have a problem with sexual harassment!"

"Sit down, Garner!" says Carson.

Garner flops back into his seat, shaking his head.

Carson thinks about what Roberts is implying. They don't need any investigations into their department. Those kinds of investigations find what they want to find.

"Can't we just cut her some slack?" Roberts continues. "If any of us lost our partners, we'd want some time to try to process it, wouldn't we? All she's doing is seeing if she can find any reason for the girls to leave town so suddenly." He looks at Garner. "She'll probably be back within a week or two with no more answers than you. After all, if you've done your job properly there won't be anything else to find. So where's the harm?"

Carson knows he has to be seen to be a caring boss, especially with the female employees. Otherwise they'll rise up against him and put one of their own in charge. He throws his pen on his desk and relents. "Listen, I don't have a problem with her investigating the case but if she doesn't find anything within two weeks, Detective Garner, you need to close it until we get any new leads. And explain your reasons to the girls' nearest and dearest. We need to stop them going to the press and bad-mouthing us every five minutes."

Garner gets up and storms out of the office, leaving just a lingering smell of tobacco behind him.

"Thank you, sir," says Roberts. As he turns to leave, he looks back and adds, "You know as well as I do that Valdez is a better detective than Garner. Sure, I know you two are old friends who've worked together for years, but you need to give her a chance to shine. She could be a real asset to this department, and therefore to you, if people like Garner cut her some slack. His outdated attitude toward women sucks and he could get the department in a whole lot of trouble if he doesn't improve."

Carson knows he's right, but he also shares some of Garner's attitudes. "Listen," he says, "we're from a different generation than you and Valdez. When we were your age female cops didn't answer back and they certainly weren't better shots than we were. We're being overtaken by political correctness. It just takes us dinosaurs a little longer to catch up, that's all. It doesn't make us bad people."

"I understand that," says Roberts. "But you need to catch up quick. Maybe we should get someone in to train the team on equal opportunities?"

Carson's mood darkens. "Don't be stupid, Roberts. I'd be the laughing stock of the police force if I made my employees attend something like that. I thought you were busy? Get out of here."

He notices Roberts shake his head as he leaves. He won't go as far as organizing equal opportunities training but he does need to make sure Garner stops arguing with Valdez. Someone like her could get them all into trouble.

CHAPTER TWELVE

Detective Garner arrives home early after leaving the station in protest at Chief Carson's decision to let Valdez take over his case. He's in a foul mood that not even a joint could improve and he slams his front door shut loudly behind him, so everyone knows about it.

His wife doesn't even look up from the TV. She's used to his moods and she's concentrating on *Days of Our Lives* too much to be bothered to ask him who's upset him this time. She has a constant air of despondency about her and Garner can't find the energy to care.

His grown-up son, however, comes running down the stairs like a child greeting Santa at Christmas. He blocks Garner's entrance to the kitchen.

"Hey, Dad!" He leans in close to Garner's face. "Can we go for a drive? Mom says she's had too much wine to take me out."

Garner looks at him and sighs heavily. Travis is twenty-six years old, skinny, greasy and creepy. He rarely washes, doesn't work, and can't interact with strangers.

Garner and Shirley had always hoped his behavior could be the result of some kind of mental health problem or learning disability, as that would mean whatever's wrong with him isn't their fault. But their family doctor believes there's nothing wrong with the boy, which means he's just a loser. Which probably means it *is* their fault. Maybe they should have sent him on more play dates as a young kid, but no one wanted to play with him. Not after he set fire to the school. He was an outcast from age six.

Garner's not sure how much his wife knows, but he suspects Travis has unhealthy interests. And when they tell him no, he explodes. They've learned to tip-toe around his moods, to keep things easy.

"Not now," he says. "I've only just got home."

"I know but I really want to go out," whines Travis.

"Tough. I need to eat. You'll have to wait."

His son's greedy smile falters and he looks like he wants to start trouble. He must think better of it because he storms upstairs without a word instead. He doesn't slam his bedroom door, so that's a good sign.

Garner watches him go and his heart sinks. He wishes they never had a child, and he doesn't even feel sorry for thinking it. He knows they're going to have to live with him until they die because he'll never move out. Not voluntarily. That's not to say Garner doesn't have feelings for his son. But his feelings are confused. His feelings are bordering on grief for the child Travis should have been.

Garner's phone rings. It's Lloyd Peterson, his business associate.

"We've got a great game lined up for tomorrow night," says Lloyd. "Everyone's coming and everyone's up for spending some proper dough. Will you be joining us? I need a chance to win back the money I lost to you last time." He laughs.

Garner cheers up. "You can try, my friend. You can try."

"So, you're in?"

"I'll be there by the time it starts, don't you worry. Get the good rum ready." As he ends the call, he turns and comes face-to-face with Shirley.

"So you're going out gambling with your friends again tomorrow night?" she asks with a blank expression.

"Listen, I work hard and I need downtime. You don't know what it's like being a cop. What we go through every day. You'd want a night out too if you were me."

She curls her lip into a snarl. "I *do* want a night out. You can't keep leaving us alone, Alan. I don't care how much money you win, or how many expensive watches you bring home. You should be helping us, not deserting us all the time. Your son needs you to be a proper father to him."

He can't listen to her. He feels guilty enough already. "I'm going out. If he acts up, tell him I'll take him out another time. I might not be back tonight so don't wait up."

He opens the front door fast, so that neither of them can make him stay. This time, Shirley slams it shut behind him.

CHAPTER THIRTEEN

Lone Creek, Colorado

Dean slept for nine hours straight. He didn't even change his clothes or get under the bed covers he was so tired. After waking just before six in the morning he went straight for a slippery jog with Rocky, around the freezing grounds, and then got in the shower with the temperature turned up high. He finally feels like he has a reason to get up early again now he's working on a serious case.

After reviewing the photos from Hannah's camera, he knows now that something bad has happened to at least one of the girls. Although they've not seen the photos from Hannah's camera, he doesn't know how the local PD can conclude the girls voluntarily left town. It's a ridiculous theory even without the photos. Something doesn't add up.

He heads downstairs for an early breakfast, taking Rocky with him. They're greeted by Delilah as they enter the restaurant.

"Morning. Is it okay if Rocky sits under my table? I don't like to leave him in my room for too long."

Delilah's stern, wrinkly face melts at the sight of Rocky and she becomes uncharacteristically friendly. "Of course it is. We'll just say he's one of those emotional support dogs if anyone complains. You look like the type to need one. Are you staying another night?" She bends down to fuss Rocky, who laps up the attention.

Dean ignores the insult, hoping that was her attempt at humor. "We'll be here a while."

"I'll tell Nathan to make sure he keeps all the uneaten sausages to one side for you, boy."

Rocky licks her hand as she talks, and Dean looks at his dog with a surge of pride. With such a dysfunctional upbringing, having a neglectful and abusive drug addict as his original owner, it really is a wonder Rocky didn't turn into an aggressive animal. Instead, he couldn't be more trusting.

"You know," says Dean, "wherever we go, he gets fed better than I do."

"That's because he's cuter than you," she says. "Take a seat. You're early, so breakfast will be a half hour or so."

"That's okay, I have things to do." He points to his laptop. He takes the seat by the window that Eva used at dinner last night and looks around the room for her. She must still be in bed. Possibly nursing a tequila hangover. It's empty in here except for an older couple who look up and say good morning to him.

Delilah silently places a cup of black coffee on his table and leaves to help her husband in the kitchen.

Rocky settles under his chair, sniffing all the old food stains on the carpet, as Dean opens his laptop. He starts by sending Jackie Walker a quick email to let her know he's arrived and hopes to be able to start speaking to the employees today. Then he starts researching the missing girls on social media. He's always surprised by how much personal information people willingly give away to anyone who wants to read it.

He starts with Jodie's Facebook account. He locates the correct Jodie Lawrence by checking the workplace listed for all the results. Once he finds her, he's relieved to see everything is set to public so it's all open for him to view. Her

photos show she has dyed, bright red hair and green eyes —
although that could be contact lenses as they're unnaturally
green. He supposes she could've used a filter.

Jodie's tall, with strong shoulders and toned arms. She
looks like she could be a swimmer. He scrolls through her
photos, of which there are hundreds. She appears to be either
kissing or hugging a different person in every photo. She also
clearly likes smoking pot. That could mean there's a drug
dealer in the mix. He wonders whether she owed someone
money and they came to collect.

Lots of comments from friends sit unanswered on her
timeline. People asking where she is, and prayers that she's
safe. He reads some of the responses from others under these
comments but apart from some attention-seeking trolls, there
are no clues about what's happened to her.

Jodie describes herself as *a lover of life and wannabe model*.
Dean checks out her friends next. There are over one thou-
sand people listed so he does a manual search for Hannah
Walker's name in her friend list, but it doesn't come up.

That's interesting. He doesn't think he would go on a
long trip with someone he didn't consider a friend.

Jodie's Instagram page is surprisingly set to private.
Perhaps she has a different set of friends on this site. Friends
not suitable to share on Facebook. He does a quick internet
search to see if anything else comes up about her but, other
than articles about her high school basketball successes, he
finds nothing.

Nothing really stands out about Jodie other than she
likes smoking pot and has a lot of friends.

Dean wonders whether the detective in charge of the
case managed to get into Jodie's private messages on either of
her social media accounts. They could hold all sorts of clues.

He doesn't notice Delilah approaching him with a
cooked breakfast until she clears her throat. She waits while
he moves his laptop to one side and, as she places it in front of
him, he inwardly cringes at the amount of grease everything
is swimming in.

"Thanks, that looks great."

"Sauces are over on that table behind you," she says before handing Rocky a fat pork sausage. "Here you go, sunshine."

Rocky's tail thuds against the floor in delight.

Dean gets up and grabs some napkins to dry some of the oil off of his eggs and sausages, trying to be discreet so as not to offend Delilah. It may be swimming in oil but it all tastes good. He eats quickly so he can start researching Hannah next.

He tries every social media site he can think of but not one of them produces results for the Hannah Walker he's looking for. It's unusual for someone that age not to use at least one social media site. Maybe she uses an alias to keep things private.

He's about to give up when he decides to do a more general search of her name. What comes back shocks him.

"Wait. She did *what*?"

Rocky must hear the excitement in his voice as he gets out from under the table to sit next to him, ready for action. There are many British newspaper articles about Hannah Walker. He's only seen one photo of her that Jackie emailed him, but it's definitely the same girl in all the newspaper articles. The only difference is she's a little younger in these. He scrolls back to the first link and clicks on it.

The Hampshire Daily Echo
4th August 2015

 Local girl, 15, questioned about the murder of Katie Sewell.

 We can exclusively reveal the name of the local 15-year-old girl who has been questioned in relation to the death of Katie Sewell, also 15. Katie was found dead at the bottom of a cliff in a local quarry a week ago and police are currently questioning Hannah Walker about the suspicious death.

 Sources close to Katie's family allege Hannah was with her best friend at the time of her death and failed to report it to the police. She also failed to call for medical help, which could have saved young Katie's life.

When asked for a statement, the investigating officer, Inspector Foster, told us: "We can't comment on the details yet as our investigation is ongoing, but this is a tragic and avoidable death. We await the coroner's findings and no one has been charged in relation to Katie's death."

Dean leans back in his seat and thinks about the implications. If Hannah was involved in the death of her best friend back home in England three years ago, could she be involved in Jodie's disappearance now?

He may have to look at this case from a different angle.

Maybe they weren't killed or abducted by a stranger or a guest. Maybe relations got so bad between them that Hannah snapped, did something stupid, and then fled town before getting caught.

He looks up to see Eva approaching him. He still doesn't want her to know why he's really here so he quickly closes his laptop.

She raises an eyebrow. "Porn? At this time of the morning?"

He laughs, surprised at her joke. "The breakfast of champions."

She rolls her eyes. Rocky jumps up at her but she stops him from slobbering her hands by gently pushing him away.

"Join me for breakfast?" asks Dean.

"I've already eaten. I've been up since four."

"Wow." He's impressed. He thought he got up early today. "What were you doing up at that time?"

She looks annoyed. "Mind your own business."

He realizes he's managed to irritate her again. He picks up his laptop. "I've finished my breakfast anyway. I guess I'll get out of your way."

As he stands, she touches his arm. "Look, I'm sorry. I don't mean to bite. I'm having trouble sleeping and it makes me even more of a bitch than I usually am."

He feels for her. He remembers how exhausting insomnia is. Just after his brother died, Dean went without sleep for almost a month straight. It made everything harder to deal with. Just making himself a hot drink became overwhelming, which meant he regularly went thirsty and hungry because he just couldn't deal with basic self-care.

"Everyone's allowed to feel tired, you know. That doesn't make you a bitch; it makes you human." She looks away and he can't read her expression. "Are you sticking around for another day?" he asks.

She nods. "I have to."

He waits for her to explain why she has to but she just stares back at him. He's frustrated at her short answers. He knows they're strangers but he's just trying to get along. She doesn't want to disclose anything. Maybe she thinks he's a journalist from a local paper. He thinks about it for a second and then makes the rash decision to level with her. Two heads would be better than one, after all.

"Come with me," he says as he walks out of the restaurant.

"Where to?" she asks.

"My room."

"No way!"

"Eva, I have something I want to tell you."

"Well, tell me here then. I'm not going into a stranger's hotel room. I'm not stupid!"

He stops and turns to face her. "It has to do with Hannah Walker and Jodie Lawrence."

Her smile falters and her face shows she's conflicted. She looks defiant, like she's ready to deny knowing those names, but then her professional curiosity must take over because she beats him upstairs with Rocky running a close second.

As she approaches his room, Eva says, "I would prefer we did this in my room but as you have the last room they cleaned together, I want to see it."

So she *is* a cop. Dean's glad. He thinks they could help each other find some answers. This is good for Hannah's mom. And Eva will have access to the reports from the original investigation. He didn't know the girls also helped with housekeeping. He thought they just worked the check-in desk, but it would make sense that everyone does a little of everything in a place like this.

As he unlocks the door to his room he feels excited to have someone to work with again. He hasn't enjoyed working alone as a PI. Sure, he's had Marilyn to run things by, but nothing beats having a partner or a team around you. He's hoping Eva feels the same way.

As he turns to let her follow him into his room, he can tell she doesn't.

CHAPTER FOURTEEN

"What do you think you're doing lying to law enforcement?" Eva demands, hands on hips.

"Whoa!" says Dean with his hands up. "How could I possibly know you're a cop when you didn't tell me? All I know about you is your name — assuming Eva *is* your real name — and the fact you're not getting a lot of sleep lately."

She scoffs. "Of course I'm a cop. Why else would I be here and not ski?"

"I don't know," he says. "I noticed a poster in the lobby for a ghost tour and thought maybe you had a love of the paranormal."

She looks like she wants to punch him. "Listen, I don't have to explain myself to you because *I'm* the detective here. Who the hell are you supposed to be? You're clearly not an accountant, I can tell that."

Dean sits on the bed. "Wow, that's actually a compliment. I would hate to look like an accountant."

"It's not supposed to be a compliment," she says, clearly not enjoying his sense of humor. "You better tell me right now who you are, or I'll arrest you under suspicion of abducting the two girls." She rests her hand on her weapon.

Dean knows she won't use the gun on him. He rubs his face and looks over at Rocky who's watching with interest.

"My name's Dean Matheson and I'm a private investigator. I'm here for the same reason as you."

She laughs. "You're a private dick? The one Jackie Walker threatened to hire?"

"Right. Why are you laughing?"

"Because PIs are pathetic! They're just wannabe cops who aren't good enough to make it in law enforcement, or they've been kicked off the force for being incompetent. Show me your PI license."

Dean stands. He begrudgingly digs out his license from his wallet and shows it to her.

She gives it a good look. "Let me guess, you didn't make it through the police training so you set up business on your own?"

It's his turn to be angry now. "Actually, *Detective*, I spent five years as a corrections officer in a prison and three years as a police officer. I've worked with some of the best detectives around, and I know that no one from *my* department would ever stop working this case without finding these girls." He thinks of sloppy Detective Miller and ignores the fact that he would have done just as bad as Eva's team. Detective Jones would have found these girls weeks ago.

Eva doesn't look impressed but she does look intrigued. "You were a cop? Then why the hell are you playing at being a PI now? Did you get fired?"

"Of course not. I just had . . ." He trails off. He's not sure how to explain the whole sorry mess he left behind in Maple Valley. "I guess I had a run of bad luck."

She moves closer. "What kind of bad luck? Mental breakdown?"

"No!" he exclaims. Although, if he really thought about it, maybe he did experience a breakdown, and that's why he didn't realize sooner what was going on.

"Well, what then?" she says. "It would take a lot for me to leave the force, but then I'm professional and obviously a lot tougher than you."

"I lost some people, okay? Within months of each other. But I wouldn't expect you to understand how that affected me, since you're more professional than I am."

He's surprised to see her look ever so slightly concerned. "Who did you lose?"

"Why? What does it matter to you?" he says, sitting on the bed again.

She moves closer to him but she doesn't sit down. "I'm sorry, I didn't realize."

He looks up at her face and sees she's being genuine, so he confides in her. "First, I lost my brother to suicide. Then I lost my wife. She was murdered." He doesn't mention their unborn baby. He can't.

She gasps but doesn't reach out to comfort him. He's glad; he doesn't need her sympathy. But it's nice for her not to be mad at him for the first time since they met.

She sits on the chair opposite the bed. "Where's home for you?"

"New Hampshire. But I moved to Vegas after everything that happened."

She thinks about it. "So, basically, you ran away from your emotions and your responsibilities as a cop."

He does a double take. "What?"

She stands. "Self-pity will only get you so far, Matheson. You have to face things head-on. Don't get mad, get even. Did you at least manage to catch the guy who killed your wife before you fled town?"

"I'm done talking about this." He stands. "Now we know why we're both really here, what are we going to do about these missing girls?"

She laughs again. "*We* aren't going to do anything. *I'm* currently investigating their disappearance. I've already had enough men screw this investigation up. I don't need another one getting in my way."

Dean thinks they should work together but she turns away from him and starts examining the room, presumably for anything left behind by the girls during one of their last housekeeping shifts. Despite her attitude toward him, Dean can't help but like her. She's direct and puts work first. But he's not sure whether he can trust her yet, so he doesn't want to tell her about Hannah's camera in case she turns out to be as disappointing as the rest of her department.

He owes it to Jackie Walker to do everything in his power to find the girls. She might not be pleased if he gives the only clue he has to the police department that has already let her down so badly. Olivia gave the camera to him and not the police. There must be a reason she couldn't trust them with it. He considers sharing Hannah's diary with her first. As a way of testing her intentions.

"Can I see a copy of the report?"

"What report?" she mumbles as she crouches on all fours to look under the bed.

Rocky thinks it's some kind of game. He jumps under the bed with her. As far as a Rottweiler can fit, anyway.

"The report your partner wrote up. Maybe I can spot something they missed."

She sits back on her knees with an amused smile on her face. "Now why would I show you that, *Mr.* Matheson?"

He ignores the dig. "How about because I have Hannah Walker's personal diary. You know, the one your team neglected to find during their search of this very lodge."

She jumps up, excited. "You're kidding? Where did you get that? Let me see."

Dean retrieves it from his bag and holds it up next to his face.

She lunges for it, putting her hand on his chest for balance. He pulls it away at the last second.

"I got this through legitimate means and you're more than welcome to read it," he says. "*If* you let me work with you on this case. I think we have a better chance of finding the girls together."

She steps back. He knows it's risky to anger her because she has way more power than him here, but she looks amused again.

"I could arrest you for withholding evidence. You know that, right?"

He smiles. "Of course I know that. I used to be a cop, remember?"

She sighs and Dean watches her, stunned that she's even considering it.

"The minute you get in my way you'll be asked to leave. Not just the resort, but the town."

"I won't get in your way. I'm as keen to find them as you are. Hannah's mother practically begged me to help so we have to do better than your partner."

"An untrained chipmunk could do better than him," she says. "But he's not my partner, just another detective at my PD." She sighs. "I need coffee. Let's read the diary downstairs."

Eva walks to the door and as she grasps the handle Dean says, "Wait until I tell you what Hannah Walker did when she was younger."

She turns with a smile. "Has no one ever told you the internet is available on everyone's computers, not just yours?"

She walks out of the room.

Dean cringes. Of course she's already looked into the girls' backgrounds. He wasn't thinking. This is a new case to him, but obviously not to her.

He knows that if he's got any chance of earning her respect, he needs to start acting more like a detective and less like a second-rate PI.

CHAPTER FIFTEEN

Eva leads them downstairs to the bar. It's almost midmorning but some guests are still eating breakfast in the dining area. Sandy's behind the bar, preparing for the morning skiers who no doubt enjoy coffees and hot chocolates after hitting the slopes.

She watches Matheson out of the corner of her eye and wonders how much to trust this ex-cop she finds herself with. For all she knows he could be someone Detective Garner's planted to keep an eye on her. Matheson doesn't seem like he's local though, and definitely not someone Garner would mix with.

Truth be told, she could really do without him and his dog tagging along with her everywhere she goes and getting in the way of her investigation, but she wants to be on the inside of whatever he manages to find out. She has no choice but to let him work alongside her for now. Managing to secure one of the girls' diaries shows Hannah's mother trusts him and he's serious about finding them.

She wants to believe his sob story about how he left law enforcement as a result of losing his brother and wife, but she has little respect for his decision. He could've just taken some time off work to deal with it, not run away to avoid it.

She has every intention of finding out what happened to her husband and to do that she needs to get her head together first. She might not feel up to being in the same room as Garner just yet, but only because it's all so fresh. She took the missing girls' case to give her some breathing space while she plans her next move. But she'll never walk away from the injustice of what happened to Frank.

Someone will pay for it.

"Eva! How are you?" asks Sandy. "Sorry for the mess. It's about to get busy in here." He has rows of cups and cutlery lined up.

"No problem," she says. "We can come back later if you prefer?"

Sandy spots Matheson and the dog behind her and his smile falters slightly. "No, that won't be necessary. Take a seat. Coffee?"

"Please." She chooses a stool at the bar.

The dog sniffs everywhere as Matheson takes a seat next to her. She watches Sandy give the dog a disapproving stare before he turns away.

"Guess he's not an animal lover," says Dean, under his breath.

"He's nice," she whispers. "Don't be mean."

Matheson raises his eyebrows. "What's this? Have we actually found someone in this world you like?"

She gives him a stern look and Sandy comes back, carrying cups and spoons.

"Who's your friend, Eva?" he asks as he sets everything down.

"He's not a friend. He's more like a stray I seem to have picked up. His name's Matheson."

Dean holds out his hand. "My name's Dean, actually. I'm just in town for a short while. This is Rocky."

Eva watches Sandy stare at Rocky again. He isn't falling for the dog's charms.

"I don't allow dogs in this room because of the food. It's not exactly hygienic, is it? I'm sure you understand."

Matheson looks surprised. Eva can tell he's never met with this reaction before. It's a good job Sandy didn't see the dog eating breakfast in here earlier.

"Sure," says Dean. "I'll take him outside. Come on, boy." He leads the dog to the double doors a few feet away from the bar and makes him sit outside on the patio area, under a heated pergola.

The dog starts licking the snow around the edges of the patio.

Eva turns to Sandy with a questioning look. "You don't like dogs?"

"Not really," he admits with a smile. "Too needy. I'm more of a horse person. So who is this guy?"

"I'm trying to figure that out myself," she says as she watches Matheson approach. She looks at him properly for the first time. He clearly works out as he's slim with toned biceps that she can see under his short-sleeved T-shirt. He's well dressed — smart but not overly so — and his black hair could probably do with a trim, but it suits him being a little messy. She likes the way it curls at the ends. His eyes are a deep shade of blue, matching the color of his T-shirt.

Eva catches her thoughts and immediately thinks of Frank, who was the complete opposite of Matheson, physically and professionally. He probably spent too long in the gym bulking up and he would never have given up his career in law enforcement. He was a cop through and through.

She looks back at Sandy and can tell he's taken an instant dislike to Matheson. Whether that's because of his dog or for some other reason, she's not sure.

"I hope you don't mind?" Sandy says to him.

"Not at all," says Dean as he sits at the bar. "It's good to put him in his place every now and then. He has a big ego."

Sandy doesn't smile at the joke. "Coffee should be ready now. Excuse me."

Dean leans forward and says quietly, "Are all the locals this friendly?"

"Maybe your sense of humor is annoying to some people."

He sits back, hurt. "Wow, you really don't like me, do you?"

She sighs. "I have no feelings for you one way or the other, Matheson. All I know is we've got work to do."

"My name's Dean."

She looks at him. He's serious. "Fine. If it makes you feel better, I'll call you Dean. Okay?"

He smiles at her. He has a nice smile. For some reason, she finds it irritating. But then, everything irritates her at the moment so it's probably not him. She's probably being too hard on the guy.

Sandy comes back and fills their cups with coffee. Eva weighs up whether she could ask him about the two missing girls without him realizing that's why she's here. If anyone knows something, he should. He employed them.

Before she can say anything, Rocky barks. Dean's off his seat and out the door immediately. She follows him when she hears raised voices.

The first thing she spots is the two jerks who tried to come onto her yesterday. The redhead, who Sandy referred to as Leroy, is holding Rocky's leash.

Eva looks at Dean. He's calm at the moment, leaning against the door, acting casual. He probably thinks he can charm his way out of this, but he didn't see the look on Leroy's face yesterday when he threatened *her*.

"Look who it is, Leroy!" says Patrick. "The skirt who kneed you in the balls!"

Dean looks over at her with raised eyebrows. She shrugs.

Leroy looks feral when he spots her. He grins and pulls Rocky closer to him.

Even if Eva wasn't a cop, she'd know this guy is trouble. He's clearly used to getting his own way around here, which is why he won't let what she did yesterday drop. She hurt his ego and he wants her to pay.

"This your dog?" he says.

Eva's unsure how to respond to keep the situation calm. She doesn't want these two hurting the dog or Matheson. As she's the only police officer here, she's ultimately responsible for keeping the peace.

"He's mine," says Dean, still calm. "And I suggest you drop his leash."

"You can shut your pie hole," says Leroy. "This don't concern you."

The dog remains still at Leroy's feet. He's a big, dense animal and probably more than capable of protecting himself. He's not showing any signs of feeling threatened. He even yawns. Eva wonders why Dean even has him if he hasn't bothered training him as a guard dog. Soppy dogs are good for nothing but slowing you down.

She looks at Leroy and then at Dean, trying to figure out how to get them out of this situation without her being reported. The last thing she wants is to be recalled back to the station so soon. Garner would love that.

"Rocky, come," says Dean.

She watches Rocky's ears rise and he moves toward his master, but Leroy pulls on his leash so hard he jerks the dog backward.

She needs to do something, fast. "Listen, Leroy." She steps forward. "Would it help if I apologized for yesterday?"

Patrick looks at his brother for his reaction.

"No. It wouldn't," sneers Leroy. "You're gonna get what's coming to you." He looks like he's retrieving something from his pocket.

Before she can even get her gun out, Dean acts.

"Rocky, attack!" Dean lunges forward at the same time as the dog jumps up at Leroy with all his weight behind him and teeth bared, growling.

Leroy's taken by surprise and knocked off his feet. Dean drops on top of him, punching him hard in the jaw. Leroy's head hits the ground with a crunch. But he's bigger than Dean and he tries to fight his way out of Dean's hold.

Eva's about to add her weight to the mix but, surprisingly, Dean punches him again and then forces his head to the ground so that Leroy's eating snow.

Patrick just watches, open-mouthed.

Rocky barks loudly but all he really did was provide a distraction. Eva doesn't know if he'd ever actually bite somebody. Maybe he would if Dean was struggling to get control of a situation.

Dean pulls out a gun, which Eva didn't even realize he was carrying, and holds it to Leroy's bloodied cheek.

"Do we have a problem here, Leroy, or can I let you and your boyfriend go on your merry way?

"Hey!" says Patrick. "I'm his brother, not his boyfriend!"

"My apologies," says Dean. "I should've known you could do better than this one."

Eva surprises herself by laughing.

Sandy appears behind her. "Should I call the cops?" he asks, with no enthusiasm.

He's obviously used to this kind of behavior from these two, despite telling her yesterday that they were harmless. She can't understand why he doesn't fire them. Is it really that hard to get decent employees around here? She wonders whether there's more to their arrangement than Sandy has let on.

Dean gets off Leroy and actually helps pull him up. He keeps his gun drawn but pointing downward. "It was a pleasure meeting you, Leroy. But if you ever touch my dog again, I'll shoot you."

Eva's surprised at his change in demeanor. She didn't think he had it in him.

Leroy spits blood into the snow in front of Dean's feet. "You two better watch yourselves. And I'd keep an eye on your dog if I were you." He spins around, pulling Patrick with him.

Sandy shouts out after them. "For God's sake, Leroy, shut up and get back to work before I fire your ass. This is the last warning you'll get from me."

As they walk away, Sandy goes back inside, and Dean gives Rocky's neck a rub.

"I'm meant to keep you out of trouble," he says to the dog.

"Who said you can go around pulling weapons on random people?" says Eva.

He stands up straight, holsters his gun, and smiles. "It's one of the few perks of not being a cop anymore. I can wave my gun at pretty much anyone with no chief of police to answer to. Don't worry, I have a permit. Now, could you fetch me some ice for my fist? I just hurt myself defending your honor."

She's glad he handled the situation himself, without her needing to get involved. Maybe he *was* a good cop once.

CHAPTER SIXTEEN

Dean sips his coffee while resting his hand in a bowl of iced water. It feels good. Rocky has been allowed in the bar now, but Sandy still doesn't seem keen on either of them.

"Nice employees you have around here," says Dean. Now he's met Leroy he understands the comment Hannah made in her diary about how Jodie was lucky not to be sexually assaulted by the guy. Perhaps he *did* force himself on Jodie at a later time. Maybe on both of them. Maybe they struggled to get away and he had to silence them.

Sandy starts putting out a hot buffet ready for the lunchtime rush later. If there is such a thing around here. The TV above the bar is showing the weather channel, with the volume low. Dean's keeping an eye on it. The state of Colorado is hidden by snow and warnings of high winds, and the attractive female presenter is highly animated.

"Don't judge us all by those two," says Sandy. "Every town has its share of troublemakers. Reliable employees are hard to come by somewhere this remote, and those two always turn up for work and more or less do as they're told. I have to take what I can get. It's not like I'm inundated with résumés of people wanting to work here. Plus, well, I feel kind of responsible for those two. They probably wouldn't get a job anywhere else around here."

"Sandy," says Eva. "You're clearly an intelligent man and you've just seen that my friend here is carrying a weapon. I expect you already know why we're here?"

Sandy butters some bread rolls and smiles. "To be honest, Eva, I guessed you were probably a cop as soon as I saw you handle yourself yesterday. I wouldn't have guessed your friend here was a cop though. No offense intended, Detective Matheson."

"None taken," he says as he takes another sip of coffee and thinks about how it is offensive. "But I'm not a cop anymore and I don't work at Eva's PD. I'm a private investigator working on behalf of Hannah Walker's mother. But we're both here for the same reason. We need to know what you can tell us about your two missing employees. And we need to know whether Leroy and his brother could've harmed them."

Sandy looks at him. "What? Don't be stupid. They're harmless."

Dean shakes his head. Nothing angers him more than people who turn a blind eye. "Harmless to you, maybe. But not to two young women who have no one watching their backs out here in the mountains. Presumably, you saw Hannah and Jodie at some point on the day they disappeared? I mean, it's not that big a resort that you wouldn't see your employees regularly."

Eva gives him a look to suggest he's being too abrupt, but he doesn't care. He's here for answers, not to make friends.

"Did you get to know them very well?" she adds.

Sandy stops what he's doing and sighs. From the looks of it, he spends all his time at the lodge so Dean knows he must've interreacted with Hannah and Jodie at some point during their stay. He probably hired them, unless he leaves the hiring up to Olivia, which is possible.

"Sure, they were nice girls," says Sandy. "They'd only been here a month or two before they disappeared. They were good at their jobs . . . Well, Hannah was better. The guests liked them both. But I've already told the police everything I know. Haven't you read their report?"

"I work with Detective Garner at McArthur PD," says Eva. "I've read his report, but he thinks the girls left town voluntarily. I'm not saying that's not what happened, but I need to find out where they are because their families are never going to rest until they know. I mean, come on, Sandy. Imagine how this feels for them."

Dean wonders if Eva or her department managed to track down Jodie's estranged family. He also notices Sandy's referring to the girls in the past tense. Is that because he thinks they're dead?

Sandy pours himself a shot of whiskey and brings the bottle over to them. He leans against the bar. Eva helps herself to another coffee.

"Like I said, they were nice girls. They were polite and having fun, and it's crazy that they've vanished. But there were no signs of forced entry into their room and apparently nothing to suggest they were abducted. I've had employees leave with no notice many times before. Not everyone's cut out for the hospitality industry. Some people think it's beneath them when they discover you have to do a bit of everything: cleaning, serving, fixing."

Dean doesn't think that's the case here. "When did you last see them?" he asks.

"The morning before they disappeared. They were excited about something. I overheard them talking about a paranormal tour they were booked on. I don't know whether it was one of the tours Olivia books — we're not the only place around here that runs them — but it wasn't for that day. It was for later in the week. After they disappeared. You'd need to check with Olivia for the specifics." He downs his shot before adding, "The British girl — Hannah — she seemed younger than Jodie. Shy and polite. Anyway, when I saw them, they were bundled up in warm clothes and leaving the lodge through the lobby. Before they left, I asked them if they were enjoying working here."

"What did they say?" asks Dean.

"I don't remember exactly, just that they were excited to be here and they thought the lodge was cool. They'd tried some snowboarding. Oh, and I remember Olivia telling me she'd driven them up to see that big hotel up in Estes Park the week before. The one that was in that horror film from years ago. So they must've been interested in the paranormal. That's what gave me the idea I mentioned to you yesterday." He looks at Eva. "About having my own ghost. I figured if people are willing to travel all the way up to Estes Park, they might travel here if the ghost was good enough. Then I might make enough dough to replace the furnace at last. I've been warned it only has one more year of life left, if that."

Eva nods and Dean can tell she doesn't think Sandy had any involvement in the girls' disappearance. Despite getting off on the wrong foot, Dean agrees that he seems like an honest, hardworking man, although not very forthcoming with the details. Probably because he has to protect his business. Dean almost feels sorry for him. He's clearly trying hard to keep this place afloat with little help. He wonders whether he owns the place on his own or whether he has a partner. If he does, they're obviously never here. Maybe it's an ex-partner who just takes their cut. Sandy continues before he can ask.

"Jodie was always trying to get me to serve them alcohol, but they were underage so I never did. They didn't mind too much. It was all a bit of fun for them. If I had any information about where they might be, I would share it. I don't need bad publicity for this place. It gets enough already."

Eva leans forward. "What do you mean?"

He hesitates. "We've had some negative reviews online these past few weeks. Mainly because the décor needs updating, but also because the kitchen employees are slow and the food isn't great. That kind of thing. Nathan and Delilah are past their prime but they're reliable. And they've worked here since the beginning of time, so what am I going to do? I can't fire them."

"How was the dynamic between Hannah and Jodie?" asks Eva. "Were they getting along okay, as far as you could tell?"

Sandy thinks about it. "I got the impression that Jodie was running the show. She was bossy and liked to bark orders at Hannah, but Hannah didn't seem to mind. She was easy-going. Like I said, they were excited and joking around. They appeared to like each other from what I saw. But then . . ."

He stops. Dean waits for him to finish his sentence but he looks like he's changed his mind.

"But then what?" he asks.

"Well, it's probably nothing, but within a minute or two of them leaving I heard raised voices outside. I was too busy to go look, and then Patrick and Leroy came in, looking pleased with themselves."

Dean says, "Are you saying you think they had some kind of altercation with the brothers?"

"Not an altercation as such, more like words. Leroy probably made a pass at one of them and got slapped away."

"*Slapped away?*" says Eva. "It takes more than a slap to stop him. I doubt two young women could defend themselves against an asshole like that."

Sandy looks at her. "The brothers came in here within minutes of the girls leaving, so they couldn't have done anything."

"What happened next?" Eva asks.

Dean can tell she's hungry for information. At least she's taking this more seriously than the rest of her department.

"I can't remember. I had a line forming at the bar because it was almost lunchtime. Sorry, my memory's not what it was."

Dean asks, "Did you ever see Jodie with a guest called Bryan?"

Sandy hesitates again. Dean can't understand why he won't trust them.

"Sure, briefly. Some of the kitchen employees were talking about her, saying she was acting . . . unladylike, shall we say, with a guest. It didn't take much to put two and two together and realize it was with Bryan. That's not the kind of behavior I condone in my establishment, but what am I going to do? They're both adults."

"Jodie is only just eighteen," says Dean. "How old is Bryan? And is he still here?"

"He's one of our few returning guests. He's left now, but he'll probably be back next year, flirting with someone else. You have to remember these people are on vacation. They're here for a good time and they like attractive employees to flirt with. But he wouldn't have done anything with Jodie."

"Do you know that for a fact?" asks Dean.

"Look, he's a charming, middle-aged guy with a bit of dough. He doesn't need to get involved with teenagers. He could take his pick of women nearer his age. If you really think the girls were abducted, shouldn't you be looking for a monster? A sex offender? Don't you have a register for those types? Although you can usually tell what they are just by looking at them, don't you think?"

Dean knows that not all monsters look like monsters. Some of the worst sex offenders he's dealt with have been people he knew; people he went to school with, who he would never have suspected. People want to believe the less attractive you are, the more likely you are to be a criminal. Juries are less likely to convict attractive defendants. Juries like their criminals to look like criminals, which is why so many people get away with murder.

Sandy goes back to organizing the buffet. "But, hey, what do I know? Maybe I'm wrong. Hell, I thought the girls would turn up with their tails between their legs, full of apologies for missing work because of some week-long party they were at. Look how wrong I was about that."

"All the same," says Dean. "I'm going to need Bryan's phone number." Eva looks at him and he realizes he's stepping on her toes. "Fine, you can call him."

"If you insist," says Sandy. "Olivia can get that for you. She can tell you more about that paranormal group too. But I'm pretty sure they'll be long gone by now."

Dean's not satisfied. Sandy's definitely withholding something. Maybe he doesn't want to get too involved in case it affects his business or reputation. This is a problem that often comes up with potential witnesses.

Sandy butters more bread. "Don't assume we're all backward around here, Mr. Matheson. Just because we're a small town doesn't mean we're all inbred and incompetent. If any of the employees knew where the girls went, I'm confident they would come forward and tell the police. Sometimes people go missing because they want to."

His blasé attitude angers Dean. "You don't have daughters of your own, I take it?"

Before Sandy can respond, Eva stands up to leave.

"Thanks for your time, Sandy. And the coffee." She drops a ten-dollar bill on the bar.

"No problem."

"Just one more favor?" she asks as she reaches the door. "Don't tell anyone we're investigating the girls' disappearance. We're not here to upset anyone. We just want to find them and be on our way."

"Understood," says Sandy.

Eva leads Dean and Rocky away from the bar and toward the lobby. Dean's about to start quizzing her for her thoughts but she grabs his elbow and leads him away from Sandy's view.

"I thought we were going to read Hannah's diary next?" he says.

"We will, later."

"What's going on?" he asks as he slips his coat on.

"I'm thinking about Detective Garner's report," she says. "He'd spoken to Olivia about the paranormal group. It consisted of three males, all in their twenties, and the tour was on the night after the girls disappeared. It was at a dilapidated hotel on the other side of town. Garner said he'd been unable to track down any of the men because the cell number they listed on their poster was disconnected and no one around here knows them. Olivia didn't know whether they had a Facebook or Twitter page and said they were just passing through Colorado. She told Garner lots of paranormal groups travel the country, film everything they do, and charge guests a fee to join them. But they haven't been questioned, even though they checked into the lodge two days before the tour, while the girls were still here."

Dean shakes his head. "How could Garner not speak to them? Did he at least speak to this Bryan guy?"

Eva sighs and keeps walking as she zips up her jacket. "Nope. You see what I'm up against? Garner isn't interested in policing. He'd rather spend his time drinking and getting high. He thinks I don't know it but he spends most of his work time pursuing other interests. I just don't know what those other interests are yet."

Dean's not surprised. He's worked with someone just like him before. "Did he even issue a state-wide BOLO and canvass the town?"

Eva shrugs. "If he did, he didn't put it in his report."

"How did he get away with any of this?" he asks, incredulous.

"He's best buddies with our chief. Oh, *and* the mayor *and* the local sheriff. They have themselves a cozy set-up and I think that's why they never liked Frank. He knew too much about something."

Dean frowns. "Who's Frank?"

Eva turns back to him with a strange look on her face. He can't tell what she's thinking. "He was one of the best police officers in the whole department," she says. "He was worth ten of the likes of Garner."

"Did he leave?"

She turns away from him. "No. He died."

She finishes wrapping herself up in warm clothes and leaves the lodge through the front entrance.

Dean wants to ask more but she's walking too fast.

"Come on, Rocky."

Rocky runs ahead of him.

CHAPTER SEVENTEEN

Eva silently curses herself. She hadn't wanted to think about Frank, never mind talk about him. Especially with a stranger. She's starting to feel too comfortable around Dean Matheson already and it's alarming to her that it feels so natural to work with him. She hears Dean and the dog catch up with her.

Dean stumbles on some branches hidden by the snow and almost falls into her as he asks, "Where are we going?"

She stops abruptly and spins around. "I tried talking to the front desk clerks earlier but none of them would tell me anything significant. They must realize I'm a cop, and I bet Garner ruined their opinion of McArthur PD." She takes a deep breath. "It's so frustrating because it's as if they all know something but they won't spill it. Although one of them mentioned Hannah enjoyed walking this trail." She nods to the left of them. "It leads up to the base of Wolf Peak. Hannah's into photography apparently, and this is obviously a picturesque area for taking photos."

They look around as they crunch through the compacted snow. It was bright earlier but the dark clouds have now rolled in, and the wind has picked up. Snow slides off the trees in heavy clumps. It feels like there's a storm coming.

Eva glances at Dean. He looks cold. His ears are bright red and he's rubbing his gloveless hands together.

"Don't you have gloves? A hat?" she asks.

"Not with me. It's been a while since I've needed them."

"Who comes to a ski resort unprepared for the weather?" she mutters. "Does your dog know how to track people and scents?"

Dean looks at Rocky who's unsuccessfully chasing a squirrel through the pine trees. "That's not something I've covered in amateur K-9 school yet. But if he smells something out of the ordinary, I'm pretty sure he'd lead us to it."

"Okay, get him over here." She pulls out a woman's white vest.

"Just call him. He'll come for you."

She rolls her eyes. "Rocky! Come."

Rocky stops in his tracks and looks at her, ears raised. The snow starts falling again, with flakes so thick they accumulate on Rocky's nose as he stands to attention.

"Come!" she says again.

He launches into a run and only stops when his front paws are on her chest, his tail wagging furiously.

She almost falls backward under his weight. "Here, sniff this." She holds the vest under his nose.

"Is that Hannah's?" asks Dean.

"It was found in her room. I took it out of evidence at the station. We have all their belongings."

Rocky grabs the vest out of her hands and runs off with it.

Eva sighs. "If he loses that, I'll blame you." She runs after the dog.

Eventually, Rocky stops, drops the vest, and rubs his face all over it, and Eva can tell he's destroying any DNA that might be on it from a possible abductor. She hopes their forensics team already got anything of significance off of it. Before she makes it over to Rocky, he spots something more interesting and runs into the thick underbrush.

She has to crouch down to follow him under the trees and through the bushes until she notices what he's excited about. She kneels down next to him.

It's a hiking boot, partially hidden by the snow. It's gray with a bright pink bootlace. She leans in to clear away the snow and notices it has dried blood all over it. Then she spots the bone protruding from the foot inside.

"Holy crap."

Rocky eagerly sniffs the boot. Eva pushes him away, but he's persistent. And heavy. He wants the bone.

"Get your mutt away from this, Matheson!" she shouts, without looking up.

When he doesn't respond she leans back on her feet, pulling at Rocky's collar. She turns her head to see where he is. "Matheson?"

He isn't there, but someone dressed all in black launches at her with a baseball bat. She instinctively turns away from the inevitable blow. She doesn't see her attacker's face as she drops forward, onto the boot.

CHAPTER EIGHTEEN

Glenburg, Colorado

After the argument with his wife, Detective Garner went to visit Tracey, his lover. He suspects Shirley knows about her and she doesn't even care. After spending all night and his day off work with his lady friend, Garner finally leaves her apartment just as it gets dark. Despite being gone for so long, he's not ready to face the music yet and go home. Instead, he heads to the casino he part-owns for the game night they have planned.

As soon as he arrives, he relaxes. The club is far away enough from where he lives and works to be discreet, so he doesn't bump into anyone from work. Other than the people who are invited to use the facilities, that is.

As he walks in, he undoes his shirt collar and his suit jacket, indicates to the young female bartender what he wants to drink, and then heads to the poker table. Lloyd Peterson and the Sheriff, Stan Bowerman, are already there and already drunk by the looks of things.

Garner intends to catch up. That's the good thing about being in on a casino. The drinks and the rooms are free. Not that he could get away with spending a second night away from home. It's a shame. The bartender is new. And cute.

"Alan, you made it!" says Sheriff Bowerman. "You're behind, buddy. Take a line and get your dough out ready!"

Garner spots the coke lined up ready for him. He helps himself, wiping his nose after. "I'll sit this game out. I need to eat first."

"Gloria!" shouts Lloyd. "Bring us some food."

Gloria, the bartender, immediately runs back to the kitchen to see what bar snacks she can fetch for him.

As well as Lloyd and Bowerman, some other men Garner recognizes are hanging around. Some are half-heartedly joining in. Others are distracted by the pretty girls walking around the casino with drinks.

"You look like you've had a rough week. Tell us all about it," says Bowerman.

"It's Valdez," he starts. He doesn't have to explain who she is as they all knew Frank. "She's putting her nose in my business. And yours."

Bowerman raises his eyebrows. "What does that mean?"

"She thinks those missing girls up at Lone Creek were abducted or something, I don't know. She won't let it rest. She's at the lodge, looking for them."

Sheriff Bowerman doesn't look bothered as he downs a shot of bourbon. "She can look all she wants. Those girls left town of their own accord. They probably shacked up with the traveling ghost geeks you told me about. Now they're too scared to tell their parents. Hell, maybe one of them got pregnant and they've gone to take care of it!" He laughs.

"I know she's wasting her time but that woman bothers me."

"Why do you let her get under your skin?" asks Lloyd.

"I don't know. She's trying to give me a bad reputation, ever since she accused me of sexual harassment. Can you believe that? Me? *Sexually harass* a woman?"

The bartender puts a rum and Coke in front of Garner, which he downs immediately.

"Get me two more."

"You've only got to look at a woman to be accused of that nowadays," says Bowerman. "And most of them should be glad of the attention."

"*Did* you harass her?" asks Lloyd, with a smirk.

Garner licks his lips. "I copped a feel. What's wrong with that? She may be a bitch but she's got a great body."

They all laugh and Garner notices the look on Gloria's face. She clearly finds them disgusting. His smile falters and he thinks of his wife and son at home. Shirley has given him that same look many times.

As he downs another drink, his cell phone rings. "Ah, shit. It's the old ball and chain."

The others playfully mock him as he declines the call. But it immediately rings again.

"Damn it," he says, standing.

"Don't let her bust your balls, big guy," says Lloyd.

Garner finds a quiet corner to take the call. "What is it?"

"Is he with you?" says Shirley.

"What?"

"Travis. Is he with you? He's gone out and taken my car. He better be with you."

Garner's heart sinks. Travis never learned to drive properly. They didn't want him to. The farther he can go, the more trouble he can get into. Normally, he only steals one of their cars when he's desperate. Last time he crashed into a tree, narrowly avoiding a line of elementary kids on a field trip.

Sometimes Garner wonders whether Travis was aiming for them.

"Jesus, Shirl. Why did you leave your keys where he could find them?"

"Don't blame *me* for this. You should've been here. You need to go and find him. He could seriously hurt himself."

"But I'm nowhere near home right now."

She sighs heavily down the line and he can picture her rubbing her temples. "Alan? *Find him.*" She ends the call.

Garner knows where Travis will be heading but he doesn't want to go there. Feeling like something bad will happen tonight, he downs his last drink and walks away from the poker game. He hears the others jeering him as he leaves.

CHAPTER NINETEEN

Location unknown

Hannah's teeth are chattering so much that it's causing her gums to bleed. But that's good because it gives her something to taste, even if only temporarily. The blood wets her dry, cracked lips, like a macabre shade of lip gloss.

Now that she's alone, she's running out of hope. It's hard to tell how long it's been since Jodie deserted her, or even how long she's been imprisoned here. If she's to trust the tally she tries to keep, it has been twenty-one days since she and Jodie were taken.

She finds it difficult to believe it's been three weeks and no one has found her yet. It must be five or six days since Jodie escaped. She should have brought help by now. Hannah tries not to consider the possibility that Jodie might not have made it very far before succumbing to her terrible self-inflicted injury.

The days merge together here because it's dark almost all day long, apart from a tiny ray of daylight that peeps through the hole in the bottom of one of the walls. The hole the rats made to come and go.

Some kind of discarded dry food, perhaps corn or cereal, in a sack over in the far corner attracts them here. She can't make out what's spilling out of the sack but she can see the rats coming and going every time they're hungry. She thinks there are just two of them, so she's named them Jodie and Hannah.

Although the rats are huge, they're not half as scary as the spiders. She's always been afraid of spiders, but here they're worse. Spiderwebs fill the shadows, so thick she can't see through them. The spiders themselves are more active at night. She hears them scuttling around and she feels them crawling through her hair and into her ears, seeking warmth.

Whether she's imagining them on her, she'll never know.

The rats are also showing more interest in her with each day that passes. She's plotting to kill the one she named Jodie as soon as it comes over to her again. Not because she's scared of it, although she is, but because she envies its freedom, just as she envies Jodie's. The rats can come and go. They choose to come back to this terrible place, but she has no choice in the matter.

She hopes her friend dies in the freezing conditions outside for leaving her alone here. She'll be losing blood and exposed to the weather, which has been getting steadily worse from the sound of it. There's no way Jodie would make it far enough to find help before succumbing to blood loss. Adrenaline will only carry her so far.

She won't be the first friend of Hannah's to die, but it would've been kinder for Jodie to stay here and die with her.

Hannah doesn't want to think about the lengths Jodie went to in order to free herself from these shackles. Luckily, their captor hasn't been here since she left, so they're completely unaware. The minute they find out, she knows they'll take their rage out on her.

That's why she's been sleeping next to the chainsaw for the last few hours. Not to use it on herself — she's always had a low pain tolerance — but to use it on the person who comes here at random intervals to torture them.

She's hoping there's enough gas left in it to cut through her captor's neck.

CHAPTER TWENTY

Lone Creek, Colorado

Dean retrieves Eva's key from her coat pocket as he holds her up with his right arm. When they get inside her room, he helps her onto the bed.

He didn't catch a glimpse of their attacker as he was struck on the head from behind. He woke up face-down in the snow with Rocky licking his neck and barking. He doesn't know whether Rocky tried to chase the person or whether he chose to stay with them the whole time. Dean couldn't see Eva until he stood up, while trying to ignore the pain in his head.

Hopefully, Eva saw who attacked them.

If it wasn't for Rocky, Dean knows he probably wouldn't have come around so soon and both of them could've frozen within a couple of hours in this weather. It's turning into a blizzard out there.

The pain in his head makes him wince again and the side of his face feels numb from the snow. He leans over Eva and checks the back of her head. There's blood all over her hair and scarf.

"Eva? What happened? Did you see who did this?"

She says something but her words are slurred. Dean leans her forward to check the laceration. Her hair is thick and dark so it's hard for him to see where the blood's coming from. He parts it all gently and she winces as he touches the wound. It's only small, but it must be painful as it's already badly swollen.

"You've got a head wound but it's stopped bleeding so that's a good sign. Ignore the amount of blood on you; head wounds always bleed more. I'll get you a compress."

Eva tries to sit up. "I'm okay. I don't know what happened though. Do you?" She must go dizzy as she leans sideways.

Dean makes her lie back. He goes to the bathroom and soaks a face towel under warm water. When he returns, he gently presses it against the back of her head as she leans her face into his shoulder. She has to hold his arm to stay upright.

"Someone hit us with something," he says. "This was obviously intentional, which is not what I'd expect at a vacation resort. My head hurts like a bitch, but at least it's not bleeding. Did you see anything?"

"Not really," she says, her words muffled by his jacket. "They knocked me out before I could see who they were, but I remember they used a baseball bat and I think they were dressed in black."

Dean's alarmed. Someone isn't happy that he and Eva are staying here. They could've been killed. "You could have a concussion. We should get you to a hospital."

She sits up then, pulling away from him and taking the compress from his hand. She slowly presses it onto her wound and winces. "No, it's fine. You must've passed out too?"

"I did, but I'm fine."

She scoffs. "Typical man. I need the hospital but you don't?"

He sighs. "You're right. I'm sorry. I'm just worried. I wasn't trying to patronize you."

"You can pour some tequila onto this towel," she says. "That'll disinfect the wound and clean off the blood."

Dean shakes his head. "Don't be stupid, that's not going to help."

She points to the bottle of tequila she brought upstairs with her after dinner last night and yells, "Pass me the damn liquor, Matheson!"

He stands. "Okay, okay! No need to yell."

He hands her the bottle, which is almost still full. For some reason, he expected her to have drunk most of it last night. She strikes him as a drinker. Most of the cops he knows are.

She pours some on the wet face towel and holds it to her head, trying not to show how much it hurts.

Dean winces as he watches her. "That's gotta sting."

She leans back against the pillows, her head holding the compress in place. He sits back down on the bed, unwilling to leave her alone like this.

"I could use a drink," he says. "Are you going to share?" He knows she probably wants him to leave but either of them could be concussed so they need to keep each other awake.

"So liquor's your vice?" she asks him as she passes the bottle.

He smiles, glad she's attempting humor. "Whiskey used to be, for a while. But before that I didn't even drink caffeine, believe it or not. What's your vice?"

"I don't have one," she says. "If I *had* a vice, my life would be a lot easier."

He frowns. "Why did you order the tequila if it wasn't to get drunk?"

"For company, I guess. In normal circumstances that would last me a month. I tried to be an alcoholic once but I can't stand the taste of alcohol."

"So take up smoking."

"What, and smell like Detective Garner? No way."

"Drugs?" he suggests.

"Too clichéd."

"Sex, then?" he says, smiling. He wonders how far he can push her.

"I wish." She doesn't take the bait.

She must be in pain because he doesn't think he would've gotten away with that before the attack.

"You have a slight temper," he says. "Maybe that's your vice?"

She gives him a dirty look. "Screw you."

He turns away, smiling. "Told you . . ." he mutters.

She tries to stand but rolls like she's going to fall off the bed. "Shit, the room's swaying." She lies back.

"Eva." He rests a hand on her arm. "Do you think this was Leroy getting back at us?"

She considers it. "Possibly. But I think Leroy would've taken advantage of me while I was passed out. If you know what I mean."

Dean shakes his head at the thought. He doesn't know how someone like Leroy stays out of prison. "We should report this to the police."

"Don't be stupid," she says. "I *am* the police. And the last thing I want is Garner being sent out here to report back that I've been attacked. I'd be switched to a different case."

He thinks about it and knows she's right. He doesn't want Detective Garner up here either. He's clearly incompetent. "Fine. Do you remember what you were looking at before you got hit?"

It seems to come back to her as she sits up straight. "The foot! Did you bring it back with us?"

Dean retrieves it from inside his coat. "It's well and truly frozen." It's in one of Rocky's poop bags to preserve the evidence. "You need to get your forensics guys up here so they can check this out and search where it was found. We need to know whose foot this is."

Eva takes a deep breath. "There's no way they'll make it up here during this weather. And I don't want them here yet. I don't know who I can trust in my department. We're finding out so much more than Garner did. I just want more time to figure this out, unhindered. We're getting close, Dean. I know we are." She glances over his shoulder. "In the meantime, we need to preserve the foot. Is there an ice box in that fridge?"

Dean opens the refrigerator door and finds the ice box. "There is. It might just fit. But first I'm going to send some photos to a friend."

"Why on earth would you do that?" She looks confused.

"She's a medical examiner. I think she can offer an opinion about how the foot was severed from the leg and maybe even how long it's been since it was cut off."

Eva leans back against her pillows. "Can we trust her?"

Dean thinks about Sheila Didcott, the woman he had an affair with after his brother killed himself. "Absolutely. She's currently living in my house."

Eva raises her eyebrows. "Oh, so she's your girlfriend?"

"What? No, nothing like that. She's just looking after the place for me while I'm gone."

He uses his phone to snap some photos of the hiking boot first, and then he pulls the tongue open to expose the gray flesh and bone inside.

"Hold this down for me so I can get a good shot."

Eva pulls out some disposable latex gloves from her purse and he realizes she came more prepared than him. She pulls the boot's tongue as far open as it will go.

Dean snaps ten photos at different angles and sends them all to Sheila with a quick message.

Need your help. How/when did this happen?

He stores the boot in the ice box. It only just fits.

"Let's hope the maid doesn't want to clean the fridge anytime soon," says Eva.

Dean's cell phone rings immediately. He smiles. He should've known Sheila would work on it straight away, no matter how busy she probably is. Although, he's hoping the death count in Maple Valley has reduced since he left.

"Hey, Sheila. How are you?"

"Well, well, well. Dean Matheson, messaging little old me. And such a romantic message too! No naked photos though. I'm disappointed."

He laughs. "How have you been?" He moves away from Eva to the corner of her room but he can tell she's watching him with interest.

"I was going to call you anyway, actually," she says. "I have some news."

The phone line becomes weak and Dean can only hear her faintly. He moves around until he finds a spot with a stronger signal. "Let me guess, you got Detective Miller fired?"

She laughs. "I wish! No, it's just that I'll be moving into my own place soon, which means you'll need to find a new tenant."

Dean's disappointed. Finding a new tenant while he's this far away is going to be a pain in the ass and he doesn't have time for it. Maybe it's time to sell the place.

"Okay, no problem. Are you telling me you finally earned enough money for that mansion you've always wanted?"

"Not exactly," she says. "I'm engaged, so I'm moving in with my fiancé."

"No shit? Congratulations, Sheila. I'm happy for you." He means it too. Their affair was never about love; it was about trying to find ways to cope with his brother's unexpected death.

"You'll never guess who the lucky man is," she teases.

Dean assumed it was someone he didn't know. Otherwise, he would've heard about it by now. "Please don't tell me it's Miller?" he jokes.

"What? As if I'd let that beast near this perfect body!" She laughs. "No, actually, it's Steve."

Her voice fades as the line weakens again. Dean thinks he heard her wrong.

"Say that again, Sheila. I'm having trouble hearing you, there's a bad signal. We've got a storm brewing here. It sounded like you said Steve." He laughs at the idea.

Her voice returns, loud and clear. "I did say Steve."

Dean's stunned. Steve Dalkin is one of his closest friends, as well as his old sergeant at Maple Valley PD. He suddenly realizes he's lost touch with most of his old friends and co-workers, apart from Detective Jones and his wife Barbara. Now he thinks about it, Steve's perfect for Sheila. He's a great guy.

"He kept that quiet! I didn't even know you two were dating."

"Yeah, well, in a town like this it's best to keep things quiet until you're sure. We've been seeing each other for nine months and I've got to tell you Dean, I'm in love."

Dean's genuinely happy for them and finds himself smiling. "That's great, Sheila. Congratulations. I'll call Steve soon. I'm stuck in the Rocky Mountains right now, trying to find two missing teenage girls."

"Does the foot belong to one of them?"

"We think so."

Sheila's tone changes. "Who's we? I thought you worked alone now, Mr. Private Investigator. Unless you mean Rocky."

Dean looks at Eva, not wanting to talk about her while she's here but unable to avoid it. "I'm helping one of the local detectives. It's completely informal. She's just humoring me."

Eva nods to show she agrees.

"*She*? Uh oh," Sheila teases him. "Is she pretty?"

Dean feels his face redden so he turns away from Eva.

"What kind of question is that? She's a great cop."

He watches Eva's reflection through the mirror on the wall. He can tell he has her full attention.

"That's not what I asked, Dean."

Sheila may only be teasing him but it puts him in an awkward position. "Yes, she is. Extremely. But that doesn't matter. Tell me about the foot."

"Look," says his friend with a sigh. "It's been two years since Linda passed away. Don't live like a hermit. You're entitled to move on with someone else eventually."

Dean's uncomfortable discussing this right now. He knows there's no way Eva would ever be interested in him. She doesn't exactly hide the fact she finds him irritating. Besides, he has no intention of being anything but professional.

He realizes then that he doesn't even know if Eva's married or seeing someone. But then, why should he? It's none of his business.

"Sheila?" he says. "The foot?"

She laughs. "Okay, okay. I'm looking at the photos now on my laptop. The flesh is well preserved. It must be pretty cold up there?"

"It is. We're in the middle of the mountains and can't go far because of the weather. We'd rather not use the local police department's forensics guys, for various reasons."

"Got it. Okay, let's take a look. Hmm. From the laceration marks around the remaining ankle flesh, and the way the ankle bone is cut, I'd say this was done using something other than a normal blade. Maybe even something with two blades."

"Okay."

"Hang on." She goes silent as she studies the images. "Yeah, it may have been something with rotating blades."

"Rotating blades?" He faces Eva again. She's petting Rocky, but still listening.

"Hold on while I zoom in. Yeah, I think I'm right but I can't be one hundred percent sure without seeing it first-hand, obviously. I'd say this was done with something like a circular saw, or some other kind of contractor's tool."

Dean winces at the thought of it. "Damn, a circular saw?"

Eva raises her eyebrows and grimaces.

"Not a good way to go," he says.

"She might not be dead though," Sheila continues. "It depends on how much blood she lost and what was done with her after this. If the only limb she's missing is one foot, she could survive that for a short while. But sick perps who torture teenage girls with circular saws are unlikely to stop at one limb. Unless she managed to kick him in the balls and then hack his genitals off, of course, and let's hope she did. In the meantime, you need to find the rest of her. Hopefully, alive and intact."

"How long ago do you think this was done?" he asks.

"There's no way of knowing without examining it first-hand because it's so well preserved. The skin is almost completely devoid of blood, but I assume you don't know how long it's been sitting in the snow?"

"Afraid not." He sighs. "Thanks for your help, Sheila. It's been good catching up."

"No problem. But before you go, Detective Jones told me he's visiting your old friend today."

Dean's stomach flips with dread. Not really wanting to ask but feeling he has to, he says, "Which old friend?"

"Lizzie Glover."

He knew Jones had been keeping track of her — he keeps track of everyone he puts away — but Dean never thought he'd actually visit her.

"At the secure unit?"

"Right. He managed to get a visitor pass at last. She declined all his previous requests, so I don't know what changed her mind this time. It should be interesting to hear what she has to say though."

Dean doesn't want to talk about her in front of Eva. Or at all, even. "Well, hopefully, a year in the hospital means she's not as messed up as she was. Anyway, thanks again. I appreciate your help."

She must sense his unease at discussing the woman. She drops the subject. "My pleasure. Good luck finding them. And, Dean? If I had a daughter go missing, I'd want you on the case."

He suddenly feels homesick. He misses his friends. "Thanks. Am I invited to the wedding?"

"Well, we haven't set a date yet but of course you'll be invited. Just make sure you bring your new lady friend."

He rolls his eyes as he says goodbye.

Eva slowly stands up. "A circular saw? That's brutal."

"I know. We need to find them, Eva. And fast." He pauses. "I've got something that might help us."

CHAPTER TWENTY-ONE

Eva watches as Dean pulls Hannah Walker's camera out of his bag and explains who gave it to him. She can't understand why Olivia didn't hand it over as evidence to Garner. She knowingly withheld something that could have helped in the investigation.

"Olivia didn't trust Garner," says Dean, putting the camera down and opening his laptop. "She disclosed to me that one of her sons has been missing for eight years and she feels it was never investigated properly."

Eva's mouth drops open. "*Eight* years? That poor woman." He disappeared before she joined the department. She can't imagine what it's like to lose a child and never have closure. But on the other hand, knowing how that feels, Olivia should have handed Hannah's camera over the minute she found it. She could've helped find the missing girls.

Something doesn't feel right to Eva. Something's going on in this lodge that everyone's hiding. "Let me see what was on it."

Dean hands his laptop over to her. Rocky's asleep next to her on the bed.

Eva ignores the throbbing in her head as she scrolls through the images. These are *not* the kind of photos you'd expect to be taken by two young women enjoying their working vacation in Colorado. The ones taken outside in the dark are downright creepy.

"Well this confirms it," she says. "Someone has them."

Dean looks up. He's sitting in the armchair opposite her bed reading more of Hannah's diary.

"Or someone *had* them," he says. "We don't know if they're still alive."

She shudders. It doesn't feel very warm in the room. Her arms are covered in goosebumps.

Dean glances at her, concerned. He gets up and pulls a spare blanket from the closet before resting it over her legs. "It's probably not too late to try to make it to the nearest hospital before the storm worsens," he says. "You don't look well."

"I'm fine. I'm just cold and tired. The heat in this place is crap." She can't help but notice Dean has taken both his jacket and his sweater off, and seems comfortable in a T-shirt, so it can't be that bad. She sighs. She can't get sick. They have too much to do. "There's no way we'd get far in this weather anyway. I bet we're already snowed in."

He looks out the window but it's already pitch-black and the snow is building around the edges. It's coming down so thick it's obscuring the light from the lanterns outside. He returns to his seat.

"Playing devil's advocate," she continues, "these last photos look to me like the camera could have malfunctioned. It's really only the head wound that suggests they were harmed."

Dean disagrees. "And the severed foot, remember?"

"Right, but until it's tested for DNA, we don't actually know that belongs to one of the girls we're looking for. There's always the possibility that was the result of a completely different situation. Still messed up, don't get me wrong, but not necessarily involving Jodie or Hannah."

"True," he says. "But come on, Eva. What are the chances? I've been thinking about those photos of the darkness, where the camera flash captured random stones and things. I think whoever was using the camera at that time, presumably Jodie based on the red hair, was using the flash to light their way. Maybe she escaped from wherever she was being held."

Eva nods. "Or, if we consider the alternatives, those photos could've been taken before she disappeared. The camera wasn't date-stamping the images with the correct date. The year on these states 2016, which means Hannah didn't set up the date and time when she bought the device. So we don't know when these photos were taken."

Dean nods.

"Let's say Jodie had too much to drink one night," she says. "She could've gone for a walk after. Let's face it, what else is there to do around here in the evenings apart from drink, hike, and ski? She might've lost her way in the dark. Maybe her head wound is a result of her stumbling over something she didn't see, rather than caused by someone else."

Dean isn't convinced. "I think if we hadn't both been hit over the head today, that would be more believable than it is now." He stretches his arms and back.

They've been stuck in her room all afternoon. Eva just wants to get out of here but she feels like she's getting steadily worse. She finds some painkillers in her purse and swallows them dry.

"My gut tells me Jodie was using the flash to light her way after escaping from whoever took her," he says. "Maybe she discarded the camera when the battery died or dropped it when she was re-captured. She could've been found by her abductor on her way back to the lodge."

Eva lies back on the bed, tiredness sweeping over her. She touches the back of her head with her fingers, feeling where the blood has matted into her hair. At least it's stopped bleeding. Dean doesn't look affected by his assault at all, which is annoying.

It's frustrating that they have no idea where the girls could be. Their abductor could have taken them out of state by now. Or they could be nearby, clinging onto life and waiting to be rescued. She wishes she'd been sent up here originally, instead of Garner.

"If she escaped and passed out," she says, thinking out loud, "she'd be dead out there on the trail somewhere. It's such a big area to search, and with the snow potentially hiding her, it would take a huge team to find her." In towns like this, it's not unusual to find missing people in the spring, after the snow has thawed.

"Let's face it," says Dean, "if the foot we found is Jodie's she couldn't have gotten very far, or traveled fast, on just one foot. She would've been crawling on her knees. Which means she would've either turned up alive or been found dead by now. I think it's more likely that she's been killed and dismembered, and the killer unwittingly dropped her foot while disposing of her body. Either way, I have to start searching for her. I can't stay in here when Hannah could still be alive." He pulls a sweater over his T-shirt. "Rocky? Come on, boy."

Rocky jumps down off the bed.

Eva tries to sit up. "I'm coming with you."

Dean goes to her. "No. You need to rest because otherwise, you're going to slow me down. I don't have time to look after you out there. I'm sorry."

His words don't sting because she knows he's right. She doesn't have the energy to go outdoors tonight. If she gets some sleep she could be up early to continue the search with him tomorrow.

"I'll ask the front desk to bring some food up," he says. "After they've been, lock your door. Whoever attacked us this morning could come back. I'm going to sneak out this time so none of the employees can keep track of me, just in case it was Leroy. I don't want him knowing you're in here alone."

"You're going to try to sneak out with him by your side?" She nods to Rocky.

The dog raises his ears and barks at them. She can't believe how intuitive he is. He always knows when they're talking about him.

Dean smiles. "Fine. I'll shoot the shit with the front desk clerk first, give them the impression we're hanging out in our rooms all evening. I'll order room service, then I'll head up in the elevator and come back down using the employee stairs." He pulls his jacket over the sweater. "I wish your department had carried out a proper search while they were here and found this camera sooner. They should have taken it more seriously. I mean, how the hell did they conclude the girls left of their own accord when all the evidence points to the contrary?"

"That's Detective Garner for you," she says. "He doesn't value women much. If it'd been one of his pals who'd gone missing, he'd throw everything at finding them. He's just a revolting person. It wouldn't surprise me if there was no investigation at all. He probably just spent his time up here drinking with his sheriff buddy."

Wind rattles the windows. It sounds like it could break through if it gets any wilder out there.

Eva worries about her new companion. If Dean gets lost on one of the trails, he could die. But she knows not to suggest he waits for morning and daylight. *She* wouldn't.

"Take my hat, gloves, and scarf."

Dean raises his eyebrows. "They're not pink, are they?"

She snorts. "Do I look like a pink kind of girl? They're still on the floor from when we got back." She thinks he would've used them whatever color they were. That's how cold it looks out there. "What about Rocky. Does he need a dog coat or something?"

"Are you kidding?" He smiles. "Rocky's from New Hampshire. He was made for this weather."

Rocky barks, excited to be leaving the room. He follows Dean to the door.

Dean turns back to look at her. "See if you can find anything in Hannah's diary. I didn't get through much of it."

"I'm on it." She picks up the diary from the end of her bed and leans back with it. She pulls out an empty page and writes her number down for him. "Before you go," she throws him her phone and the piece of paper. "Put your cell number in my phone so I can keep track of you, and add my number to yours. If I don't hear from you in an hour, I'm coming out there."

He looks surprised as he does what she says. "You must be concussed if you're voluntarily giving me your number."

She laughs. She knows she's been pretty hard on him but actually, he seems okay. Genuine even. He passes her phone back to her and she puts it on charge. "Don't use the flashlight on your phone too much, you'll drain your battery. And tell the front desk I need coffee. Lots of it. None of that decaffeinated crap, which should be illegal by the way."

Dean smiles. "Remember, as soon as you've got your room service order, lock this."

He and Rocky leave.

CHAPTER TWENTY-TWO

Location unknown

Hannah's woken by the pain in her legs. The chains that shackle her leave little room to change position. She keeps getting pins and needles and her skin is terribly bruised both below and above the chain.

She doesn't know how long it's been since her abductor last visited, only that it was when Jodie was still here. She's hoping for another day free of him. She's become numb to the conditions here because she sleeps most of the time. It's been about twenty-six days since she was taken. Almost four long, painful weeks.

When she isn't asleep, she talks to the rats. Sometimes they stop scurrying around and look at her as if they're listening. Or maybe she's imagining it. What isn't her imagination is how one of the rats is visibly rounder lately. Hannah thinks she's pregnant. She doesn't dare think about the consequences of that.

Her captor usually leaves behind bottles of water but only scraps of food. Dry bread and cereal bars mainly, which Hannah rations until his next visit because she never knows how long he'll be gone. Last time he left a chocolate bar, but he'd smeared it with rat droppings while they watched. It took a long time before she was desperate enough to eat it. Jodie had point-blank refused, but she had more fight than Hannah. She was determined to get out of here, and she did.

In the end, Hannah figured the rat droppings might kill her sooner than the man who brought them here, and that would be a blessing at this point.

Now, however, she's out of food and her stomach won't let her forget it. She sits up and stretches her back as much as she can, to get her blood flowing. Both her legs are dead. She doubts they'll ever work properly again after being shackled for so long, but she does daily muscle stretches to try to be ready should the opportunity to escape ever present itself. Her ankle is chained like Jodie's was, and there is only just enough length to the chain for her to reach a bucket he left for them to empty their bowels into. She's needed to do that less and less as the days wear on.

She checks under her makeshift bed for the chainsaw. She didn't want him finding it while she was asleep so she pushed it behind her, as far under the pile of empty boxes as she could. She pulls it closer to her now and rests against it. To know she has a possible means of attack is comforting.

The next hour goes slowly as she listens to the sound the rats make nearby, chewing through wood. They're making so many gaps in the walls that she's feeling the cold more and the wind has pushed a lot of snow underneath. It almost reaches her.

The man stripped her of her ski jacket last time he was here, for no other reason than wanting to see her suffer in the cold. She can see it slung over an old cabinet in the corner opposite her. She still has her gloves, hat and, scarf as well as the jeans, T-shirt, and hoody she's wearing, but she'd give anything for that jacket right now.

Still, she's grateful he didn't strip her completely. He's never tried to molest her either. If he does, she knows she'll go insane. She can't bear looking at him so she wouldn't be able to cope with him touching her. If he ever tried to kiss her, she knows she'd throw up.

He seems to enjoy watching them suffer. He enjoyed tying them up tightly and leaving them cold and starving out here in the middle of nowhere, and he gets visibly excited when he burns them with a cigarette lighter. Hannah looks at the burn marks all over her legs where the flame burned through her denim jeans and blistered her skin. They itch like crazy and she can feel the blisters seeping some days.

When he crouches next to her with the lighter in his hand and a menacing smile, she cries. There seems to be no reason for him to do these things other than to torture them. There's something seriously wrong with the man and she knows that if she ever makes it out of here alive, she'll see him in her nightmares for the rest of her life.

He was worse to Jodie because she gave him too much attitude. On their first day here, they were begging for their lives and saying they'd do whatever he wanted if he let them go. That was their first mistake; assuming he wanted to use them for sex. Thankfully, he couldn't be less interested in them for anything sexual.

Once Jodie figured out he'd never let her go and she couldn't manipulate him, she mercilessly teased him instead. She mockingly asked if he grew up without any friends and whether he still slept in his mother's bed. She'd told him that all serial killers are mentally ill and have secret fantasies about their mothers.

Hannah had tried to stop her but Jodie said she knew what she was doing.

The man had made her pay for it. Hannah closes her eyes tight, not wanting to think about what he did to Jodie while all she could do was sit by and watch, utterly helpless.

She falls asleep again. She dreams of her friend from back home in England. Katie Sewell. The girl who died. Hannah still misses her terribly and she knows Katie would never have left her alone here like Jodie did. She realizes that, if Katie had never died, she'd never have moved to the US in the first place and none of this would be happening.

Maybe she should've died with Katie back then. It would've been better than this horrific existence.

"Wake up. Now."

Hannah's confused. She feels a hard kick to her leg. Right where the chain is. The pain from the metal digging into her sores makes her go dizzy.

"I said, wake up. NOW!"

She quickly wakes and realizes her deranged captor is looming over her. He slaps her hard across the face, making her ear ring.

"Where is she?" he shouts, his spit hitting her face. "Where is she?"

Hannah starts crying because she knows he likes that. It soothes him. "She got away when I was asleep. I didn't see her leave. But she hasn't been gone long," she lies. "You can probably still catch her! If you're quick!"

He looks at the dried bloodstain around the spot where Jodie was shackled. "How did she get out of it?"

"I told her not to go," she weeps. "I tried to get her to stay with us!"

He turns his back on her as he inspects the floorboards and the chain, trying to figure out how Jodie got away.

Hannah sees an opportunity. A burst of hope fills her chest as she allows herself to consider escaping.

With trembling hands, she quietly turns and reaches behind for the chainsaw. She manages to pull it in front of her without him hearing. Before she pulls the cord, she has to build up the courage for what she's about to do. She could be responsible for this person's death and she doesn't know how she feels about it. But she can't bear the thought of dying out here with him.

She waits for him to turn back to face her so she can watch the chainsaw slice through his neck.

As he slowly turns and leans in, he repeats the question. "I said, how did she—"

He notices what she's holding just as Hannah pulls the chainsaw's cord. The machine screams into life, but Hannah screams louder. He reaches for the saw, blocking her, but Hannah manages to push the blades toward his face and feels his blood mist her hands.

Her captor has fast reactions. He moves his head back before grabbing the chainsaw from her. His face only has minimal damage. A large flap of skin droops over one of his eyes. Blood oozes down his face, but slowly. If it was faster, she might have some hope that his wound would kill him.

The chainsaw falls silent.

He screams at her over and over without forming words. His blood and spittle hit her in the face.

All hope is lost. She's failed at her one chance. She realizes she's going to die here after all.

When he's done screaming, he hits her across the head with the chainsaw's handle. The pain stuns her, making her vision blurred. She's surprised he doesn't slice her head off. But that would be a blessing for her, and he wouldn't want that.

He leaves without another word.

"Run, Jodie! RUN!" she shouts after him. "He's right behind you!"

Dazed, it takes Hannah a while to remember that it's been around eleven days since Jodie escaped.

CHAPTER TWENTY-THREE

Lone Creek, Colorado

Detective Garner arrives in Lone Creek just as the storm worsens. His windshield wipers can barely keep up with the heavy snowfall and the wind is howling through the closed car windows. He has the heat turned up as high as it will go but he still feels chilled.

He can't believe Travis stole Shirley's car in this weather. God only knows what state it will be in by now. He half expected to pass it on the road, upturned and smoking in a ditch. Maybe that would've been a blessing.

Garner knows Travis will be here and it makes him feel sick to think about it. He doesn't want to know what his son is up to. He just knows he has to take him home before he goes too far. There must be a reason he was so keen to get to the lodge. A new plaything to excite him, maybe.

Not for the first time Garner thinks about hightailing it out of there and starting over on his own, someplace warm like Hawaii. He doesn't know why he stays with Shirley and Travis. He doesn't love them anymore.

But he can't help feeling he owes them. Plus, he's onto a good thing with the casino, so he doesn't want to have to leave that behind. If only Travis could disappear somehow. It would be easier to divorce Shirley if Travis was out of the picture. He loved her once and he can't bring himself to leave her trapped with their son forever. Even though she seems oblivious to what Travis is really capable of. She's able to see her beloved child underneath his ugly exterior.

Garner can't. Not anymore.

The windy road that leads up to the Winter Pines Ski Resort is treacherous, but it's a road he's traveled hundreds of times because it's his family's lodge. It was left to him and his two brothers when their parents passed away twenty-odd years ago. Garner hates it. It killed his parents by constantly bleeding them dry of money. They had to work hard every day of their lives to keep it open. He watched them run themselves into the ground trying to make it profitable, but it never was. It only ever broke even at best.

His younger brother, Todd, died out on the slopes when he was only thirty-two years old. Garner's still not sure what happened there. He just knows there was a lot of blood on the slopes that day. Whether it was an accident or something else, he'll never know, and he has no interest in finding out. The coroner, an old school buddy of Garner's, ruled it an accident as a favor to Garner and his older brother, Sandy. They didn't want it going down in history as anything else. And Sandy didn't want the bad press for the business. He's just like their parents: trying to keep a resort open that should've failed years ago.

Not many people in McArthur know of Garner's history with this place. At work, only Chief Carson knows he part-owns it and that's only because they've known each other for over thirty years. Carson knew Garner's parents and he's stayed here many times for free. As for anyone else in the department, he's never told them, and McArthur is far enough away from Lone Creek for people not to find out through local gossip. He's ashamed of the place. Under its sparkling, Christmas card veneer, it's crumbling around them and Sandy's just wasting his life here.

The vehicle's headlights struggle to cut through the snowfall. Garner thinks about the casino. He's a silent partner. Lloyd Peterson and two others run the place day-to-day. Lloyd runs the side of the business that handles the drugs so that, if they're ever caught, Garner won't be held accountable and lose his job. But Garner does have some dealers working for him. He has Leroy and Patrick discreetly selling drugs to guests at the lodge.

His thoughts turn to Eva Valdez. She and Sergeant Roberts don't know about his link to the resort and it's why Garner didn't want her coming up here. She'll just read something into it because she has it in for him. He doesn't want to bump into her while he's here, so he intends to find Travis as quickly as possible and leave unnoticed. He figures Valdez will probably just be propping up the bar for her whole stay, crying about 'perfect' Frank Morgan. Frank was nowhere near perfect and, when all's said and done, he's glad Frank died. It's no great loss and one day he might even tell Valdez that.

His cell phone rings. He tries to answer it while keeping his eyes on the road and his left hand on the steering wheel. He has to concentrate.

"Garner here," he says.

"Have you found him?" asks Shirley.

He sighs. "Give me a chance, I'm not even there yet! The weather's slowing me down."

She says something else but the signal's bad so he can't make it out.

"What's that?"

She tries again but he still can't hear her. While he's distracted the car almost misses a bend and he barely avoids steering off the side of the road into the woods seventy feet below.

"Shit!" He throws his phone onto the seat next to him and shouts, "You're distracting me and I can't hear you. Hang up."

He doesn't wait to see whether she does or not. He pushes ahead through the weather. He's always hated the long drive up to the lodge. It feels like a drive through his past. That's partly why he doesn't come up here much anymore. Years ago, Shirley used to spend a lot of time here helping his brother with the housekeeping and cooking, trying to keep costs down. She was as convinced as Sandy was that it could be a nice little earner for them, and she was good at helping out.

But that meant Travis had to entertain himself. He was home-schooled after trying to burn his school down. No other local school would take him. The lodge became his playground and the employees his playthings.

Garner's not sure how much Shirley knows about what their son gets up to during all his spare time. She wasn't with Garner when he walked in on Travis tying up a seven-year-old girl in one of the empty guest rooms a few years back. But he thinks she turns a blind eye so she doesn't have to admit it to herself. That's what he does, anyway.

After all, what are they supposed to do? He can't exactly report Travis to the police. There would be a criminal investigation into his son and Garner would probably be suspended from his job while it was ongoing. If they realized what Travis is capable of, Garner would be let go, probably with no pension. That's if they didn't lock him up alongside his son. Garner would be ridiculed and he'd lose everything. And for what?

He had walked in at the right time and untied the girl. She was unharmed. She'd only been there an hour. It's not like his son's a serial killer. He just gets his kicks out of scaring kids, probably because he had no friends growing up. He doesn't know what he's doing is wrong. He's not wired like everyone else.

Garner had told Travis not to do it again and appeased the girl with some candy so that she wouldn't tell her mom. After all, isn't that what a good father should do for his son — protect him?

The wind tries hard to force his car off the road just as he finally reaches the long driveway that leads to the lodge.

He slows to maneuver some broken branches in his path and, as he does, one of the biggest trees on the ascent starts creaking loudly. Garner watches it in his rearview mirror as a long, thick branch breaks from it and falls sideways, across the narrow road behind his car. It misses by inches. That will stop him from leaving anytime soon.

He punches the steering wheel. "Dammit!"

He's probably going to have to stay the night now. It's too dangerous out here tonight to risk trying to move it. Sandy can move that and the others with the snowcat early tomorrow. It's going to be harder to avoid Valdez now though. She'll probably accuse him of stalking her if she sees him. He'll have to stay in his room, order room service and keep an eye on his son, if he can find him. If not, Travis might figure out she's a cop and stay out of her way. Garner hopes so.

CHAPTER TWENTY-FOUR

The vehicle's tires creep over the compacted snow as Garner watches the lodge reveal itself ahead. Lights shine brightly in some of the second-floor windows, which means they might make some money this winter if the rooms are starting to fill. Garner doesn't care though; he gets enough money from his casino. If it was up to him, he'd torch this place and claim the insurance. He'd happily share the payout with Shirley on the condition she takes the money and Travis while he gets to leave. For good.

He parks near the entrance to the lodge. As he gets out of his car, he spots Shirley's dark blue Ford discarded at the rear of the parking lot. He can tell it was parked by Travis as it isn't anywhere near straight.

He thinks he hears a dog barking in the distance. He can't believe someone would voluntarily go for a walk in this weather. His unsuitable leather work shoes glide over the snow. As he enters the lobby, the heat from the fire hits him and he wishes he could enjoy it. But he has to find his son.

He spots Olivia at the front desk. She doesn't disguise her contempt as she notices his arrival. He wishes Sandy would fire her ass. She's just another ghost from his past.

"What are you doing here?" she asks.

"I own the place, remember?"

She rolls her eyes. "Sandy's in the office."

"You need to tell your guests there'll be no getting out of here tonight. Road's blocked with a big-ass branch. I wouldn't be surprised if the rest of the tree comes down too."

She raises her eyebrows. "How will I get home?"

Garner sighs. He can't believe he had a relationship with this woman once. Until she turned crazy on him. "You have legs, don't you? You only live twenty minutes away."

She's quick to anger. "That's twenty minutes in a *car*, not on foot and in this." She gestures outside.

"Fine, help yourself to a room for the night."

Incredulous, she says, "I can't. I have three kids, remember? You should do, considering one of them is yours. Besides, if I stay here, I might vanish into thin air like the others."

Garner doesn't take the bait. They have a lot of history together and he knows she'll work here until either the place folds or she dies. He needs to find a way to get along. "Fine. Leave early if you want. Is there anything left to do today?"

She's surprised at his change in attitude and he knows she can't resist his offer.

"No," she says. "We waved off a group of Canadian tourists earlier this afternoon. I just need to check the housekeeping schedule and see what state their rooms are in but, to tell you the truth, we're not operating at full capacity, guestwise or employee-wise. So it's not exactly busy around here."

He nods. "Fine. Get going as soon as you're done. Wrap up warm. It's even colder than usual out there." He heads to the office just around the corner from the front desk. Maybe his brother knows where Travis is.

Sandy's even less happy to see him than Olivia was. He's sitting in their mom's favorite armchair, by the small log fire. He has a laptop perched on his knees as he stares at a spreadsheet. He's always trying to make the numbers add up, just like Mom had tried to. Garner spots the bottle of rum next to him.

"Well, well, well. The prodigal son returns," says Sandy.

"Still trying to make the finances work?" asks Garner, trying hard to keep things civil. He could do without an argument tonight.

"Someone has to. This is my livelihood. Unlike you, I don't live in the pocket of town officials who are happy to advance my career. And income."

Garner sees red. Sandy always knows how to hit the right nerve. It's funny how only family can do that so well.

"Listen, I'm not here for an argument. I've got enough problems already. I'm here for Travis. Have you seen him?"

Sandy's face darkens. "Why would he be here? I've told you before he shouldn't be here without you. Unless he wants an honest job, of course. In which case, he'll be welcome. I could put him to work immediately. Teach him the ropes."

Sandy doesn't know what Travis gets up to here because Garner has never told him. Sandy's too busy taking care of the place to notice what goes on right under his nose. Some of the employees have complained before about Travis lurking and watching them. But miraculously, no one has ever made a formal complaint or, God forbid, called the police. Not yet anyway.

Garner doesn't want to think about the employees who quit with no notice or disappear without their belongings. He's not responsible for them. He can't even keep tabs on his own son. He thinks of the two girls who recently vanished. But he's not ready to let his mind go there yet. They probably skipped town with the paranormal guys. He'd found nothing to suggest they were taken against their will. Leaving their belongings behind doesn't mean anything.

Today's kids live in a throwaway society where everything's replaceable. He'd bet they're living it up in California by now and are too scared to tell their parents. One of them was a runaway and probably a bad influence on the British girl.

"One of your co-workers is here," says Sandy. "She said her name's Eva."

Garner sighs. "I know. I'm avoiding her. Just don't be too helpful or bend over backward for her. She's got it in for me."

Sandy looks surprised. "Really? I like her. She seems nice. Intelligent."

"Whatever. Have you told her we're related?"

"No. I didn't think you'd want me to, since you're so ashamed of this place. Maybe if you were proud of the business, we'd be more successful. It wouldn't hurt for you to help out around here once in a while and promote it to your many acquaintances."

"Hey, I do help out," he says. "I've pumped plenty of money into this dump."

"Sure," says Sandy. "And you resent every single cent."

"It's wasted money, that's why."

Sandy takes a sip of his drink. "Take a seat, Alan. We need to talk."

Sandy pours him a straight rum, no ice. They've always had the same taste in liquor.

It warms Garner's chest as he downs it but he doesn't take a seat. "Is it about this place?" he asks.

"This place isn't going to last much longer." Sandy looks up at him. "The building's falling apart quicker than I can repair it and we rarely get return guests anymore. But that's not what we need to talk about. Why would Travis be up here, alone? Where's Shirley?"

Garner sighs. He sometimes wishes he could confide in his brother about his concerns about Travis, but he'd be horrified, especially if he found out about that girl Travis tied up on the premises. Sandy's not a cop so he doesn't see the daily reality of how bad people really are. If he accepted everyone had a bad streak, he might help Garner manage Travis. But Sandy lives in a ski lodge where everyone's happy because they're on vacation. They've left their problems and their secrets back home.

It must be a nice life for him.

"He stole Shirl's car. You know what he's like; he loves this place because he spent so much time here as a kid."

"But where does he go?" asks his brother. "I never bump into him on these little adventures he has. You'd think he'd visit his uncle while he's here."

It's true that Travis likes Uncle Sandy. Sandy always had more patience with him, and he really thought Travis would work here when he graduated. But Travis didn't graduate. He just withdrew from everything and pursued his own interests. They don't even get together as a family for Thanksgiving or Christmas anymore. There's too much tension because of the lodge, with Sandy believing Garner doesn't pull his weight and Garner believing Sandy should sell up and get out. But also because Garner's embarrassed for his brother to see how odd Travis has become.

"I don't know what he's thinking or doing when he's here. He's not right, Sandy." Garner helps himself to another rum and shakes his head. "That kid's not right." He's on the verge of spilling everything. It's a lot for one person to cope with and it's going to come out sooner or later.

Sandy stares at him. "He's your *son*, Alan. Sure, he's different and he's reclusive at the moment. He needs to make some friends. Hell, he needs a girlfriend, or a boyfriend. That would change everything for him."

Garner shakes his head. "No. He's not interested in anything like that. He doesn't like being touched. He's started wearing gloves at home so he doesn't make physical contact with anyone. A new symptom of his weirdness."

Sandy's shocked. "I hadn't realized things were getting so bad. He needs help, Alan. Take him to your doctor and get another psych evaluation. He needs a second, or even a third opinion. You could stop it from getting any worse. Maybe they'd prescribe something that could help him?"

Garner downs another drink and places his empty glass on the side table. "It's too late for that. They don't prescribe medication for what Travis has."

"But—"

Garner cuts him off. "I've got to go find him. Oh, and there's a huge branch down on the road outside. It's blocking us off. I wouldn't be surprised if there are more down by now too, maybe the whole tree."

Sandy runs a hand through his hair. "Dammit. Think it can be moved with the snowcat?"

"I don't know, it's a big son of a bitch. Anyway, I'll help you in the morning, but me and Travis are going to have to stay here tonight. Is my usual room okay?"

Garner used to come here with various different women until Olivia told his wife. Shirley threatened to leave him, which would've meant it would just be him and Travis at home. That was a risk he wasn't willing to take. So he tries to be more discreet now by keeping his lady friends away from Olivia's prying eyes whenever he can. The casino's good for that.

"Probably," says Sandy. "It's not like we're full. But check with Olivia."

"I've sent her home. She was whining about not being able to drive back because of the roadblock so I told her if she set off walking now, she'd be fine."

His brother shakes his head. "You should've gone with her. That's a long walk in the dark for a woman on her own, especially in this weather."

An almighty crashing sound makes them jump. The lights in the office flicker before cutting out.

Sandy jumps up from his seat. "We've been hit by something."

"Sounds like another tree. Got any flashlights?"

"In the store cupboard next to the front desk."

They open the office door and are confronted by darkness.

"Looks like the power's out everywhere," says Garner.

"Great. I'll sort this out. You find Travis. He used to be afraid of the dark."

Garner snorts at the irony. Now the dark is afraid of him.

CHAPTER TWENTY-FIVE

Dean smiles to himself at the irony of how he was missing the cold New Hampshire winters when he was in Vegas. He'd give anything for some hot sunshine right now. Even Rocky's slower than usual, trying to propel himself forward in the blizzard. Maybe he shouldn't have brought the dog out this time. Greg had told him Rocky should take it easy. But Dean thinks Rocky would probably prefer to keep having fun for as long as possible.

Rocky spots a small animal running through the trees and barks excitedly several times, although he doesn't run after it.

After leaving Eva's room Dean went to the front desk but there was no one there, just a sign saying *Be right back!* He didn't want to wait so he left a note with Eva's room service order: *any hot food and lots of coffee. Room 28.*

There weren't many guests walking around but he could hear music and laughter coming from the bar and restaurant area. There's nothing else for the guests to do tonight but eat and drink.

Dean didn't pass anyone as he left the lodge and headed toward the trail. At one point he heard what sounded like a tree crashing down somewhere in the distance, and he wondered whether to head back rather than risk being hit by a falling tree. But Rocky was way ahead of him at that point.

The cold is bitter against his face so he pulls Eva's hat low, over his eyebrows. Once they reach the part of the trail that's thick with trees, the wind pulls back, unable to reach them. They're protected from the thickest snow too, although they have to dodge what's falling from the canopy. They've almost reached the spot where Eva found the severed foot.

Dean slows to look around, not just for clothes or the other boot; he's looking for any outbuilding that could be hiding the girls. It's too dark to see very far ahead of him.

Realizing he's out of breath, Dean stops to take a break and check on Rocky. "Rocky? Come."

The dog sits next to him, panting. Dean rubs him all over to keep both of them warm. He can feel the snow dampening his shoes. He sighs, disappointed that he hasn't made it very far yet and may have to turn back because of the weather. He doesn't want to wait until morning, even though rationally he knows he's probably not going to find anyone out here tonight. But finding them tonight instead of tomorrow could be the difference between life and death.

Rocky's ears lift suddenly, and he stands up, looking back the way they came. He barks forcefully. Dean hears the snow crunching.

Someone's coming. He has his gun under his jacket and, thinking about what happened to him and Eva this morning, he touches it, ready.

"Who's there?" he shouts into the dark.

The crunching stops. Whoever it is heard him. Rocky barks louder. The crunching starts again and Dean can make out a figure walking toward them. He can't tell who it is because they're wrapped up head to toe in dark clothes.

Rocky runs up to the person and they stop to pet him. They shake their hood off and Dean recognizes Olivia.

"What are you doing out here?" he asks. "Surely you don't need a cigarette this bad?"

"This is my route home." She rubs her gloved hands together as she talks.

"You don't drive?"

"The road's blocked with fallen branches. We're trapped here." She gives a strange laugh that suggests she's been trapped here for years.

"We'll walk with you then," he says. "No one should be out alone tonight."

"You are," she says. "At least I have a reason."

He gives her a sideways glance as they walk. Rocky's closely following them. It's not as cold in the woods. "Tell me about the girls. What are they like?"

Olivia smiles. "They're lively and fun. Hannah was quieter than Jodie, more sensitive too. She wants to be a horror writer. She's into the paranormal and stuff. So am I, a bit. I like psychics and paranormal shows. But she reads about it too and wants to study it alongside writing. You'd think she'd be a goth with the things she reads and the music she listens to, but she's not. She's your typical girl next door, looks-wise. Jodie's more noticeable." She stops to take a deep breath before continuing. "Some people paint Jodie as the bad girl, but she's not. She's had a tough life and I defy anyone with her upbringing not to be looking for love in all the wrong places. Unfortunately, there are plenty of men ready and willing to take advantage of a vulnerable girl like her. That makes them the problem, not the girls."

Dean agrees. "I don't know if you looked at the photos from Hannah's camera but they suggest something bad has happened to them, Olivia. What do you really know about it?"

She stops. Dean notices tears on her face.

"What do I know? That's a joke. Everything's an illusion here. People come for a dream vacation but they end up leaving with nightmares. That's if they're lucky enough to leave at all." She turns to him. "You want to know what I've learned after living in Lone Creek all my life? I know the snow bleeds here, Mr. Matheson. I know there have been a lot of so-called accidents and people going missing over the years, and the police don't care. You can't blame them really, because no one knows whether they were suicides, murders, or worse."

He's taken aback. "What's worse than suicide or murder?"

She turns away and walks faster, shouting over the wind. "Your loved one vanishing. Having no body to bury. Never finding answers. That's worse than anything else."

Dean reaches out to stop her and then rests his hand on her back. "Olivia, I'm going to stay here until I find answers. I just hope that involves finding out what happened to Aaron too."

She breaks down. Dean hugs her to him.

Talking to her is frustrating because she clearly has some insight into what's going on at the Winter Pines Ski Resort, but she's emotionally trapped and too afraid to say, so she's talking in riddles. Maybe she thinks she'll get her son back if she toes the line. But she said it's already been eight years since Aaron went missing. How much longer would the people responsible make her wait?

Rocky barks to get Dean's attention. He's not doing well; he looks sluggish and cold. They need to get back.

"Let's get you home," he says to Olivia. "If it's okay with you, Rocky needs to get inside to warm up. We won't stay long."

She nods.

CHAPTER TWENTY-SIX

After walking the rest of the long, windy route in silence, Olivia leads them into the charming town. Everything looks like it's been designed with Christmas in mind. Twinkling lights and orange lanterns glow around them, and the whole place is covered in a white blanket of snow. Dean counts fourteen different stores in this part alone, the stock ranging from ski wear to fancy chocolates, with some stores boarded up with realtor signs outside.

A few dedicated shoppers are still out, browsing the store windows, but most of the stores are closing for the evening.

As he passes a street light, he notices a missing person poster for the girls. Only the top half remains and the ink in their photos has bled, fading their images. Olivia sees him looking at it.

"That's the last one. All the others were pulled down soon after they were put up. People don't like outsiders to know our town has itself a problem."

Dean looks at her. He can't believe no one here wants answers about the girls.

Olivia stops at some external steps that lead to an apartment over an outdoor clothing store. He follows her up and inside.

What Dean notices first about Olivia's apartment is the size — it's small — followed by the mess. Clothes and toys cover the floor. Still, the apartment is warm and he feels his hands slowly coming back to life.

"Excuse the mess," says Olivia. "The kids spend a lot of time alone and I'm usually too tired to clean up when I get home from that place."

He smiles. "Listen, it's warm. That's all we need."

Three children appear from one of the two bedrooms: two young girls and an older boy. They stare at Dean for a few seconds and then he's instantly forgotten for Rocky, who's already found a warm spot in front of an electric heater.

The two girls run over to him and, without waiting to find out whether he's friendly, they launch at his neck and hug him tight. Rocky wags his tail and then collapses onto his back so they can rub his stomach. The boy joins them. Rocky hasn't been around kids much, not since young Emily Gordon was his playmate, but he's gentle with them. Dean finds himself wondering how Emily's doing these days. She was about the boy's age when her mom died. He keeps meaning to reach out to her but he's worried he'll remind her of what happened to her mother.

"Can I get you a drink?" says Olivia. "Whiskey? Hot chocolate? Irish coffee?"

Dean smiles. "Hot chocolate would be great, thanks. I won't stay long. I just need to send a few messages."

Olivia disappears into the kitchen and Rocky's content with the kids around him, so Dean sits on the couch and texts Eva.

Too cold to do much and we had a diversion downtown. Heading back soon. Order me and Rocky something hot from the kitchen.

He looks at the TV. The news channel is flashing up weather warnings for their area. Looks like the storm is only going to get worse over the next twenty-four hours.

His phone buzzes in his hand. Detective Jones is calling him. Dean doesn't want to ignore him, so he gets up to find

Olivia in the kitchen. "I've got to take this call. I hope you don't mind?"

Olivia hands him his drink. "Nope. I've got to start their dinner anyway."

He chooses a seat in the corner of the room, away from the kids who are still fussing Rocky and paying him no attention. Answering the phone, he says, "Hey, Jones. How are you?"

"You're a hard man to get a hold of. I've been trying all evening."

"We're in the middle of a blizzard with sub-zero wind chills according to the news right now. Cell phone coverage isn't great so I may lose you."

"No problem," says Jones. "I just wanted to update you on my visit with Lizzie Glover today. I hear Sheila told you I was going. Are you okay to talk?"

Dean hears Olivia banging around in the kitchen, so he knows she isn't listening. Still, he's not keen to hear what Jones has to say. "I am for now. How did it go?"

He hears Jones sigh.

"That bad, huh?"

"It was . . . strange," says his friend. "She's put on a lot of weight since we arrested her. I know by the time the lengthy trial had finished she looked different, but she's even bigger now. I guess she's got nothing else to do all day but eat. Well, that and talk to her shrink. She was calm too. She didn't seem agitated by seeing me again after all this time. I'd have thought she'd still be mad at me for helping you catch her."

"She's probably heavily medicated," says Dean. "That can cause weight gain too. Did she say why she finally accepted your visitor request?"

"Well, I'll get to that. We had an interesting talk. She said she knows what she did was wrong and she understands why she's locked up. But to tell you the truth, it felt like she was just paying lip service and repeating what she's heard her shrink tell her. There was no emotion behind any of it. She didn't show any remorse for her victims. But I wasn't there to break her balls and rehash it all; I was just interested in how she was getting along. I wanted to get a feel for what the officials were thinking more than anything. I don't want them falling for her crap and releasing her before she makes it into a proper cell."

"Right."

"And her main doctor, or psychiatrist, or whatever the hell they are, came in while I was there. You could tell he wanted to make sure I didn't upset her."

"Well, sure, I can understand that," says Dean, leaning back in the chair. "If you upset their patients, they're left to deal with the aftermath."

"Right. But I didn't like him at all. Kept putting his hand on her shoulder like some weird signal that he was there for her. Creepy. But I've never been to therapy so what do I know? That's probably how they do things. You should've seen her when he walked into the room. You'd think she was in love with him by the way her face lit up. Until she asked about you, anyway."

Dean's stomach flips. "What do you mean?"

"Well, Barbara thinks I shouldn't tell you this part because you'll just worry about it, but I think you can handle it." Jones snorts. "It's actually funny in a tragic kind of way."

Dean doesn't want to hear it. If he could politely end the call now, he would. He's moved on so much since she was convicted that he hasn't allowed her any space in his head. But now it feels like she's sitting in the same room as him. He swallows but doesn't say anything.

Jones continues. "I was getting up to leave, said thanks for seeing me, yadda yadda yadda, and then she looked at me all doe-eyed and teary. She said, 'Detective Jones, when is Dean coming to check me out of here?'" He laughs. "I mean, can you believe that shit?"

Dean's palms are sweating. "*Me*? Why would I check her out? I helped put her in there!"

"I know, right? Get this," Jones continues. "She said she's ready for the wedding and she's waiting for you to pick her up

149

to drive her to the church. She has her dress all picked out of a bridal magazine. The page was stuck to her wall with tape."

Dean doesn't want to ask but he can't help himself. "What wedding?"

"That's what I asked," says Jones. He hesitates. "She said she was going to be the new Mrs. Matheson. She genuinely appeared surprised that I didn't already know."

Dean leans forward and goes cold all over, despite the warmth in the small apartment. Rocky gets up and walks over to him, leaving the children disappointed.

"It's only then that I noticed the ring on her finger," says Jones. "It was a child's green plastic ring, like out of a Christmas cracker. She started fiddling with it, as if you gave it to her and it's the symbol of your damn love or something!"

Dean can't find the words to convey what he's feeling. He can't believe what he's hearing. He feels like he could vomit.

"Matheson?" says Jones. "Are you okay? Just remember she's in a secure psychiatric unit. She's there for a reason. She can't get to you."

He knows that, but he's still creeped out. He thought she would've moved on by now. How could she think he wanted to marry her? After everything she did to him and his wife. She's obviously still delusional. Whatever they're giving her in that hospital clearly isn't working, which is worrying.

"I'm fine," he whispers. "Did she say why she thought that?"

"No. Her doctor wrapped things up at that stage and then he had to rush off to see someone else so I didn't get a chance to speak with him. Don't let it bother you, Dean. I just wanted you to know she's clearly in the right place and if she keeps spouting things like that she'll be in there forever. Which, believe me, is a good thing."

He's right. She'll never be allowed out. Dean feels slightly better. Not knowing how to process what he's heard and wanting to change the subject as quickly as possible, he asks, "How's Barbara? Is she out tonight? Normally she's taken the phone off you by now."

Jones chuckles. "Yeah. Ironically, she's up at the secure unit. Ever since she found out I'm due to retire again soon she's been volunteering up there. In the mother-baby unit. It's like she doesn't want to spend any time with me."

Dean smiles. He remembers how Jones used to drive her crazy before he came out of retirement. Barbara used to be a midwife, so it makes sense she'd want to volunteer with babies. She's all heart, that woman.

"She's only doing it to help someone out for a month or two and initially she loved it," says Jones. "But she sometimes gets a little emotional over the women who can't take care of their babies. You know, the ones where CPS only let them see their babies once a week. Some of the women are so medicated they can't understand why their little ones are taken off them after the visit. And there are others who don't even remember having babies. It's tragic. But Barb's doing what she can to help them."

"Good for her."

"Yeah, except she's caught a bug up there and is fast coming down with the flu. I told her she should stay home and get some rest but you know what she's like. She says she's volunteered for admin duties while she's ill, so the babies aren't at risk of catching it. I just hope I don't catch it. I'm picking her up soon. Anyway, did you—"

Dean looks at his screen. The call has ended. He tries calling Jones back but he can't get a signal. He slips his phone into his pocket. "We better get back soon, Rocky." He sips his hot chocolate as Olivia's son tentatively approaches him.

"My mom says you're a cop."

Dean smiles at him. "I used to be a cop. Why, is that something you'd like to do?"

He nods.

"What's your name?"

"Dominic."

"Well, Dominic, if you want to be a police officer you need to work hard at school and start noticing everything that happens around you."

"You mean start watching people?"

"Kind of. If you notice something that looks suspicious, keep watching. But make sure people don't know you're paying attention. Bad guys don't like being watched, so you have to do it carefully."

"Okay. Will I get a gun?"

"You will."

"Have you got a gun?

"I have." Dean can tell Dominic wants to see it, but he's got to go. "That shouldn't be the only reason you become a police officer though."

"It's not," says the boy. "I'm going to find the baddies who took my brother. I want to stop Mom from crying. I'm going to make them bring Aaron home."

Dean doesn't know how to respond to that. He puts his hand on Dominic's shoulder and gives it a squeeze.

Dominic turns and sits in front of the TV as Dean takes his empty cup to the kitchen.

"Thanks for the drink. We're going to head back now. I want to make it back to the lodge before the storm gets any worse."

He sees four plates of sausages and oven fries lined up ready for the family's dinner. Olivia hands him a bag of cooked sausages.

"Sustenance for your walk back. You be careful out there."

"Thanks. They're Rocky's favorite. Look, if there's anything you think would help me find the girls, just give me a call." He writes his name and his cell number on the notepad hanging from her fridge. "No one would find out it came from you. I'd be discreet. I have that luxury because I'm not a cop."

She smiles wearily and he takes that as his cue to leave.

Once outside, Dean remembers he messaged Eva but he hasn't received a reply so he sends another one.

Everything okay? On our way back. Should be there in just under an hour.

The signal strength is so weak it won't send. He has to hope it'll get through while he's on the move.

Rocky's sniffing the bag in his hand so he digs out a sausage for him and then puts Eva's hat and gloves back on. The kids wave from the window and he can hear them shouting, "Bye, Rocky!"

"Come on, boy. Let's get back."

CHAPTER TWENTY-SEVEN

When Dean and Rocky finally make it back to the lodge, the snow is drifting into the entrance, filling the corners of the doorway. It's so heavy Dean had to light some of the way back with his cell phone. The battery gave up as they made their way through the parking lot.

It's warm in the lodge. His face tingles as the blood returns. Rocky veers straight for the fireplace. Dean follows him and warms his hands. He suddenly realizes the fire is the only light source. He looks around. Nothing's on, not even the TV over the front desk. The power must be out everywhere. There are no employees to be seen.

He carefully makes his way to the staircase, trying not to bump into anything. "Rocky!"

Rocky follows as they head upstairs in the dark. The hallway to his room is pitch-black with no emergency lighting, just the fire exit signs are lit. They have backup batteries for this scenario. He feels his way along the wall until he reaches what he thinks is Eva's door. He knocks, not wanting to just walk right in. There's no answer.

"Eva? It's Dean."

Rocky starts pawing at the door. Dean tries the handle. It opens. He'd told her to lock it after him.

"Eva?"

He pushes the door open and Rocky runs inside with a bark. He loudly sniffs the room, nose to the carpet.

Dean can't see much but he quickly notices a bad smell. It could be the leftovers of her room service. He walks to the side of the bed where she was resting when he left, to see if she fell asleep, but he can tell it's empty because there's no one under the bedspread.

He finds her cell phone plugged into its charger on the nightstand and tries to operate it. It didn't charge fully but there's enough juice left to run the flashlight. It takes his eyes a few seconds to adjust after he switches it on. He shines it around the room, trying to see if she's sleeping somewhere else. But the room's empty.

"Maybe she's gone to help sort the power," he mutters. He doesn't think Eva would sit and do nothing if she thought the guests would be scared or at risk of hurting themselves in the dark.

Rocky jumps up on the bed and starts barking. As Dean spins around to see what he's barking at, the flashlight illuminates a large pool of blood that covers half the bedspread.

Alarmed, Dean shouts, "Rocky, get down!"

Rocky drops to the floor as Dean leans in for a closer look. Blood spatter covers the headboard too.

He tries not to panic but it's clear something terrible has happened to Eva. He draws his weapon and runs to the door to lock himself in while he considers the options.

He opens Eva's phone to see whether she contacted anyone after he left. It's not protected with a code or password, which surprises him. The last call she made was to someone listed as *Sgt. Roberts*. Dean doesn't remember her mentioning her sergeant before, only Detective Garner, so he doesn't know if this is someone she trusts.

He opens her web browser and finds three open tabs, each one showing a different newspaper article about a guy called Officer Frank Morgan. They say he was killed in the line of duty. This must be the cop Eva mentioned briefly.

But what's this got to do with the blood? He skims the first article.

Officer Morgan is survived by his wife, Detective Eva Valdez, also from McArthur PD. She declined to comment. They had no children.

His shoulders drop. "Oh, Eva." She lost her husband. And recently. The articles are all dated the end of November. Why didn't she say anything? And why is she back at work so soon?

But Dean knows why. When he lost his wife, he only took a little over a week off work. Once the funeral was over, he needed something to distract him from the pain and shock of what had happened. He thought it would do him good to throw himself into an investigation, but returning so soon meant he couldn't do his job properly and he put people in danger, most of all himself.

He looks at the blood on the bed. Could Eva have been overwhelmed with grief and self-harmed? Some cops do it to cope with the stress of the job. Add to that a recent bereavement and it would be heartbreaking, but understandable. Dean's annoyed with himself for leaving her alone. He shines the light at the blood spatter again.

No. If it was caused by a self-inflicted wound she'd still be here, dead or dying.

Someone's hurt her.

He brings up Sergeant Roberts' number on her phone and calls it before he can worry about whether or not this person is someone Eva trusts. The signal is stronger here than when he was at Olivia's. The phone rings just once before it's answered.

"Valdez?" A male voice answers.

"Is that Sergeant Roberts?" asks Dean.

"Who is this? And where's Eva?" The man's tone changes immediately.

"My name's Dean Matheson. I'm a private investigator working for the family of Hannah Walker. Eva and I have been working together but she's gone missing."

He hears Roberts switch his TV off and drop the remote control. "Whoa, back up. Where are you calling from?"

"I'm staying at the Winter Pines Ski Resort, with Eva. When we realized we were both here for the same reason, we started working together. But earlier today we were attacked out in the woods, on the property, and Eva was hit harder than me but doing okay. I left her in her hotel room and when I got back, she was gone, and her bed's covered in blood." He takes a breath. He's probably not making a lot of sense.

"Okay, I'm coming up there," says Roberts. "I can be there in a couple of hours."

Dean shakes his head. "You won't be able to reach us. The storm's so bad here that I've heard there are trees or branches down, blocking the roads. Bring a team as soon as it clears, and I'll keep you updated while I still have a working cell phone."

Roberts hesitates. "Listen, I don't know you from Adam, and for all I know you're the one who's hurt her. How can I trust you?"

Dean sighs. "I used to be a cop. Contact Captain Brown or Detective Jones at Maple Valley PD in New Hampshire and they'll vouch for me. But in the meantime, as this could be a life-or-death situation, do you want to tell me what you and Eva were discussing tonight?"

There's a slight pause before Roberts replies. "Well, she didn't tell me she was attacked earlier, that's for sure, but that's typical Valdez. She was telling me she might have evidence the girls were abducted but she didn't want me to tell anyone in the department yet in case Detective Garner gets involved and shuts her down."

"What is it about him that bothers her so much?" asks Dean.

"Where do I start?"

"I don't have time to get into it now if it's a long story. Every second I spend talking to you is time away from finding Eva, and I suspect whoever has her also has the girls."

"Jeez, she's always getting herself into trouble."

"What's that?" says Dean.

"Valdez. She's always getting in trouble. She's like a dog with a bone."

That's a quality Dean admires in her and he would think her team would too, given she's a detective. "Look, if there's something you know that can help me find her, you have to tell me. She's told me Garner didn't give a crap about the girls when he was investigating the case. Could there be a reason why?"

"Possibly. I agree he's not trustworthy. Do you know about her husband?"

"Only what I've just read online. Killed in the line of duty. He must be the great cop she told me about."

Roberts scoffs. "Frank was an okay cop, I guess. But he wasn't as perfect as Eva thought he was. There's a lot she doesn't know."

Dean can't get into that right now. He needs to be out looking for her. He doesn't need to know about her private life. "We'll have to pick this up another time. I need to find her. Come up as soon as the roads are clear, but don't bring Garner. I get the impression he could be more of a hindrance."

"You got that right," says Roberts. "Keep me updated as much as you can. Are you armed?"

"Yes."

"Good. Use it if you need to."

"Roger that."

Dean hears something outside the door. Rocky runs over to it, sniffing the gap underneath. Whoever it is could've been listening into his conversation with Roberts. Dean silently walks to the door and grabs the handle, gun at the ready.

He swings it open and raises his weapon.

There's an almighty clamor and a woman screams. "Don't shoot! Don't shoot! It's room service!"

He can make out a young girl in the dark hallway, probably about nineteen, wearing a kitchen apron over her blue uniform. He looks at where the food and tray landed on the floor. Rocky devours what smells like mac and cheese. Dean's stomach growls with hunger.

"Well, it *was* room service," she says.

"Why didn't you knock?" he says. "What were you doing just hanging around?"

"I didn't know if I had the right room! It's so dark and I knocked the coffee over on the stairs so I don't even have your full order. Plus it's cold because the power's out so I couldn't keep it hot. I figured you'd rather have it a little warm than nothing at all. I'm sorry!"

Dean suddenly realizes Eva went missing before the room service order was noticed and delivered. Which means it wasn't anyone from the kitchen or front desk who took her. Whoever it was must've been watching them after they'd returned from being attacked earlier. It's got to be Leroy and his brother. Leroy had told them to watch their backs.

The girl looks at him. "Are you going to make a complaint? Please don't. They'll fire me. Or worse."

"What do you mean worse?"

"Well," she hesitates. "They could make me wait on Travis."

Dean frowns. "Who's Travis?"

They both turn in unison as someone runs up the stairs toward them.

CHAPTER TWENTY-EIGHT

Eva's exhausted. Her nerves are shot and she needs to eat before she passes out. Her body is operating purely on adrenaline right now, making her legs and hands shake.

As she runs up the stairs in the dark, all she can think about is how much trouble she's going to be in. She knows no one will have her back in this sorry situation and Chief Carson will probably use what she's done as an excuse to fire her. She misses a step in her haste and falls into the railing. Her ribs make contact with the wood and a shot of pain goes through her.

"Son of a bitch!" It wakes her enough to find her last ounce of strength to continue up the stairs, slower this time.

She stops as she reaches the top step because she hears a strange noise scurrying toward her, like some kind of over-sized spider. Goosebumps spread up her arms and she takes a step back as it nears.

Before she knows it, Dean's dog is all over her, licking her face and doing circles in excitement.

"Okay, boy, calm down. Jeez, anyone would think I was your mother."

"Eva? Is that you?"

She hears Dean at the end of the hallway so she heads toward him, relieved he's back. The dog runs alongside her, jumping up at her every fourth step. It's extremely annoying, or maybe adorable. She can't decide which.

Dean rushes toward her and shines a light in her face, then he frantically traces it over her body, front and back. He gently touches the back of her head and then looks at his fingers. "How the hell are you still standing?"

"What do you mean?" she says, trying to get rid of the light blindness from her eyes. "Aside from being ravenous, there's nothing wrong with me." She notices the girl. "Who's this?"

"I'm Laura, from the kitchen." The girl passes her, carrying a tray.

Eva's stomach growls. "Nice to meet you, Laura. I'm Eva. Is the kitchen still open?"

She stops. "We can't cook with anything that needs electricity but we have plenty of bread, soup, and canned goods in the pantry. Want me to rustle something up for you?"

"That would be amazing. I'll come down to the restaurant shortly. Give me everything you've got. And coffee. Definitely coffee. You've got a gas stovetop, I take it?"

"Sure have." Laura smiles. "I'll boil some water in a pan."

Eva grabs her arm before she leaves. "Make it a big pan."

Laura laughs. "No problem."

As she leaves, Eva turns back to face Dean. He's holding the flashlight downward now so she can see his face. He looks incredulous and stressed.

"What's the matter with you?" she asks.

"Eva! What the hell's going on? Where have you been? Whose blood is that on your bed?"

She realizes he must've thought it was hers and that's why he's acting weird. She's touched by his concern. She doesn't think anyone in her department would've been this worried about her in the same situation. Well, maybe Roberts.

"It's okay. It's not mine. Why? Is there a lot of it?" She walks past him and enters the room. "I can't see a thing. Where's my phone?" Dean hands it to her and she assesses the bed. "Whoa, he's a bleeder."

"Eva?" says Dean. "What happened here? I thought you were dead! I even called your sergeant to tell him about what happened earlier, and that you'd disappeared."

She panics. "You called Roberts? He's not coming up here, is he? We haven't found the girls yet and he'll take me off the case. There'll be an internal investigation into the shooting, and I'll be screwed. We can't let that happen because I know who took Hannah and Jodie!"

"Whoa! Slow down!" he says. "First of all, what shooting?"

Eva sits on the armchair opposite the bed and downs a shot of tequila, straight from the bottle. "Leroy. He's dead. The asshole came for me earlier. Anyway, I need to eat before I collapse. You must be hungry too?"

Dean looks shocked but he also looks ill. His face is alarmingly pale and he isn't cracking jokes. She reaches for his forehead. It's clammy, but when she touches his hands they're freezing cold. "Conditions are bad out there, huh?" she says as she rubs his hands to warm them.

"The worst. I need to eat too. I gave all the sausages to Rocky."

She doesn't know what he means about sausages and just hopes he's not delirious. She leads them both downstairs. "I'll explain everything as we eat."

The restaurant and bar are lit up with candles on every table and some battery-operated lanterns. A few other guests are at the bar talking to the young bartender, asking about the power cut. Eva overhears the bartender explaining Sandy and some others are in the basement, trying to find enough portable generators to keep the guests warm tonight. The furnace needs electricity to run so this place will turn cold fast.

She opts for a table for two next to the window and Dean sits opposite her. It's almost midnight now so they can't see outside. The darkness out there hides everything apart from their reflections in the glass. Eva thinks how the solitary candle in the middle of their table makes it look like they're out for a romantic meal.

162

"So tell me," says Dean. "What happened with Leroy? And where's his body? It wasn't where you shot him."

Laura comes over to them with two large mugs of steaming hot coffee. "I'll bring sandwiches in a minute. Do you both eat meat?"

They nod and their stomachs growl in unison. Laura heads back to the kitchen and Rocky sprawls on the floor, half under their table, leaning against Dean's legs.

"Keep a hold of the cup in your hands," she says. "You need to bring your temperature up. I can't have you flaking out on me, Matheson. Not now."

He does what she says, which makes her smile. Then she remembers what happened with Leroy and her stomach flips. Her hands haven't stopped shaking since she shot him, and that's not all down to having low blood sugar. He's not the first person she's shot in her role but it's never something to be proud of. She warned him, *twice*. He should have backed down. "He must've seen you leave because within minutes he was in my room," she says.

"I told you to lock up after me."

"I was going to, once my room service had been delivered."

"What did he do?" asks Dean.

Eva shudders. She's not sure whether it's because she's cold or because of the look she saw on Leroy's face.

"He said something lame like, 'I told you I'd get you, bitch.' And then he came for me. He was quick and I was drowsy. He flipped me over on the bed unbelievably easily, and he started tearing at my clothes. I was putting up a good fight, but he flipped me like I was a pancake, it was that easy for him. That guy was *strong*. I think it's because he was running on anger. I was genuinely scared for a minute there. Especially when he managed to undo my jeans while pinning me down."

A look of horror passes over Dean's face as he realizes where this is going.

"It was awful because I couldn't breathe. He was so heavy." She swallows, thinking about what could've happened

163

next. "He pushed my face into the pillow, digging his hands into my hair. When he felt the dried blood he must've wondered what it was because he was momentarily distracted, so I was able to reach for the heavy lamp from the nightstand. I swung it at him as I turned around. I heard the crunch as it broke his nose. It was incredibly satisfying."

Dean shakes his head. "I should never have left you alone. It's not like I achieved anything out there."

She takes a sip of coffee and it tastes amazing. It's still scalding hot but she doesn't care. "Listen, I'm a cop. These things happen. I don't need you or anyone else to rescue me, protect me, or whatever you want to call it. Risks like this come with the job and I'm okay with that. I wouldn't do it if I wasn't."

He looks at his coffee. "I know you don't need protecting. Doesn't mean I can't wish I hadn't left you alone."

She takes a deep breath. "Anyway, breaking his nose really must've pissed him off because that's when he pulled out a knife and stabbed me."

Dean looks up. "What? Where?"

"Just my arm. I've bandaged it. It stings but it's a shallow wound. I just need to keep changing the bandage, so it doesn't get infected."

Dean snorts. "Damn, I wish I worked with you all the time."

She feels herself blush.

"Is that why you shot him?" he asks. "Because he stabbed you?"

"No. He came at me with the knife again and I could tell he wasn't going to stop until I was dead. He had that crazed look in his eyes that drug addicts get, you know? He must've been high on something. That's when all the lights went out because of the power cut, so I managed to get away from him, into the bathroom. But he jammed his foot in the door before I could lock it. My gun was in the bathroom on the vanity, so I grabbed it and I warned him, Dean. I said if he didn't back down, I'd shoot him. The son of a bitch just laughed at me!

He was controlled purely by rage at this point." She lowers her eyes. "I warned him once more because he was getting in and I knew I couldn't hold the door forever. First, I fired a warning shot at the sink, and then everything went quiet. He released the door and I heard him take a few steps backward. I could hear his nose whistling from where I'd broken it. At that point I thought he was going to leave."

She takes another sip of coffee as her throat has gone dry.

"But when I opened the door, he lunged at me out of the darkness so I had to shoot. I had to assume he had the knife in his hand. I tried to shoot low, to just take out his leg or something, but I think I got his crotch."

Dean stifles a laugh. This wouldn't normally be a laughing matter but after the day they've had, she gets it.

"He fell back onto my bed and just stayed there, still. I tried to stop the bleeding and rouse him because, let's face it, it's easier when they don't die. Much less paperwork. But he must've bled out fast, judging by the bedspread. I must've hit an artery."

Dean looks her in the eye. "You were totally justified in shooting him. You gave him two warnings. What kind of idiot ignores that?"

"The kind who's used to getting his own way," says Eva. "The kind who thinks women are theirs for the taking and we'll just accept it."

"Where is he now?"

"In the bathtub. I packed him with ice from the machine on the first floor."

Dean looks surprised. "I guess with the power out, he'll stay cold for a while. But he can't stay there forever. Make sure you put the *do not disturb* sign on your door. The last thing we need is housekeeping walking in on that." He sips his coffee. "You know, this probably isn't the first time he's tried to rape someone. In fact, in her diary Hannah mentions how Jodie was lucky not to be assaulted by him."

Laura comes over and places two huge sandwiches in front of them, with potato chips and salad on the side. "We had a beef joint going cold," she says. "I've put in as much as I can. Also, I found some canned dog food for your dog and added some beef on top. Hope that's okay?"

Dean looks up at her. "He'll love it. Thanks, Laura. We appreciate it."

Eva watches as Laura puts the bowl down in front of the dog. He wags his tail as he eats.

"He's a noisy eater," she says before looking at Dean. "I agree that this won't be the first time Leroy has tried this with a woman. Which is why I'm convinced he took Hannah and Jodie. We just need to find where he took them."

Dean considers it. "You're probably right. But wouldn't Sandy or the rest of the team know what he was doing?" He takes his first bite of food and she can tell he's relieved to be eating.

"It's a small town, Dean. They protect their own. And they can't risk losing visitors by having scandals reach the papers. Everybody is complicit. They just want to keep their jobs and their livelihoods. But yeah, we obviously need to interview the employees next."

As she bites into her huge sandwich, her taste buds savor the flavors and she can't eat fast enough. They eat in silence for a while, stopping only to sip coffee.

"I walked Olivia home earlier," says Dean when he's finished. "She alluded to this place being trouble. She said there have been several disappearances here over the years."

Eva's eyes light up. "Maybe Leroy didn't just rape people. Maybe he was a serial killer?"

Dean finishes his sandwich and looks at her funny.

"What?" she asks.

"I'm sorry about your husband."

She suddenly feels sick as her appetite disappears. "How do you know?"

"I had to use your cell phone as mine was dead. I saw the articles you had open. What happened?"

She sits back in her chair, using a napkin to wipe her fingers. "All I know is that Frank got a call-out to a disturbance

166

at a convenience store. I was told he was stabbed by a junkie outside. That's where they found his body. By the dumpster, like a discarded piece of trash. No one told me until he was already in the morgue."

"*What?*" He frowns. "That's terrible. You should've been called to the scene. Have you checked the crime scene photos?"

She shakes her head. "There aren't any. Apparently, the camera malfunctioned after the photos and footage were taken. It wiped everything."

Dean's not buying it. "Can't they be recovered? Don't you have a digital forensics person for that kind of thing?"

She nods. "They said recovery was unsuccessful." Eva believes they either didn't try hard enough or they didn't want to recover them because someone was paying them not to. "To make matters worse, Frank shouldn't have attended the call-out alone. The cop he was partnered with wasn't feeling well. A sudden migraine, apparently. The supposed junkie was never found, and the surveillance tapes from the store don't cover the spot where it happened. It's all a mystery. One that's too convenient." She sighs. "But when I say that out loud the whole department turns against me."

Dean looks angry. "If you want me to, I can look into it. Once we finish here."

She looks at him, surprised and touched that he would offer to help her. "Thanks, I appreciate the offer. But you wouldn't be allowed access to anything you needed. Chief Carson would make sure of that. I have to find out for myself. Frank was a great cop and an amazing husband. I owe it to him to get answers."

And she will get those answers. No matter what it takes.

CHAPTER TWENTY-NINE

Garner's watching Eva in the restaurant. She's with a man he doesn't recognize. They look cozy. He's half tempted to go over there and ruin their dinner. But it's not worth the trouble and he still hasn't found Travis. He walks into the kitchen, looking for food. It's empty of employees apart from one pretty blonde girl he's only met once before, when he came up to investigate the missing girls. He can't remember her name. She's busy making sandwiches so she doesn't hear him approach.

He walks up behind her and leans in, pressing his body against hers. "Is that for me?"

She jumps against him which makes him laugh. He moves away.

"Why did you do that?" she says, clearly annoyed.

"I'm the owner of this place and I can do what I want. Just remember that. Technically I'm your boss."

Her manner changes from angry to worried. "Sorry. You took me by surprise. You can have it if you want?" she offers. "I can make more."

He takes the sandwich from her and eats as he talks. "How do you like working here?"

She hesitates to find the right words. He knows she probably wants to say she hates it here, but can't.

"It's okay, I guess," she says. "I like Sandy. He's a good boss. And the guests are nice. Usually. Sometimes we get good tips."

"But?"

She looks at him. "It's just a bit creepy. Especially in the dark like this. I'm scared of the dark."

He scoffs. "Aren't you too old to be scared of the dark?"

She turns away from him and goes back to buttering the bread. He rolls his eyes. Women are so easily offended these days.

"Well, if you need someone to stay with tonight, to keep the ghosts away, I'm in room eighteen. I can keep you warm during the power outage."

She glances at him, horrified. It pisses him off. She should be all over him if she wants to keep her job.

"I room with my friend who works here. We'll be fine." Then she adds, "Thanks," as if she realizes she shouldn't upset him.

"Whatever." He watches her work while he finishes the sandwich. She has a weird tattoo on her neck, under her ponytail. But she has great legs. They're curvy and slim. "Do you know someone called Travis?"

She looks up, grimaces, and then puts two and two together. Sandy must've mentioned to her at some point that Travis is his nephew. "Is he your son?"

"Yeah. You know him then?"

She turns away, but not before he notices the disgust on her face. He wants to backhand her for it but he has to remember he's a cop and he can't risk getting reported. Not that he thinks she'd tell anyone. She's meeker than a mouse.

"I've met him a couple of times."

"Yeah? What do you think? Is he someone you'd date?" he teases.

"I don't date men."

Garner's surprised. He would never have guessed. "Shame," he says. "You could've been my daughter-in-law. We could've been close."

169

She turns around fully and the terrified look on her face tells him he's gone too far. He's taking his anger for Travis and Valdez out on her.

"Shit, I'm just messing with you. I'm trying to find him. Know where he is?"

She relaxes. "I thought I saw the back of him earlier today. He was heading out of the lobby. He didn't look like he was wearing the right clothes to be out in this though. I almost ran after him with a coat but . . ." She stops.

"But you didn't want to talk to him, right?"

She slowly nods. "Sorry."

He puts his plate down. "I don't blame you, honey. Neither do I."

He turns around and leaves the kitchen. Viewing his son through the eyes of others is tough. If other people are noticing how odd he is, it's bad.

CHAPTER THIRTY

Olivia opens her front door to an unexpected caller. The wind almost tears the door from her grip as it blows wide open, but there's no one standing there.

"Great. Now I'm hearing things."

She closes it again and goes back to watching late-night TV, low, so the kids don't wake. Dominic is asleep under a blanket on the couch, and the girls are in their room. Her small heater is struggling to stay on as it keeps cutting out. She worries about the cost of their electricity bill this month and pulls a second blanket over her legs.

There's another knock at the door. She waits to see if it's just the wind playing tricks on her. It's followed by a much louder banging, which wakes her son.

"Mom?" he says, bleary-eyed. "Who is that?"

"Hush, don't wake the girls."

She struggles out of her seat and goes to the window, afraid to open the door again. Something about that knock feels menacing.

She can't see the doorway from the window so she's going to have to open the door. Maybe it's the private investigator, back with more questions. She likes him and what he's trying to do, so she opens the door.

As soon as she sees who's standing there, she knows she's made a big mistake. Possibly the last mistake of her life. She tries to slam the door shut, but it's too late. He's in. He pushes her backward and she falls down, onto the heater. Her hand sizzles as she reaches behind her and touches the metal bars that cover the exposed elements. The pain is instant.

She always feared this day with Travis would come. She suddenly regrets never leaving Lone Creek and finding a safer place for her children to grow up. But she didn't want to leave without Aaron. What if her boy returned one day and she wasn't here for him?

Dominic shouts at Travis and she's trying to stop herself from screaming out in pain. She's thinking of her girls. They don't come running to see what's happening, thankfully. She can picture them in their room, huddled together, scared.

"What do you want, Travis?" she says, trying to remain calm. The tremor in her voice gives her away. "Leave us alone! Haven't you done enough damage to our family?"

Travis stands dead still in the center of the room, in that hunched way of his. He looks like a man-reptile hybrid. His eyes dart around the room and his tongue emerges from his mouth occasionally. She's always thought he looks like he's never been through puberty, but the years are aging his body regardless. He has an old man's curved back and a severe, pointy nose.

She's never known what's physically or mentally wrong with him — even his parents don't know that — but she knows what he's capable of so she can't find any sympathy for him. Right now his face is all bloodied and a large flap of skin hangs over one of his eyes. Dried blood is smeared over his face. Whether it's a combination of his and someone else's, she doesn't know. She doesn't *want* to know.

This is bad. He's been on some sort of rampage. He must've finally snapped.

He looks at Dominic but speaks to her. "I saw you walking through the woods with that man earlier. Did you bring him here?"

Travis is going to assume she told the private investigator about him.

Her heart sinks and she cups her burned hand to her chest. It stings so bad she just knows it's going to weep for days.

She shakes her head. "I didn't tell him anything. He hasn't got a clue what's going on. Neither do I! He was just walking me home from work and then I asked him to leave."

He looks at her now and grins. It's not a nice grin. She can see the saliva forming in the corners of his mouth and wonders whether that's the last thing her son saw before he died. If Travis was humane enough to kill him, that is. She goes dizzy with the pain in her hand. Her skin is quickly blistering, filling with translucent pus. All she wants to do is run it under some cold water. She wonders whether she'll be alive long enough to visit the hospital. How she'll afford the medical bills.

"What was he doing here?" he asks with a sneer.

She panics. "He took a call! From, er, I don't know who it was from but it was nothing to do with you! It looked like he was given some bad news or something. He went all pale and miserable."

It's clear Travis doesn't believe her. He walks past Dominic who's standing in front of the couch where he was sleeping. Travis covers her son's face with his hand and shoves him backward as he passes. He enters the kitchen.

Olivia prays he isn't getting a knife. She gets Dominic's attention and whispers, "Get ready to run. Slip your shoes on quietly, now. Then head for the front door and don't look back. I'll find you."

He shakes his head. "I won't leave you."

Her heart breaks. "You need to get help. For me and your sisters. *Don't look back.*"

Dominic's eyes fill with tears and he silently nods, slipping his shoes on as quietly as possible. He has a sweater next to him on the couch and he pulls it over his head, tears silently spilling down his innocent cheeks. He looks at the front door. She can tell he's building up the courage to make a run for it. He's a good boy. If she can save even one of her children, that's better than nothing.

The thought brings a sob to her throat. *What will Travis do to her girls?*

Travis shrieks in the kitchen. He starts smashing things up.

"Go!" she shouts. Dominic takes his cue and stands up, but his legs must buckle beneath him from fear as he falls backward and has to try a second time. The short hesitation gives Travis time to notice what he's about to do as he returns from the kitchen. Travis grabs Dominic.

"What's this?" he shouts at her.

In his other hand, he's holding the notepad from the fridge. It has the private investigator's name and number on it.

Her heart sinks. She knows it's all over now. For all of them.

"That's my landlord's number."

His black eyes glow with hatred. "Your landlord has the same name as the man staying at my dad's lodge. It's him, isn't it? The cop."

He must've checked the guest list at the lodge. She didn't think he had the brains for things like that. She stands up, ready to face whatever he's going to do. She needs to make time for the kids to escape.

"Travis, calm down. I'll do anything you want me to."

Her cell phone buzzes, causing a distraction. Travis forgets about Dominic as he searches for her phone.

Olivia shouts "Run!" as she leaps forward. She doesn't stop to check whether Dominic escapes. Instead, she starts hitting Travis with all her strength. He's small and skinny so she easily overpowers him with her extra hundred pounds. She forces him onto the floor.

He tries to get up but she has his hair in both her hands and is banging his head against the floor over and over. Then she pulls the flap of skin off his face, making him howl in pain.

174

She doesn't hear her girls react and can only hope they've slipped out so they don't have to witness this.

She's going to kill Travis. For Aaron. She doesn't need to know what he did to her son all those years ago. She finally faces the devastating truth that Aaron can't still be alive. So she's going to get revenge.

She climbs off him to find a sharp object to stab him with but when she turns back she sees he's pulled out a gun. It's one of the antique revolvers Sandy keeps in the display case next to the front desk, along with a selection of old hunting rifles. She recognizes it because she's dusted it for the last twenty years. Never once did she think it would be used to kill her.

Dominic cries, "No!"

They both turn to him. Olivia's heart sinks as she realizes he didn't escape when he had the chance. He's paralyzed with fear at the front door.

"It's okay, honey," she says. "You run along now, like I told you."

Travis smiles. "You better get a head start boy, because I'm going to hunt you down and do what I did to your brother."

Dominic's eyes widen. He finally flees.

Olivia can only hope he finds somewhere to hide. Tears run down her face. All she can do now is pray Travis has some humanity in him somewhere. She looks at him. He's pointing the gun at her face. Her only chance to get out of this alive is to let him in on a secret.

"Travis? Listen to me. You don't want to hurt him."

"Yes, I do." He grins.

"No, you don't. Dominic is your *brother*. Your half-brother. Me and your dad had a relationship years ago. You wouldn't want to hurt your only brother, would you?"

He momentarily looks confused, then conflicted. She takes that as a good sign.

"You could be friends, the two of you. If you treat Dominic right, he'll look after you."

It's as though Travis doesn't hear her. He's frowning. "Is this where my dad spends all of his spare time then? With *him*?"

"What?" She frowns. "No, we never see your dad." She can tell this isn't working. He's too far gone. "Travis. Think of your father. He'll lose his job and you'll go to prison. Think how much this will hurt him."

Travis is no longer grinning. His expression is pained. "My father hates me and I hate him."

He shoots her four times, but she's dead with the second bullet. The one that goes through her forehead.

CHAPTER THIRTY-ONE

When they've finished eating, Dean suggests they go upstairs and try to get some sleep so they can be up early in the morning. They need to speak to Bryan, the guest Jodie Lawrence was flirting with, and they need to interview the employees. He's especially keen to interview Sandy in more depth. The guy should know what his employees and guests are getting up to and it's time he took some responsibility for Leroy. They also need to conduct a proper search of the grounds, in daylight.

They stop outside Eva's room.

"You can't sleep in there with a dead body in the tub," he says. "You know that, right?"

She chews her lip. "I could probably just grab a key for another room from the front desk. No one would even know," she says.

"That would make sense if we knew for sure that Leroy's brother isn't going to come looking for you. He must've realized by now that Leroy's missing and put two and two together."

She scoffs. "I doubt it. Something tells me Patrick isn't very bright. Besides, I really don't think he's in on this with Leroy. He's not as aggressive."

Dean nods. "You know, I don't think Leroy took the girls."

She raises her eyebrows.

"If he was some kind of serial killer, he'd be onto a good thing in this town because no one seems to care when people go missing. And the local cops are incompetent, no offense, so would he really risk losing his cozy set-up by raping someone like you, who can clearly fight back and look after themselves?" Dean doesn't believe so. "He obviously went too far with you, probably farther than he's ever gone with someone else. But that's because he felt you burned his ego and he didn't have the intelligence to cope with that like an adult. Which suggests he's as dumb as his brother and incapable of covering his tracks with anything more serious, like murder or abduction."

She thinks about it and sighs. "I don't know. I guess you could be right. That would leave us with Bryan and the paranormal guys as suspects. Or someone else here. Maybe even Hannah, if the newspaper reports about her are to be believed. She could've flipped out on Jodie for all we know. Jodie could be her second best friend to die in three years . . . I don't know, my thoughts just keep going around in circles. This place is so odd."

He nods. "You can say that again."

"For now though, I need to sleep." She looks at her door but doesn't move to open it.

"Stay with me and Rocky," says Dean. "I can sleep on the floor and you can have the bed. You know it's best if we stick together tonight. The only person I trust in this place is Laura. Even Olivia's hiding something."

He can tell she doesn't want to stay in his room. She obviously values her privacy.

"What if I take another room," she says, "and Rocky comes with me? He can listen out for any intruders, right?"

Dean smiles. He thinks that's the first time she's referred to Rocky by his name instead of *the dog*. "Are you kidding? This dog would sleep through an air raid."

He's not lying. Rocky has trouble waking once his head hits Dean's pillow. He'd never make a real police dog.

Eva opens her door and they wait for the smell of Leroy's body to hit them. It doesn't, but they can smell his blood drying on the bed cover.

"You must've used a lot of ice," he says. "He should be fine for another day with the power out. But you still can't sleep in there, Eva."

"I know. Let me grab my things and open a window."

"Grab the hiking boot from the ice box too. I'll pack it with ice in my sink for now."

"I'd forgotten about that. I won't be long."

"Okay. I'll leave my door unlocked for you while I fetch ice."

She spins around. "Where do you think you're going? There's a dead body in here and the lights are out! You'll wait for me here and hold the door open."

Dean's surprised. He didn't think she'd spook this easy.

"I'm fine with shooting assholes, but I've always been afraid of the dark," she explains. "Don't you ever watch horror movies?"

He laughs. "I used to when I was younger. But I'm surprised you do if you're scared of the dark."

"Well, I do, and the first rule of horror movies," she whispers as she enters the room, "is that the dead always come back to life."

She's enveloped by the darkness as he listens to her moving around inside.

"Grab my cell phone while you're in there," he says. "I left it on your nightstand when the battery died."

* * *

Once Eva has dumped all her things in the corner of his room, she changes into clean, warm clothes in the bathroom and sits on his bed.

179

Dean notices she brought the half-empty bottle of tequila with her and is swigging it straight from the bottle. He doesn't blame her; he could do with a drink too. He sits on the large armchair near the TV. He thinks he could sleep here comfortably if he uses the coffee table to raise his feet. Laura gave them spare candles and two flashlights from downstairs, so the room is softly lit.

As the power's out he can't charge his phone so he opens his laptop instead, which still has an hour's battery power left. He has some emails that have come in during the day. One is from Hannah's mom. He needs to update her tonight.

He also has an email from Jones to say sorry they got cut off earlier and to apologize for disclosing what Lizzie Glover had said about their supposed wedding. Dean smiles. Barbara would've made him do that. Jones also explains Barbara's flu is getting worse so he's been on nurse duty since she got home and she keeps summoning him into their bedroom with an annoying bell. God, he misses them.

"Okay," says Eva. "We have a severed foot. We know there was tension between the girls. And Hannah's camera shows someone outside in the dark with a head wound. The photos on it suggest a couple of possibilities. They could've gotten lost on the trail in the dark, maybe after drinking a little too much, or they could've been chased out there, or they could've been escaping from wherever they were taken."

Dean nods. "The last two sound more likely now we know what this place is like."

"Agreed." Eva continues, "Also, I read some more of Hannah's diary before Leroy interrupted me, and she mentions the girl who died when she was living in England. It was her best friend at the time and the newspaper reports suggested Hannah pushed her off a cliff. That's a serious allegation. So it's possible we've been looking at this all wrong and Hannah is a potential suspect, not a victim. Because if things went bad between her and Jodie, and let's face it, her final diary entry certainly suggests that, then Hannah could've killed Jodie and run away after."

180

Dean sighs. "I guess it's a possibility. Did you ever track down Jodie's relatives?"

She shakes her head. "Detective Garner tried to locate them but drew a blank. Once I'm back at the station I'll try looking for them."

He's glad it's not up to him to notify them of their daughter's disappearance. "I need to speak to Hannah's mom," he says. "She's emailed me to ask for an update. She couldn't get through on the phone." He checks his watch and sees it's almost one o'clock in the morning. He knows the parents of missing children rarely sleep well so he's guessing she'll answer the phone. "Let me try calling her now."

Eva takes another swig of tequila.

He smiles. "Careful, you'll get drunk."

She rolls her eyes at him and throws him her cell phone. Then she lies back on the bed and reads some more of Hannah's diary while Dean calls Jackie's number. He hopes he can get through to her.

Jackie answers on the second ring. "Hello?"

"Ms. Walker? It's Dean Matheson."

"Oh, Mr. Matheson. I'm so glad you called. I've been worried sick. The storm is all over the news. Are you alright?"

"Yeah, me and Rocky are good. We're struggling to get out much because of the cold, and we're trapped here until the roads are cleared, but we're at the lodge so it's fine. I wanted to give you an update."

"Okay, let me sit down."

He realizes she's bracing herself for bad news. He paces the room as he talks.

"I haven't found them yet, Ms. Walker. But I'm working with a different detective from McArthur PD and we're both pretty certain the girls didn't leave town of their own accord."

"I knew it!" she says. "It might sound strange to you but to have that confirmed is such a relief because now the police department has to send more people to find them, don't they? What about the FBI? Shouldn't they be involved in kidnapping cases?"

Dean has to manage her expectations. "The problem is, no one can get up here right now because the roads are blocked and the weather isn't letting up, but we're working hard to find them. We've been given a camera that we've been told is Hannah's."

Jackie gasps. "Are there any photos on it?"

"There are, and they're not the kind of photos I'd expect to be on there, if I'm honest. They start with photos of the girls at the lodge, enjoying themselves, but they turn into photos taken outside, at night. I'll email them to you once the power's restored. I think one of the girls was using the camera's flash to light her way through a mountain trail. We're not sure whether they got lost in the dark, or whether they were . . ." he hesitates.

"Tell me, please. Anything is better than not knowing."

"Sure. I'll be completely honest with you then. I think the girls were abducted by someone local and the photos are of them either being taken somewhere or escaping from somewhere."

Jackie starts crying.

Dean glances at Eva who looks sleepy. She's clutching the bottle of tequila to her chest.

"I'm sorry it's not better news," he says. "We'll find out more later today, once the sun's up. I'm sure of it." He thinks about the foot and doesn't know whether to tell her or not. Without knowing whether it's Hannah's or Jodie's, he could upset her for no reason. He decides to wait until after their search, later today. They might know more themselves then. "I need to ask you about Hannah's past. Is that okay?"

She takes a deep breath. "I knew you'd find out eventually. I didn't keep it from you on purpose, I just didn't think it was relevant."

He raises an eyebrow. "I don't know, her best friend from school gets killed and, according to the newspaper articles, Hannah was present, but she didn't report it. That's pretty relevant."

"She didn't hurt Katie, Mr. Matheson. She was there when Katie died but the shock of witnessing it made her react poorly. She came home and went to bed. She didn't tell anyone what happened, so by the time Katie was found by a dog walker, it was too late to save her. Hannah still has nightmares about it and she regrets her actions. But she was a fifteen-year-old girl who'd just witnessed her best friend's death."

Dean takes a deep breath. He hadn't expected that scenario at all. "You don't think she could be dealing with PTSD from that incident and maybe acting out of character at the moment?"

"No, because she's been doing so well since we moved to the States and away from all the negative press. The coroner ruled Katie's death a tragic accident. Hannah was cleared of any involvement. But the press wouldn't let her forget it. Since we've been over here, she's moved on with her life. It was three years ago now. She wouldn't hurt Jodie. I know it. They may argue occasionally, but don't all friends?"

Dean doesn't know what to believe. Sometimes parents either don't know or won't admit what their children are capable of.

'Sure," he says. "We'll continue with the assumption they were abducted. We'll be doing a thorough search of the grounds and property later this morning. If they're here, Ms. Walker, we'll find them."

"Thank you so much. You've already done much more than Detective Garner. I'll relay everything to Hannah's dad."

He ends the call and looks at Eva. She has her eyes closed. Rocky's next to her on the bed. Dean crouches on the floor and gently takes the tequila bottle from her hand. It's almost empty.

She opens her eyes and looks at him. Then she smiles. "I like you." She reaches out and touches his face, her fingers stopping on his lips.

Dean smiles. "You're going to regret telling me that tomorrow," he whispers before standing. "Goodnight, Eva."

She closes her eyes and falls asleep immediately.

Dean retreats to the armchair. He thinks he's going to miss Eva when this is all over.

CHAPTER THIRTY-TWO

Garner can't find Travis anywhere inside so, as a last resort, he puts his coat back on, pulls on a pair of Sandy's boots, and leaves the lodge. It's not snowing as heavily now as it was when he arrived, although it's still bitterly cold. He can't believe Travis would be stupid enough to go out in this weather, and at this time of night, but he has to check.

Shirley's car is still where Travis left it, already iced over. Garner looks toward the road that leads out of here and wishes he could just drive away, tree or no tree. Let Travis do whatever he wants. He pulls out a joint and cups his hands around the lighter's flame. It takes a while to catch but when it does, Garner takes a deep breath in. He instantly feels warmer and his shoulders relax.

He starts walking up the trail that leads to Wolf Peak, not knowing where else to look. He knows there are some old cabins up there that haven't been used for years, except as storage. He considers the possibility that Travis might have stumbled and frozen to death out here and feels a pang of guilt for thinking that would be a blessing.

After just ten minutes he's already exhausted and the joint is finished, any light relief now evaporated. He stops to check his watch; it's almost two in the morning. He should be in bed or he's going to be exhausted for work later. He curses Travis under his breath and throws his cigarette butt into the snow. Movement in the corner of his eye catches his attention. Someone's emerging from between the pine trees, about to cut across the main path.

Garner shouts, "Travis? Is that you?"

The person stops and Garner's heart thumps harder in his chest. Whoever it is, they're carrying a child over their shoulder. It looks like a boy and he appears to be unconscious. Garner hopes it's just a guest who took an ill-advised walk in the snow to wear his son out. But in his heart, he knows who it is and what they're doing.

Slowly, he approaches. "It's me, son."

Travis slowly backs away and yells, "Leave me alone!"

The menace in his voice makes Garner stop. Travis never raises his voice to him. He knows he'll be backhanded if he does. Things must be bad. And what's wrong with his face? Is that *blood*?

"I asked you to bring me here," shouts his son, "but you left me at home instead. You never do anything I ask!"

Travis makes a break for it and carries on in the direction he was originally heading, this time moving faster.

After a few seconds' hesitation, Garner follows. He's not as fast as his son but he pushes through the heavy snow, which seems determined to slow him down. He stumbles on a tree root. His ankle painfully bends the wrong way.

"Dammit!" His voice echoes through the trees. His ankle feels sprained. It hurts when touched. "Damn you, Travis!" he yells.

Garner realizes he's finally reached the end of his rope. This needs to end.

Tonight.

He pulls his foot free from the root and stumbles on after his son, with one hand on his holster.

CHAPTER THIRTY-THREE

Their room is freezing and Dean struggles to sleep, even under bundled layers of clothes. In total, he manages just a couple of hours. He looks over at the bed, envious that Rocky's keeping Eva warm while he's left out in the cold.

He tries to make out the time on his watch. 6 a.m. He gets up and goes to the bathroom, quietly closing the door. It's dark in here but he manages to empty his bladder and brush his teeth. He's glad he can't see his reflection. It's not like he cares much about his appearance, but he feels exhausted so he must look a mess. His chin feels like sandpaper and is starting to itch because he needs to shave, but it'll have to wait.

Trying to figure out which clothes are his in the dark is difficult but he manages to layer up. Not wanting to waste time lying awake, he's hoping he can make a head start somewhere, either by interviewing the employees, if any are around this early, or by searching the premises for signs of the girls. Now he has a proper flashlight it'll be easier to navigate his way.

He stops by the bed and looks down at Eva. She's breathing heavily, on the verge of snoring. He knows she'll be annoyed that he's going without her but she won't be much use if she's still exhausted. It's going to be a long, uncomfortable day out there. She had it much worse than him yesterday so the more recharged she is, the more she can help them both. He makes a quick note on the complimentary pad next to the bed.

Couldn't sleep. It's six a.m. and I'm heading downstairs. I'll be looking around. Rocky will find me when you're ready.

He puts the pencil down. He wonders if Eva will remember what she said last night. He doubts it.

Rocky raises his head to see what's going on so Dean puts a finger to his mouth. The dog snuggles closer to Eva. Dean's confident Rocky would attack anyone who tries to force their way in here, if he wakes up in time.

Hopefully, now Leroy's dead, she's a little safer. Until Patrick finds out she killed his brother, that is. Not wanting to think about it too much, Dean leaves.

The first person he bumps into downstairs is Sandy. He's at the front desk, which is lit up with lamps.

"Morning," says Dean. "I see you managed to find some generators."

Sandy looks up but he doesn't smile. He looks exhausted. "Yeah. No thanks to my team. They've all suddenly disappeared."

Dean thinks of Leroy's body decomposing in Eva's bathtub and he's not sure whether it's time he mentioned it. He'd rather have some backup from Eva's sergeant before he starts scaring the employees and guests. He decides to withhold that information for now. He slipped the *Do not disturb* sign on her door so no one should find Leroy by accident. He realizes he needs to speak to Sergeant Roberts again to see when he's going to get here.

"Sorry," he says. "I should've volunteered to help but I was distracted. Can I do anything now?"

"Maybe later," says Sandy. "I'm hoping Leroy and Patrick turn up soon. And my brother's here somewhere."

Dean nods. "Could you get me Bryan's full name and contact number? I need to speak to him today, to rule him out as a suspect."

Sandy searches the computer at the check-in desk and writes down a number with an area code Dean doesn't recognize. "Bryan Mason," he says. "Here you go."

"Thanks." Dean looks around the dimly lit lobby and spots several people curled up in sleeping bags around the log fire.

"Are they guests?"

Sandy nods. "They said they were too cold upstairs."

"Wish I'd thought of that."

Sandy steps out from behind the desk. "I need to clear the road. Some of the guests should be leaving today."

"That's something I can help you with," says Dean.

"It's fine. My brother's going to help. He needs it cleared so he can get to work."

"He doesn't work here?"

"No."

Sandy clams up and Dean knows he won't get any more out of him.

"I need to interview you at some point today," he says. "I have unanswered questions."

Sandy doesn't appear concerned. "Fine. It'll have to wait though. I need to find my brother. He's another one who's dodged his responsibilities this morning. Even Nathan and Delilah haven't made it in, but they live on the other side of town so at least they have an excuse. Sometimes it feels like I'm running this place single-handedly."

Dean lets him go and wanders into the restaurant. Laura and a young man are preparing the tables for breakfast.

Laura smiles as he approaches her. It looks like she's wearing fifteen sweaters.

"Have you been up all night?" he asks.

"No, I went to bed for a couple of hours. But we couldn't sleep." The young man joins them. "This is my roommate, Marshall."

"Hi, I'm Dean."

Marshall nods. "Hi. We only have cereals and sandwiches on offer today, I'm afraid. We're saving the soup for lunch and dinner."

"That's fine, I'm not hungry yet. I wanted to ask you both a few questions if that's okay?"

They share a look.

"What's the matter?" asks Dean.

"It's about Jodie and Hannah, isn't it?" Laura looks over Dean's shoulder as she talks.

"Right," he says. "I'm a private investigator hired by Hannah's mom. Do either of you know or have any suspicions about what happened to them?"

Marshall says, "I never met them because I was hired to cover their shifts after they disappeared, so if it's okay with you can I get back to work? Some of the others haven't made it in yet, and they probably won't, which means it's going to be crazy busy today. Especially in the kitchen."

Dean thinks he's telling the truth. "Sure." He walks Laura to a dining table and they sit opposite each other. "You won't get into trouble for talking to me. I'm sure Sandy wants to find out what happened just as much as I do. It can't be good for business having their disappearance hanging over the place."

Laura looks at her hands. "It's not Sandy I'm worried about."

Dean's concerned. Someone is intimidating the employees here. "Anything you can tell me will help because we don't know much at all."

She takes a deep breath. "Hannah was my friend. I mean, *is* my friend. Jodie was okay, I guess. But she was more outgoing than me and Hannah and she never bothered asking how I was doing or whether I needed help. It was all about her. She liked attention. She was funny though; she always had everyone laughing."

"There's some suggestion that Jodie went off with a guest after dinner that last day she was here. Do you know if that's true?"

Laura nods. "Yes, she did. His name was Bryan Mason. He was the kind of guy who wants people to think he's rich, but really the watches and the designer suits are fake, you know?"

Dean nods. "I know the type."

"I think Jodie fell for it. He was kind of attractive and a big flirt with all the employees, even with Marshall. But he was married. He comes here regularly apparently, but this time he didn't bring his wife."

"Do you know if anything happened between him and Jodie?"

She thinks. "They headed into town after dinner, probably so he could buy her some of those fancy chocolates. About two hours after they left, I saw Jodie return on her own."

Dean's surprised. "So she was seen after leaving with Bryan. That's good to know."

"Right. Bryan shouldn't be a suspect in my opinion. He's harmless. When I last saw Jodie she was smoking, which isn't allowed inside, so Sandy told her off. He said she had to smoke around the back of the lodge, so the guests don't get a bad impression of the place."

Dean leans forward. "Did she come back in after her cigarette?"

"I don't know because I finished my shift on the front desk and went up to my room soon after she left. I checked in on Hannah first as I had to give her back the scarf she'd let me borrow."

"So you saw Hannah that night too?"

Laura looks confused. "How come you don't already know this? I told the police everything."

"Was it Detective Garner you spoke to?"

"Yes, him and the sheriff. But the sheriff only came once and I could tell he wasn't interested. Someone said he's due to retire in a few weeks, so maybe that's why."

Garner couldn't have written any of this in his report or Eva would've told Dean about it. "So what was Hannah doing when you saw her?"

Laura thinks back. "She was sitting on her bed, writing something in her diary. She never spent much time online compared to the rest of us and was always writing or taking photos on her camera instead. She didn't really care about social media. She didn't want anyone knowing too much about her."

Dean assumes that's because the UK press probably follows her movements closely, thanks to her best friend's death.

"Her hair was wet so she must've just had a shower," says Laura. "Anyway, she told me she was mad at Jodie. Not for the first time."

"For ditching her for Bryan?"

"Right. She thought Jodie wouldn't be back that night so I told her that Jodie was outside, smoking. She said she might go down and speak to her before she disappeared again, but I don't know if she did. I was tired from a long shift, so I didn't feel like hanging out. I went to my room and never saw them again." Her eyes fill with tears. "If only I'd stayed with her and watched a movie, or something. She wouldn't have gone out and they might both still be here."

He touches her hand. "Laura, there are a thousand ways things could've gone differently but none of them are your fault."

She wipes her eyes.

"Tell me honestly," he says. "What do you think has happened to them?"

Looking away she says, "Olivia told all of us we can't talk about the rumors."

Alarmed, Dean says, "There are rumors? What, that the girls are dead?"

"They have to be dead after this long, surely?" she asks. "Don't you think so?"

"I don't give up until I know for certain. Because what if they are out there somewhere, Laura, and they need rescuing? We can't just give up on them. Imagine it was you who was missing. You'd want everyone to keep looking until you were found, wouldn't you?"

Laura nods. "You're right." She lowers her voice and rubs her hands together like she's trying to warm up, or comfort herself. "You need to find Travis. If I were you, I would definitely check if he has a solid alibi for the night they went missing."

"Okay, I will. But who's Travis?"

With a glance over her shoulder, she says, "I'm sorry, I can't tell you anything else because I'll be fired if anyone finds out I even mentioned him. I feel terrible but I really need this job. If I lose it, I'll be homeless."

Dean hides his disappointment. "I understand. Don't worry, I'll find him."

"Okay, but don't be obvious about it. No one here can know you're looking for him. They might tell him."

"Got it."

She visibly relaxes then. "Is that detective your girlfriend?"

Dean smiles. "No."

"She's so pretty. How do you know her?"

"I met her here, and she's determined to do a better job of finding your friends than Detective Garner managed."

Laura sits up straight. "He's horrible. He really creeped me out last night." She notices Sandy coming toward them and stands up. "I've got to get back to work now, sorry."

Dean thinks he hears her wrong so he lets her go. Did she mean he creeped her out last *time*?

Sandy approaches him. "I could really do with some help moving the debris off the road out front if you meant what you said earlier? I still can't find anyone. They must've had a wild party last night and forgot to invite me."

Dean gets up. "No problem."

CHAPTER THIRTY-FOUR

Eva wakes to the dog licking her face. She sits up and pats him on the head. A quick scan of the room tells her Dean's not here. She sees the note on the nightstand and sighs as she reads it. "Does your dad always want to be the hero?"

Rocky barks, excited that she's awake. He gives her his paw over and over again like he wants something. She's never owned a dog but she's pretty sure he wants food.

"And he didn't even have the courtesy to bring us breakfast in bed, did he?"

She sits up and swings her legs out of the bed. Rocky jumps down but stumbles as his back legs hit the ground. He looks off-balance. She frowns. Maybe his legs were asleep. He settles in front of his food bowl.

With a raised eyebrow she says, "If I give you food are you going to bring me coffee?"

He barks again, unsure what she's talking about, but he can tell she's playing with him.

Eva shivers and resists the urge to get back under the covers. Her mouth is dry from the tequila and she doesn't remember falling asleep. She pulls her coat on and finds the dog food. Not sure how much food is enough, but figuring he's a big dog so he'll need a lot, she fills his bowl to the top.

Rocky gulps it down.

She laughs. "You'll get hiccups eating like that."

It's light outside and her phone tells her it's almost eight a.m. She feels the back of her head, which is dry but still painful. At least her headache's gone, and she feels better for the deep sleep. She could really do with a shower to wash the matted blood out of her hair but the power's still out. She looks out the window and can see it's finally stopped snowing. There are even a few people on the slopes already. She doesn't know what attracts people to skiing and the very real possibility of breaking their legs when they could be relaxing on a beach somewhere hot, reading a good book instead.

Out of the corner of her eye she spots someone in the distance who looks out of place. He's pacing backward and forward on the edge of the woods, like he's talking to himself. She leans into the window to see him better.

"Wait. Is that . . . ?"

Her eyes must be playing tricks on her. She rubs the condensation from the cold glass and looks harder. It looks like the back of Detective Garner, but that doesn't make sense. He's not here.

It can't be Matheson, since he's taller and slimmer than this person. She squints and almost has her nose pressed to the glass. Her breath steams the window. It's no good. He's too far away for her to tell whether it's Garner or not. She has to investigate.

"He'd better not be spying on me."

She throws on all her extras; scarf, hat, and gloves, thankful that Dean left them behind for her. She plugs her phone in to charge, just in case the power comes back up while she's gone. It still has some battery left and she notices a text from Sergeant Roberts. She messaged him last night to say she wasn't in any trouble and that Dean jumped to the wrong conclusion.

I need an update, Valdez! No one can get up there because a delivery truck has tipped over on the ice, spilling all its contents and blocking the road. I'll be there as soon as I can. Haven't notified the chief but can't hold off forever. Call me ASAP.

She quickly texts him back to put his mind at rest.

Don't worry about me, I'm fine. Think we're onto something. Get up here but don't trust the employees. We have a body. Not the girls. Power cut, no battery left. Will call when I can.

Her phone starts ringing immediately, as she knew it would, but she needs her battery so she declines it. Fatally shooting Leroy is something that's best relayed to Roberts face-to-face. Her stomach flips at the thought of it and she worries about the reaction she'll get from Chief Carson and Leroy's family. She'll need to move his body at some point if Roberts doesn't make it up here. That'll mean asking Sandy if she can use his freezer when the power gets restored.

He's going to freak out.

Rocky's still eating but Eva wants to get outside. Dean won't be happy if she leaves him in the room but she'll come back and get him once she's checked whether that really is Detective Garner. She picks up her gun and slides it into the holster.

"Be good, Rocky."

He doesn't even look up from his bowl as she leaves.

The lobby is empty as she walks through. A selection of complimentary sandwiches and cookies sit on the front desk. More importantly, there's a large pot of hot water next to cups filled with instant coffee granules.

"Hallelujah."

She pours some hot water into one of the cups. It's only just warm enough to dissolve the coffee granules but it contains caffeine so that's good enough for her. She downs it, grabs half a sandwich, and eats it as she walks through the lobby to the outside. Cold chicken salad. Not her first choice but it tastes okay.

Outside, the wind has died down and the sun is out. It feels good on her face, warm even. She can hear some commotion in the distance, near the entrance to the parking lot, and can see a snowcat trying to move a fallen tree. Good, that means if the truck Roberts mentioned is cleared quickly too, he might be able to get up here before nightfall and he can help her with the whole Leroy mess.

She turns right and heads for the woods behind the lodge. It takes twenty minutes of fast walking to track down the man she saw from her window, and he's still some way off. He's walking away from her, farther into the woods. Wearing a black coat means he's easy to track against the white background.

She speeds up to follow him, needing to run at times. He's acting strangely, zig-zagging instead of walking straight, and talking to himself loudly. She can't make out what he's saying. It makes her not want to confront him because he looks suspicious. Maybe it's not Garner. It could be a guest. She follows him from a distance.

When they're much deeper into the woods and she can no longer see the lodge behind her, he suddenly stops and screams.

"Damn you, Travis! Why are you like this?"

She recognizes his voice. This is definitely Garner. She looks to see who he's talking to but there's no one else around. Her hands start sweating and she has to take her gloves off. Distracted, she forces them into her coat pocket as she crouches behind a tree, not wanting him to see her.

"What the hell is he doing?" she mutters.

He screams again before moving on. He must be having some kind of breakdown to be acting this way. She'd feel sorry for him if he wasn't such a dick.

She considers how to handle the situation and is tempted to ignore it and let him have his breakdown in peace while she returns to the lodge. She turns her head to look back the way she came. She's already come so far and her curiosity gets the better of her. She can't resist following him to see what's going on.

Eva's only ever seen Garner cocky or arrogant, never emotional, so something's definitely wrong. She has to follow him. She puts her hand on her holster, drawing comfort from the feel of her weapon.

She moves forward quietly, trying to avoid stepping on branches or falling over. She's glad she didn't bring the dog now, as he would've given her away. But she'd prefer to have Matheson with her right now, to confirm how weird Garner's acting, if nothing else.

Garner clearly knows where he's going as he's on a mission now. He's moving forward at a faster pace. Eva's surprised he's fit enough to walk this fast, what with all the cigarettes he smokes. He appears to have a slight limp.

Having not been this deep into the woods before, it makes her a little nervous. She doesn't know whether to stop and turn back. She could get Matheson. But that would give Garner time to leave.

Garner disappears into the white background. A minute or so later she notices a large wooden building ahead that looks like it could be for used storage. She can tell there was once a well-worn pathway leading up to it that has become overgrown. The path still has an outline made of logs but the snow's hiding most of them.

The closer she gets, the more run-down it appears. It would be the perfect place to hide someone. She gasps at the thought and ducks behind another tree, needing time to think. What's Garner doing out here? How would he even know about this place? Unless . . . He could be trying to find the girls again. Maybe he's trying to solve the case before she does, so he doesn't look so sloppy. He'd hate it if she proved him wrong and found the girls before him. He'd never live it down at work.

Is that why he's here? She doesn't know what to think but she knows she can't go in there alone. She decides to wait here for a while to see if Garner comes out. If he's discovered something bad he'll need help and she can reveal herself, but if he's here for more nefarious reasons, it's best he doesn't know she followed him.

After waiting twenty minutes in the bone-chilling cold, she finds it too uncomfortable to stay crouched. She needs to move around to get her blood flowing again. She stands up and looks back the way she came. She needs to either go and see what Garner's up to or head back to the lodge and fetch Matheson.

She hears a branch snap behind her. Before she can move, someone puts their hand over her mouth and a gun to her temple.

CHAPTER THIRTY-FIVE

Dean watches Patrick approach as he and Sandy use the snowcat to try to move the biggest of the fallen branches off the road. Patrick must've abandoned his car and walked most of the way, as he's panting and red in the face.

"Sandy? Have you seen Leroy anywhere?" asks Patrick.

Sandy jumps out of the vehicle. "Nope. I was hoping you'd know where he is."

Patrick rests his hands on his hips. "He said he had a woman waiting for him yesterday, but I haven't seen him since and I don't know who he meant."

Sandy ties a rope around a fallen branch just as Marshall walks over from the lodge and joins them, to see how they're doing.

Dean thinks they can handle this without him now Sandy has backup, so he excuses himself when he notices Patrick staring at him. He doesn't want the guy to suspect he and Eva had something to do with his brother's disappearance.

Sandy doesn't even look up. "No problem. Thanks for your help."

As Dean heads to the lodge, he notices the sky is darkening overhead. The wind's picking up too, and out of nowhere, hail starts pelting down. He thought the storm was over but it looks like it's coming back with a vengeance.

Inside, he runs upstairs to the second floor and along the corridor. He opens the door quietly in case Eva's still asleep. Rocky slowly walks over to greet him.

"Hey, boy."

He looks around but Eva's not here and his nose picks up an awful smell. He follows it to the bathroom and discovers Rocky was unable to hold himself.

Rocky backs away with a look of shame.

Dean feels bad for him. "Are you kidding me? Didn't she take you out before she disappeared?"

Rocky wags his tail but still looks sheepish.

"It's not your fault. It's okay." He strokes Rocky's head and then cleans up the mess. Checking the dog's food bowl, he asks, "Did she at least feed you before she left?"

The bowl's empty but the kibble has moved from where Dean left it so he has to assume she did. He looks around for a note but there's nothing. He picks up both their cell phones and chargers so he can charge them in the restaurant, where the generators are. Then he opens the door.

"Come on, boy. Let's get some fresh air."

Rocky descends the stairs a little slower than usual then runs ahead and out through the lobby. He probably needs to relieve his bladder this time.

Before Dean makes it through the lobby, he sees two young girls silhouetted against the snow outside. They walk in slowly. They're not dressed suitably for this weather. It looks like they're wearing pajamas with jackets. No hats or snow boots, just mittens on their hands. As he gets closer to them, he realizes they're crying.

He rushes over and kneels in front of them, recognizing them instantly. These are Olivia's girls. They're shaking from the cold and the taller girl, who must be only nine or ten, has blood on the front of her jacket. He checks her head for cuts.

"Hey, it's okay. Come here." He takes them by their hands and leads them to the fire so they can warm up. Their small hands are freezing. "Where's your mom?"

They both cry harder and he can't get anything out of them. He has a bad feeling about this.

Rocky runs back inside looking pleased with himself. He sits next to the girls. The younger girl stops crying and hugs him. He licks her hand gently.

Dean hugs the older girl to try to help her relax. "It's okay, sweetie. It's okay. Take your time. You're safe here."

When her sobbing finally slows, she steps back and looks at him.

"My name's Dean," he says. "Do you remember me and Rocky from yesterday?"

She nods.

"What's your name?"

"Kristen."

The younger girl says, "I'm Susie."

He smiles at them. "There. Now we know each other. Kristen? Can you tell me what's happened?"

She nods and says, "My mom." Her teeth are chattering badly and he can tell she can't find the right words yet. He rubs her arms.

"Is your mom okay?"

She shakes her head. "She won't wake up."

Perhaps Olivia's had an accident. "Do you know why she won't wake up?"

Susie speaks up. "Because of the hole in her face."

Dean tries to hide his shock. They must be mistaken. "What kind of hole?"

Kristen says, "A bullet hole."

Holy crap. "Do you know who shot her?" he asks.

The girls exchange a look and hesitate to answer.

"If you tell me, I can make sure they don't hurt anyone else," he presses.

Kristen looks at him. "It was Travis."

That name again. "What about your brother, where's he?"

"Dominic ran away. We heard Mom telling him to run," says Kristen. "But we couldn't find him."

Dean stands and frantically looks around. Laura's walking through the lobby so he calls her over. She recognizes the girls immediately. "Hey, Kristen. What's wrong, sweetheart?"

Dean takes her to one side. "Laura, listen to me. I need you and Marshall to get all the guests and employees together inside, in one room, including anyone on the slopes. Try to keep them in the restaurant and entertain them with food and drinks. Tell them there's an emergency situation but don't freak them out. Just make something up."

Her eyes widen. "What's happening? Have you found Hannah and Jodie?"

He needs her to do what he says and to take it seriously, so he has to confide in her. "Olivia's dead. The girls said Travis shot her. And Dominic's missing."

"Oh my God!" She swallows.

"I need to find Eva and then she and I need to find Travis. Laura, you have to tell me now, who is he?"

She doesn't hesitate this time. "He's Sandy's nephew. He's creepy as heck, and Olivia told me when she was drunk once that she thinks he took her other son years ago. Aaron."

Dean can't believe what he's hearing. "And Sandy knows about this?"

She shakes her head. "I don't know. Sandy's nice, Mr. Matheson. He's much nicer than his brother."

Dean thinks back to what Sandy said about his brother. "I thought his brother didn't work here?"

She grimaces. "He doesn't, thankfully. He's a detective, but he shouldn't be. He's almost as horrible as Travis."

Dean's confused. "If he's a detective, then why didn't he help with the investigation into the missing girls?"

Laura frowns. "He did. Sandy's brother is Detective Alan Garner. I thought you knew that."

Dean blinks. This is wild. Detective Garner owns the lodge where Hannah and Jodie went missing. Why didn't Eva tell him? Maybe she didn't know. She can't have known. He doesn't think she would come up here knowing Garner owns this place. Unless this is some kind of personal vendetta for her.

He wonders then whether she's withholding information from him. Has she been using him this whole time, not disclosing everything she knows? When Garner closed the case and concluded the girls moved on to a different town, is that because he was hiding something himself? Or was he simply trying to protect his business?

Dean doesn't know what to think. He wishes someone had told him about this sooner.

"So Travis is Detective Garner's son?"

"Yes."

He rubs his face. "Yesterday, when you said Sandy's brother freaked you out last night, did you mean Garner was here? Last night?"

"Right. He came into the kitchen but I haven't seen him since. He asked if I'd seen Travis."

"But Travis doesn't live here at the lodge?"

"No, he lives with the detective down in McArthur. They don't come up here that often, not that I'm aware of anyway."

"But they were definitely both here yesterday?" he says.

She nods. "Definitely."

Dean's worried. This is bad. "Have you seen Eva this morning?"

"I saw her head outside, but I don't know what direction she went after turning right at the doors."

"How long ago was that?"

"About an hour, maybe."

He spins around to check on Olivia's girls. They're seated next to Rocky in front of the fireplace, holding hands. He hasn't got time to comfort them.

Sandy, Marshall, and Patrick walk in. Marshall heads straight to the kitchen. Patrick's still complaining about Leroy ditching him for a woman.

Dean takes a step forward. "Sandy? Can I speak to you for a minute?"

Sandy looks stressed but he comes over. "We moved the biggest branches but there's a damn tree down now too and the weather's getting worse so we've had to stop."

"We have bigger problems," says Dean. He waits until Patrick walks away, out of earshot.

Sandy notices the girls. "What's going on?"

"Olivia's dead. They said Travis shot her."

Sandy stares at the girls in disbelief. "What? Why would he do that? They must be mistaken."

Dean tries to read him. Could he really not know what's going on right under his nose? "I don't have any answers yet, all I know is that your employees seem to be terrified of your nephew, Hannah and Jodie are still missing, Dominic's now missing, and Olivia is dead. Whatever you've been turning a blind eye to for the last few years needs resolving. Right now. Where's your brother?"

Sandy looks dazed and devastated. He sits on the arm of one of the couches and Laura places a hand on his back. "I . . . I don't know," he says. "I saw him last night, but he said he had to find Travis."

"What's wrong with Travis, Sandy?" says Dean. "What's going on here?"

The guy looks like he needs to lie down. "He's just different, that's all. Introverted. He doesn't interact with people much and maybe he acts younger than his years, but I can't believe he'd hurt anyone. Unless he's been pushed too far. His dad is pretty hard on him. There's a lot of tension between them, but I didn't think things were this bad."

Dean can see Sandy isn't going to be much help to him. "You and Laura need to get everyone into the restaurant and keep them there for their protection. Take all the generators and heaters you have and try to keep everyone warm. I need you to check that all guests and employees who should be here, are here. If any of your team haven't turned up for work because of the storm, call them and check they're safe."

He thinks about Leroy but he can't worry about that situation right now. The wind is shaking the windows and the lobby has gone dark. He hears hailstones pelting the roof.

"Just tell them it's for safety purposes because of the storm. And tell them help is on the way."

203

Laura looks at him hopefully. "Is there help on the way?"

Dean thinks of Sergeant Roberts. He hopes he's finding a way to bring a team up here. They need all the help they can get. "Yes. Sandy? Is there anywhere Travis likes to hang out when he's up here?"

Sandy tries to think. "I didn't even know he was here until Alan told me last night. He must have a hiding place, I guess, because I never see him."

"If you didn't bump into him inside yesterday, is it safe to assume he could be in one of the smaller cabins outside?"

"Yeah, I guess. He'd be freezing out there though. None of them have power because we never fill them anymore."

Dean springs into action. "Okay, get everyone inside the restaurant. This could end badly, and I need as many people out of the way as possible."

Sandy looks alarmed. "You wouldn't shoot him, would you?"

Dean sees red. "Listen to me. If he's hurt Eva, or anyone else for that matter, then yeah, I'm gonna shoot him. He's dangerous. You should've told me who your brother was, Sandy. If I'd known sooner, this could've ended differently."

Laura drags a dazed Sandy away with one hand and Kristen with the other, who's still holding Susie's hand. "Come on, everyone. Let's get something to eat."

He's grateful Laura's holding it together. He looks down at Rocky, who's alert and ready for action. He shakes his head. "Not this time, boy. I can't drag you back outside in this weather."

Rocky shakes his head, snorts, and digs his paw on the ground. He's arguing with him.

Dean smiles. "Don't be belligerent. You need to stay with those little girls. They need you. And there's food in there . . ."

Rocky barks but Dean stands his ground. He can't risk exposing Rocky to this weather again because he was exhausted when they got back from Olivia's. Besides, Dean doesn't know what he's up against yet. Rocky saved his life once but he's not willing to see him get hurt again. He's too old to survive another bullet.

He points after Laura and the girls and says, "Go."

Surprisingly, Rocky does what he's told.

Dean grabs one of the few remaining sandwiches from the front desk as he hasn't eaten yet and he knows he's going to need the energy for searching outside in this weather. He takes it with him as he walks to the doorway. From the coat stand he grabs a thicker and longer coat than the one he owns and puts it on. Then he grabs someone's hat and gloves.

He feels Rocky's eyes on his back as he heads outside and into the storm.

CHAPTER THIRTY-SIX

Dean passes some guests heading inside on his way out. It looks like they won't need to be rounded up as they've realized the weather is turning bad again. He looks for Eva among them but she's not here. He doesn't know what Garner or Travis look like but he's pretty sure they're not among the crowd either because these guests are carrying skis or snowboards.

He feels for Eva's cell phone in his coat pocket. It still has some charge so he huddles against the wind in the doorway and phones Sergeant Roberts to see where their backup is.

"Eva?" says Roberts as soon as he answers.

"Sorry, it's Dean Matheson again. Things have taken a turn for the worse up here and we could really do with that backup I asked for. This phone's battery is about to die. Where are you?"

"I've driven as far as I can but I've been stuck waiting for a delivery truck to be recovered. Someone else turned up in a cab just after I arrived. They've offered to show me a trail through the woods to get up to the lodge. Apparently it isn't too far to walk from here. We've been walking for about ten minutes so far, but the conditions are slowing us down. Is Eva okay?"

"I don't know. I hope so."

"What the hell's going on up there, Matheson?"

"I don't have time to fill you in on everything but I've just learned that Garner's son has killed an employee and both he and Garner have gone missing. I could really do with two things, and quick. First, a description of them both, and second, armed backup as soon as possible."

Roberts gasps. "I didn't even know Detective Garner had a son."

"Yeah, well, I doubt I'd tell too many people about him if he were mine."

"What's Garner even doing up there?"

"My guess is cleaning up after Travis, unless they're working together. How soon can you be here?"

"I'm—" Roberts doesn't finish.

Dean hears a loud gunshot from the other end of the phone. He has to hold it away from his ear. "What the hell?" It takes a minute for his ear to stop ringing. "Roberts?" he says, resuming the call. "Sergeant Roberts? What's going on?"

There's no answer.

Dean hears breathing on the line, as if someone has picked the phone off the ground.

After a few seconds, the call ends.

Dean stares at Eva's phone, stunned. He just heard someone shoot Sergeant Roberts. "What the hell have I been dragged into?"

He runs back inside on shaky legs to plug both cell phones in to charge. Now he knows there's no backup coming he has to make one more call before he can go and find Eva. He must look like a shell-shocked mess because the guests, who are enjoying themselves in the rapidly warming restaurant, scramble to get away from him as he stumbles in.

He takes a deep breath and tries to act normal. He doesn't need anyone getting scared right now. His hands shake as he plugs in the cell phones. He uses his to phone Detective Jones.

Jones answers quickly. "Dean, I'm so glad you phoned, I've been trying to reach you. It's Barbara, she's not well."

"What's wrong with her?" He tries to keep his voice steady. He had hoped he could ask Jones to contact nearby law enforcement to bring backup, but Jones sounds too upset. Dean realizes he's going to have to figure this mess out himself.

"We're not sure. We're in the hospital and even the doctors don't know what's going on. All I know is it started with flu and got steadily worse." Jones gulps back tears, which shocks Dean. They can't lose Barbara, she's too young.

"She'll pull through, surely?"

"I don't know. I really don't like the way the doctors are looking at each other. Can you come home?" asks Jones. "I wouldn't ask if I didn't think the situation warranted it. I can book you a flight. She might not make it out of this, and you need to be here. You're like a son to her. To both of us."

Dean swallows the lump in his throat. It's terrible timing for this to happen. "There's a storm here. No one can get in or out. But the minute the roads are clear and I can get to an airport, I'll come back."

He feels guilty for not being able to fly out immediately, assuming all flights aren't grounded. But could he, even if the storm had subsided? What about Eva, Dominic, and the missing girls? He's torn but he can't give up on Eva. At least Barbara has her loved ones around her. Eva could be dying somewhere alone right now.

Jones sounds desperate. "I understand. It's just that, well, she looks so helpless. She looks like she's already gone."

"Don't say that, Jones. She's tougher than you know. And she's in the right place. She'll pull through this. You just stay with her and keep talking to her. I'll be there as soon as I can."

Jones sighs and then clears his throat, trying to get it together. He changes the subject. "Have you found the girls yet?"

Dean shakes his head. "No. But I'm close. Someone else has gone missing now, one of the detectives. Jones, this isn't a good situation out here. I think a cop was shot dead while talking to me on the phone."

He regrets telling him as soon as the words are out. He's only going to worry about Dean now too.

"What are you talking about?" says his friend. "Organize some backup immediately."

Exhausted, Dean rubs his face. "It's the storm, and the secrets around here. I don't know who to trust. I don't know if I'm up to this. I'm completely isolated from any reliable backup right now."

"Listen to me, Matheson." Jones changes his tone, becoming stern. "Get your shit together, arm yourself, and find those girls. You only have to trust your instincts. I've told you that before. You're a trained police officer and you need to finish whatever's going on up there because right now, you're their only hope."

Dean knows he's right but it's a lot of pressure. He's only a PI now. He shouldn't be in this kind of situation. He suddenly wishes he was back in Vegas looking for stolen dogs.

Jones softens his voice. "Dean? You can do this, you know. Me and Barbara . . ." His voice breaks at her name. "We believe in you. You're going to make one hell of a detective one day. But not if you don't start believing in yourself."

Dean nods. "I'm on it. In the meantime, get me some backup. But not from McArthur PD. They're corrupt. Call the FBI if you have to. And you keep Barb alive, Jones. I'll be there as soon as I can."

"Wait, Dean?"

"What?"

"You better not get shot up there."

"I'll try not to."

They hang up and Dean pulls his shit together, as instructed. He's not going to dwell on Barbara's health. She'll be fine. She has to be because Jones needs her.

In the meantime, he has to get out there and find Eva. He spins around.

Rocky's sitting to attention right behind his legs.

Dean shakes his head. "No, boy. It's horrible out there. Your adventure's over."

The loudest bark Dean's ever heard from the dog takes him by surprise. Even the guests look over at them. Rocky follows it up with a second one in case Dean didn't get the message the first time.

Dean takes a deep breath. "Okay, okay. Jeez, there's no need to cause a scene . . ."

Rocky runs ahead of him as they leave the lodge.

CHAPTER THIRTY-SEVEN

Eva frantically looks around her to see what she can use to get out of these cuffs. She still can't believe Garner has actually handcuffed her.

This is serious. He's lost it.

Her head throbs from where he slapped her hard, near her right eye, leaving her vision blurred for a while. She managed to elbow him in the nose after he struck her, so his nose is dripping blood, but he has a look in his eye that tells her he's not playing by the rules anymore. She knew he hated her but she can't believe it's come to this. He's a desperate man right now, and she knows he's capable of anything. She has to drop the attitude and try to stop him from whatever he has planned.

The wooden building he dragged her into has no power but the shutters are open on the windows, letting in limited daylight. She can make out all the dust and decay. This place hasn't been used in a long time. A large rug is frayed around the edges, probably from rats using it as bedding for their nests, and there are thick spiderwebs everywhere.

Spiders.

Eva can't bear them. Even in her current predicament she has time to shudder at the thought of being left here in the dark with what must be some *huge* spiders.

Garner's pacing the room and muttering under his breath.

She has to think fast to try to get him out of his current state. "Garner? If you tell me what's going on, I can help you get out of this mess."

"Shut up!" he yells. "I'm trying to think."

His pacing kicks up dust from the floor that settles in her lungs, making her cough. He threw her onto the floor earlier, with her hands cuffed behind her. She hasn't risked getting up while he's acting volatile.

"There's nothing bad enough that can't be reversed yet," she continues. "Chief Carson likes you, so he'd just suspend you for a week or so and then you'd be back on the payroll. I won't press charges for the slap. Hell, I probably deserved it. I know you've been waiting forever to do that, right?"

Like hell she won't press charges. She's going to make sure he sees the inside of a cell. Friend or no friend, Chief Carson is going to wish he'd never met Garner once she's done with them both. She'll find out what their little side projects are and she'll take them down. The thought of revenge gives her strength. She moves onto her knees and slowly stands, trying to balance herself.

Garner turns to face her but he doesn't seem to care that she's standing now. "You deserve a lot more than that, Valdez. You and your greedy husband."

She gasps. She can't believe he would bring up Frank when he's holding her like this. She has to resist rising to the bait even though she badly wants to shoot him. She has to do everything by the book, otherwise she won't be able to take him down for abducting her. She takes a deep breath and releases it slowly and quietly.

Stay in control.

"What's happened here, Alan? What's so bad that you'd risk your job like this? I can help. Let's put the past behind us and work together. We're on the same side, remember?"

He looks like a man who needs to talk about his problems. But she can tell he thinks better of it because it's her.

If anyone else was standing in front of him right now, she suspects he'd open up.

Over the sound of the wind whistling through the cracks in the wood, she hears a boy scream, "Help!"

She looks around. "Who was that?" she asks.

Garner gets his gun out and then runs his left hand through his hair. He looks like he's trying to come to terms with terrible news.

She hears the boy's voice again before it's muffled by something. Or *someone*. It was coming from under the building.

"Garner? Who's down there? And why are you out here? You have to tell me everything right now so that we can help whoever that is."

Garner won't open his eyes, but he's making a strange sound into his hands.

She rolls her eyes in frustration. She can't have him falling to pieces on her while she's cuffed and helpless.

"Damn it, Garner. We're police officers and we're supposed to help people! There's a child down there crying for help. If you won't uncuff me and let me go down there, then you need to go and help that boy yourself."

He looks up at her then, with his bloodshot eyes. "It's too late for him. It's too late for all of us. We all have to die."

She's startled by his words. Was it Garner all along who took those girls? Is he a pedophile? A serial killer? He shouldn't even be in Lone Creek. He should be in McArthur. She wishes Roberts would hurry with the backup. Things are escalating too quickly. She needs to make time for Roberts or Matheson to find her.

"Alan, listen. Just take me down to wherever the boy is and let me assess the situation. *He's still alive.* That means it's not too late to turn this around. It will be so much worse for you if someone dies here today. There's no way to come back from that and remain a cop."

He looks wild now. "You want to *assess the situation*, Valdez?" He walks up to her and holds the gun against her face, pointing upward. "The situation is that I have the misfortune to have a son who gets his kicks through torturing little kids. And there's absolutely *nothing* any of us can do about it!"

He pulls back and turns away, leaving his spit to dry on her face.

Eva's shocked. Her legs start shaking and her mouth goes dry. This is much worse than she could ever have anticipated. She vaguely knew Garner had a grown-up son but she doesn't know anything about him. He doesn't talk about his family with anyone at work. Could he be exaggerating? Is this just a family drama that's gotten out of hand?

With a shaky voice she says, "Alan, please uncuff me. I'll go down there and take a look. Whatever happens to me, happens. But I can't help anyone with these cuffs on."

He looks like he's considering it so she continues. "You can keep your gun trained on me the whole time and you don't have to come down. But please let me try to help the boy. You'd be a hero then. I can tell everyone how you found him."

Garner looks at her and then slowly retrieves the handcuff keys from his coat pocket. He spins her around and tries to uncuff her but he's shaking too. Whether because of the cold or because of what he's witnessed, she doesn't know.

When she's certain the cuffs are unlocked, she lunges backward and headbutts his nose using the back of her skull. The pain is immediate and she thinks she might pass out. But it passes and she hears Garner drop to the floor. He didn't even cry out in pain.

Checking the back of her head for blood and trying not to think of her medical bill when she finally gets out of this town, she moves quickly. She looks around for a gun, hers or Garner's, but it's too dark to see anything on the floor. What little daylight there was is quickly fading. The weather is closing in on them again. The sun has vanished and she can hear something hitting the building hard. Hail.

She feels his pockets for her gun but it's not there.

"Dammit!"

She can't waste time searching for it. She looks around the room, trying to find a staircase to the basement. There's nothing in here. She walks into what was once a kitchen and she spots a closed internal door. She puts her ear against it and hears a boy sniveling.

He's down there.

She grabs a piece of wood that looks like it was once a leg from a dining table and then slowly opens the door. The difference in light up here compared to down there will give her away to anyone watching. She won't be able to do this unannounced.

"Hello?" she shouts down the stairs.

"Help me!" The boy shouts back. "I'm here!" He starts sobbing.

"Are you alone down there?"

"No. I'm here too."

A girl's voice, older than the boy's.

Eva's taken aback. She wasn't expecting that. Could it be one of the missing girls? Surely they can't still be alive. A shiver runs through her as the hairs on her arms stand up. She feels like she could cry when she realizes the girls could make it home alive. But their fate rests in her hands and how she handles this situation.

She realizes then that she had been convinced they were dead.

Before she thinks about it too much, she slowly descends the steps. "I'm coming down."

Too late, the girl shouts, "Be careful! There's someone else down here!"

She makes it down two steps before Garner creeps up behind her and pushes her down the rest of the way.

Eva hears her fellow captives cry out in dismay as their hope fades, just as she does.

CHAPTER THIRTY-EIGHT

Rocky's following a scent. Dean's surprised because previous attempts to teach him how to do this failed. He just hopes it's not a squirrel they're tracking.

The heavy hail stones can't get to Dean in the woods but he can hear thunder rumbling behind the menacing gray clouds. If there's lightning, he's in the wrong place and may need to fall back until it clears. He's no good to anyone dead.

Rocky barks, eager for Dean to hurry and catch up. Dean can feel the sandwich he ate trying to come back up because of all the running and the shock of what happened to Sergeant Roberts. But he runs faster, regardless. The tree branches hit him in the face more times than he can count. Eventually, Rocky stops. He doesn't bark this time, he just turns to look up at Dean.

Dean stops. "Is she here?" he whispers.

Rocky sits.

Dean tries to look through the trees and manages to see what looks like a private cabin, similar to the others nearer the lodge. This one, however, is much farther away. It's big and must have been charming in its time, but it's dilapidated now, proving Sandy right when he said the guests have stopped returning. Once word gets out to the press about

Olivia and Leroy's deaths, Sandy might find he needs to close the entire resort for good.

Dean watches Rocky get up and walk a few steps. He digs around with his nose and pulls out a single black glove that's half buried. Is it Eva's? It could be anyone's, and from any time. Gloves are probably the most frequently lost item of clothing ever, especially at a ski resort.

Rocky drops it at Dean's feet and barks low. It's Eva's then.

Dean draws his weapon and removes his borrowed hat. "Go back now," he says to Rocky. "You've done your bit."

Rocky doesn't understand so Dean points back the way they came. "Go get help."

Rocky always appears to know what the pointing means. He runs away, in the direction they came from. Dean's relieved. This is going to be stressful enough without Rocky getting in the way of another bullet.

He presses on, keeping low. As he approaches the building, he can see it's windowless on the side he's facing, so he should be safe from view. He approaches the front porch and stops to listen for voices. He hears shouting coming from inside, but it's faint out here. He can't make out who the voices belong to. Slowly, he climbs the front steps and stops outside the door. He can't see anyone in the front room through the smudged window, so he tries the door handle. It turns. He opens it quietly and steps inside.

The voices are louder now. They're a mixture of male and female and one of them is crying. He looks around the room and spots a gun half hidden under an old window shutter. He picks it up and releases the magazine, which he stuffs in his right pocket. He checks for a live round in the chamber and empties the one bullet into his hand before adding that to his pocket. The empty gun goes into his left pocket. This takes just seconds and when he takes his next step the rotten floorboards beneath him creak and the voices stop.

He looks down. That's where they're coming from then; the basement. That means they'll see dust fall between the cracks in the floorboards as he moves. He stands completely still as they listen. It doesn't take long for the voices to start up again.

Realizing this way is too dangerous because they could shoot up at him, he gently treads back the way he came and goes outside. He needs to find an exterior entrance to the basement.

The cabin is exposed to the weather because it's in a clearing and not fully under canopy. When a lightning bolt flashes through the sky above him and breaks a huge branch off of one of the pine trees nearby, he knows he needs to find shelter. He can't waste time out here or he could be struck any minute. The thunder that follows is so loud he feels the porch vibrate under his feet. The storm must be directly overhead.

Trying not to slip on the thick ice on the porch, he steps off it and walks to the right side of the building. That's when the downpour starts. Cold, hard rain. He's drenched within seconds. He doesn't want to put his hood up as it could obscure his view and he needs to be able to see everything right now. He protects his gun from the downpour by holding it under his coat. He has to ignore the chill that immediately seeps through his soaked clothes.

When he reaches the back of the building he finds steps leading down to a door. It can only be the basement door. He quietly makes his way to the bottom and tries to peer in through the dirty glass panes.

He can't see anything, but he hears Eva. He's sure of it, even though he can't tell what she's saying. Relief washes over him. At least she's still alive.

The door is padlocked on the outside but there's also a large, low window with just a screen covering it. The glass behind it is long gone from years of disrepair. He slowly pulls back the screen, just an inch at a time, stopping every few seconds, gun at the ready. He's thankful there's no sunlight to give him away. He takes a deep breath and doesn't stop to think how badly this could go. He carefully and silently climbs in through the window. His elbow catches on a shard of glass sticking out of the bottom left corner of the window frame. He has to ignore the pain but he feels the warm blood immediately run down his skin.

Trying to concentrate on the dark exterior, he realizes it must be a large basement as he can't see anyone on this side of it. Dean manages to slip in and go unnoticed thanks to a dividing wall. There's some old wooden furniture down here, as well as what looks like discarded landscaping tools and damp boxes. It's almost as cold in here as it is outside.

Something moves on the floor to his right and he has to stop himself calling out in shock. His eyes have adjusted to the dim light now.

It's a girl. She only looks about sixteen and she's impossibly thin. She's huddled with her arms around her knees, probably trying to keep warm. She's desperately trying to get his attention then she puts a finger to her mouth to tell him not to make a sound. That's when he notices the chain around her ankle.

What the hell is going on here? The bruising around the chain looks so painful he winces before he can hide his reaction. She ignores it and points beyond the wall.

Dean silently mouths a question. *How many people?*

She holds four fingers up, then adds another and points to herself. There are five other people in here altogether including the girl. Dean's alarmed. He can't take down three assailants on his own. Not unless Eva can get free and help him.

He gives the girl a thumbs up.

Silent tears fall down her pale face.

His heart breaks at the sight of her. He thinks it's Hannah Walker but he can't be sure; she looks so different from her photo. She doesn't have red hair, so it's unlikely this is Jodie. Dean realizes just how much is riding on what he does next. If he messes this up, she's a dead girl.

He looks around and notices another set of chains near her. This one sits empty on a large, dark stain. This must be where Jodie was kept. He thinks of the foot in the sink in his hotel room. Jodie's foot.

But where's the rest of her?

CHAPTER THIRTY-NINE

Dean waits silently so he can figure out who's here and who he needs to train his weapon on when he shows himself.

"You don't have to be complicit in this, Alan," Eva says. "There's still time to do the right thing. You said you didn't know he was capable of doing something like this until you found him out here with Dominic. You said you didn't know Hannah was down here all along, so this isn't your fault."

He's relieved to hear she sounds strong. She can't be hurt. Alan must be Garner's first name. He dares to poke his head around the corner of the dividing wall, just for a second.

Unfortunately, Olivia's son gives him away when he registers total shock at seeing him and cries out for help. Dean has just enough time to check who's standing where before he comes out with his weapon aimed at who he believes to be Detective Garner. The guy has blood seeping from his nose and drying on his chin. That must be down to Eva.

"Put the gun down. Now," he says to Garner.

The other man in the room, if you can call him a man, is holding Dominic, and when Dean appears, he pulls the boy toward him and starts making strange noises. He sounds like an overexcited monkey in a zoo. But, as far as Dean can tell, he's not carrying a weapon. This has to be Travis.

Garner has his gun pointed at Eva and he doesn't move when Dean walks over to her. "I recognize you," he says. "You and Valdez were having a nice romantic dinner together last night in the restaurant. Moved on from Frank already, Valdez? That didn't take long. Has this one been keeping you warm on your little skiing vacation?"

Dean doesn't dare take his eyes away from Garner but he can tell Eva is mightily offended. He hopes she keeps her cool, otherwise they could all get killed here and no one would ever know the truth about what happened.

Garner and his son could get away with this.

"Don't you dare mention Frank," she says through gritted teeth. "He was a better cop than you'll ever be. You've proven that here today."

Garner smirks at her and Dean wishes he wouldn't. Maybe he doesn't know what she's capable of.

"Come on, Valdez! Wake up and smell the coffee! Frank wasn't a good cop. He got killed because he was greedy."

Eva steps forward and the freak in the corner laughs way too loud. He wants blood. He actually wants to see his dad shoot her. He's such an odd-looking creature. Dean can't age him and he doesn't want to look at him. He can't imagine what it's been like for the girls to be trapped in the dark with this person. If ever there was a better likeness for the boogeyman, Dean's never met him.

Olivia's son is doing well, considering. He's standing as still as possible but his eyes are darting around like he's ready to make a run for it should the moment present itself. Dean prays he doesn't misjudge the timing and get them all killed.

"Eva," says Dean. "Nothing he says can change the truth about Frank. You know who he really was. Don't give him the reaction he wants."

Garner laughs and he almost takes his aim off of Eva, but not quite. That's all Dean would need. To distract him for one minute so he can shoot him in the arm or leg.

"Actually, I can say plenty about Frank. Did you know, for example, that he was part-owner of a thriving casino, along with me?"

Dean senses Eva's confusion without having to look at her.

"What? No, he wasn't," she says. "I would've known. He'd never go into business with the likes of you."

Garner laughs again. "You see! You don't know anything. You were living with a man who helped us launder over six hundred thousand dollars last year, all through our casino! He had all the right contacts, that's why we let him in on it. I will say he was a good crook, that's for sure. As for being a good cop . . . not so much."

Dean quickly glances at Eva. Her cheeks are red and she looks like she wants to jump on Garner, but she also looks unsure of herself for the first time since he's met her. Surely Garner can't be telling the truth?

"So when you told me earlier that I should've known what my own son was up to in here with these kids," says Garner, "how about you should've known what Frank was up to when he was *working late*." He raises his voice. "How about you stop accusing me of sexual harassment when your own husband was the biggest skirt chaser in Colorado? *McArthur's worst kept secret* we used to say. Except it was the best kept secret from his *detective* wife!" He shakes his head. "And you still don't understand why everyone in the department thinks you're an asshole!"

Dean sees Eva moving forward from the corner of his eye, so he pulls her toward him using his free hand. He keeps his eyes on Travis and Garner. "Don't fall for it. He could be lying to upset you."

"I'm not lying!" scoffs Garner. "You can ask anyone! Even Sergeant Roberts knows but he never had the balls to tell you."

"Is he in on it too?" she whispers.

"Roberts? Are you kidding me?" He laughs. "He's incorruptible, that one. Squeaky clean and dull. He heard the rumors of course, and came to visit us at the casino, unannounced. But he didn't find anything. He'd have to be in law enforcement a lot longer than he has been to find any fault with me. Then he was distracted by Frank's timely death."

Dean's desperately trying to think of a way out of this. He's alert to every single movement from every person in the room. Travis is sitting now. He's pulled the boy onto his lap, clearly enjoying the show. Dean can see his hands aren't touching the boy inappropriately so he doesn't have to worry about him too much just yet. He needs to get Eva to focus on getting everyone out of here alive.

"Eva, what's been going on in here? Is that Hannah Walker behind us?"

Eva comes out of a daze and looks at him. "It is. Travis abducted Hannah and Jodie. He's probably been taking kids and teens for years. He's a psychopath and a sexual predator."

Travis jumps up then, dropping the boy to the floor. "No!" he spits. "No, I am *not*! I don't want anything to do with them like that. That's *disgusting*!"

They hear a timid girl's voice behind them. "He tortured us. He burned us and made us eat food covered in rat droppings. He's evil!" Hannah finds her voice as she recounts how she was taken. "He found us outside the lodge, arguing. He told us we had to go with him to help him with something. Jodie didn't want to but I persuaded her because he's Sandy's nephew and I didn't want to get fired. But once we'd walked for a while, he wouldn't tell us what he needed help with and we both realized he was leading us too far away from the lodge. Jodie tried to run past him, to get back, so he tripped her up and hit her over the head with a baseball bat he'd been hiding under his coat." A sob escapes her. "The back of her head was bleeding and she was unconscious. I said I'd willingly go with him, to buy some time until I could escape, but he hit me too. When we woke up, we realized he'd dragged us somewhere. My back was bleeding for days and I have patches of hair missing from where it must've been torn out by branches as he pulled us along, one at a time."

Dean realizes it was Travis who attacked him and Eva with the baseball bat outside. He must've been trying to scare them off.

The freak is laughing. "And all along you were this close to the lodge. Close enough to get help! But, poor baby, no one came for you. No one cared!"

Hannah's face contorts. "What? I'm near the lodge?"

Dean doesn't take his eyes off the others to glance at her but she sounds devastated. It must be gut-wrenching to find out she was so close to potential help all that time.

"Does that mean Jodie made it back safe?" she asks.

He can't bring himself to answer and Eva makes moves to comfort her but Garner shakes his gun, reminding them who's in charge. Somehow, he looks as disgusted with the situation as they are. But it's no wonder they weren't found if the perp's father was the one in charge of the investigation.

Dean looks at Garner with disgust. "You covered for him. You knew they were rotting out here, you piece of shit."

Travis laughs and claps his hands together like a seal. "He *is* a piece of shit." He picks Dominic up off the floor and hugs him close. It makes Dean feel sick, so he can only imagine how it makes the boy feel.

Garner shakes his head. "I didn't know they were here. I haven't been in any of these old cabins for years. No one has. I had no way of knowing he'd ever take things this far."

Because of the look on his face, Dean believes him. He genuinely looks like he can't believe he's related to Travis. "So, what, you just didn't ask any questions? And you never did a proper search, did you? You were too scared of what you'd find. You must've known there was something seriously wrong with your son but you just left him to entertain himself, right?"

Garner doesn't reply. He's clearly struggling with his own emotions.

Dean wonders how the guy could ever move on from this, knowing what his son has been doing to these kids. Travis is probably only abducting kids because he doesn't have the physical strength to overpower adults. That's obvious just from looking at him. He would have thought Jodie, tall and athletic, could've overpowered him, but he had a baseball bat to control her. Maybe something else too.

"Garner?" asks Eva. "I know you hate me, so you're capable of saying anything to upset me, but please be honest for once in your life. Was any of that true about Frank?"

Dean's heart sinks. She shouldn't be focusing on this right now. It's going to affect their chances of getting everyone out of here alive. He needs her to help him get control of this situation.

Garner points his gun a little higher, at her head. Dean's hands are sweating and his arm is aching, making it hard to hold his gun.

"We all have secrets, Valdez. Frank had as many as me. He got too greedy and he had to go."

"What do you mean?" She takes a step forward and Dean puts his arm up in front of her, to act as a barrier. He's not going to let her get shot.

Garner's eyes narrow. "You really want to know what I mean? Okay then. Frank wanted more than his fair share. He was stealing it right out from under us. When I found out and confronted him, he said it was because he wanted out. He wanted to sail off into the sunset with a wad of cash and no responsibility. He said he'd tell the chief everything that was going on if I didn't let him get away."

Even Dean can see where this is heading. He has to stop this. Eva's shaking next to him. She clutches Dean's side.

"What did you do?" she whispers. Somehow, there are no tears.

Garner continues. "He reached for his weapon when he realized I wouldn't let him take the money and run. I couldn't let him get away with screwing us over. So I did what I had to do to survive. I couldn't shoot him without the bullet being traced back to me, so I stabbed him until he bled to death. He left me no choice. I got an acquaintance to dump his body by the convenience store."

Dean's stunned at the lack of emotion in Garner's delivery. This is a human being he's talking about.

Before he can stop her, Eva pulls her gun from his coat pocket. She must have felt it while she was using him to hold herself up.

She raises it to Garner's eye level and fires a shot.

Nothing happens because Dean emptied it of bullets. She screams in frustration and throws the gun at the detective's face, hard. It hits his already damaged nose, enraging him.

Dean pushes her out of the way of Garner's aim. Eva's breathing heavily. He hopes she's not going to suddenly leap up.

Travis starts yelping with delight and tugs hard at Dominic's hair, ripping it out in handfuls. Dominic's crying and trying to pull his hands away.

Garner looks at Travis but his gun stays pointed at Dean. His face is filled with hatred for his son. "You leave that boy alone, Travis. I'm only going to tell you once."

Dean's surprised. Perhaps he *isn't* okay with what his son does.

"You mean my brother?" spits Travis.

Dominic looks up at Travis, horrified. "Wh-what?"

"That's right! Your mommy told me a secret before I killed her. She told me you're my brother! We share the same daddy. That means we can share a room and play together forever and there's nothing you can do about it. You can sleep in my bed with me." He ends with a high-pitched, menacing giggle.

Dominic looks mortified. Dean isn't sure if he already knew his mom was dead but that, mixed with the prospect of sharing a gene pool with this monster, is threatening to tip him over the edge.

Disgusted, Garner says, "Shut up, Travis! Why do you have to be so screwed up? I'm embarrassed to call you my son!"

Travis' smile slides downward and his eyes shine menacingly. He pulls the boy's hair hard, in retaliation. "You love him more than me, don't you?"

Garner shakes his head in disgust. "I don't love you at all, you damn freak." He turns and shoots Travis straight through the heart.

Travis is dead before he hits the ground.

"No!" shouts Dean.

But it's too late. The gunshot blast deafens them for a while before all eyes are on Garner. If he's capable of killing his own son, he's capable of killing them. Dean raises his weapon and is about to squeeze the trigger but Garner beats him to it.

He places the gun's barrel against his own temple and shoots himself.

He falls to the floor. Dead.

Eva gasps.

Hannah and Dominic scream. The boy slides to the floor and bursts into tears.

Eva goes straight to Hannah so Dean hugs the boy. He holds him to his chest and repeats, "You're going to be okay," over and over. They're both shaking.

Eva hugs the girl. She turns to Dean with a look that suggests none of them are ever going to be okay again after all this.

CHAPTER FORTY

Eva sits in the kitchen with Dean, Hannah, and Dominic while Laura prepares food for them. They're segregated from the other guests and employees, who are in the restaurant, as they don't have the energy to answer questions right now. Eva's physically and mentally exhausted.

Sandy joins them and he looks downcast as he takes a seat next to Eva at the large island in the middle of the kitchen. Having learned what his brother and nephew did, he doesn't attempt conversation.

Eva didn't believe Dean at first, when he told her that Garner and Sandy are brothers. They're so different. She's annoyed that Sandy withheld it from her, but it's clear he feels responsible for everything that's happened at his family's resort. She doesn't think he was involved in any of it, but it's unclear how much he knew or suspected. That'll come out in the formal investigation, once backup finally arrives and they can all get the hell out of here.

Sandy looks like a broken man. She's going to have to keep a close eye on him. The next twenty-four hours could go either way. He might feel he has nothing left to live for.

"I'll have to tell Shirley soon," he says.

"Is that your brother's wife?" asks Dean.

Sandy nods.

"You'll also need to tell Leroy's parents that their son is dead," he says.

Sandy looks up, shocked. Laura gasps.

Dean explains. "He tried to rape Eva. He had a weapon and he didn't stand down, even after she warned him he'd be shot if he continued."

Eva had forgotten about that after everything else that's recently happened. A horrible feeling of dread returns to her stomach.

Sandy leans forward and puts his head in his hands. "I haven't told you this, because it's not exactly something I'm proud of, and to tell you the truth, I thought it was none of your business, but Leroy and Patrick are our nephews too."

She shares a look with Dean. This family is messed up. Hannah and Jodie couldn't have picked a worse place to work.

Sandy sighs. "My younger brother, Todd, was their father. He died years ago so I took the boys in when they were young. Their mother moved away and remarried. She didn't want them. Said they were unnatural. I never knew what she meant. They worked hard around here and that's all that mattered to me. Patrick's different to his brother, less arrogant, but he's easily led."

That explains why Sandy never fired Leroy and why he closed his eyes to so much of what was happening in this place. It was out of some misplaced sense of family duty. Eva thinks his heart was in the right place but he ignored it all for too long. "How did Todd die?" she asks.

"Good question," he says. "After everything that's happened, I'm starting to think Leroy had similar issues to Travis. He was the only person with Todd when he died out there on the slopes. We assumed it was an accident, or maybe suicide, but it wouldn't surprise me now if . . ." He doesn't finish his thought. He doesn't need to.

Eva doesn't know if evil can run in a family, but Leroy and Travis were similar in many ways. They did whatever

229

they wanted without caring about who they hurt. And neither of them knew when to stop. She's never dealt with anyone as wicked as them, especially Travis, but she thinks if she
talked to any convicted serial killer, she'd find they shared
similar traits to this pair.

Some people are just born bad. They don't need a reason
to be that way.

Laura speaks up. "Jodie said Leroy tried to rape her a few
weeks before she went missing. I told her to tell the police.
She said she told Detective Garner when he was staying over
with his wife one time."

Sandy shakes his head. "That wasn't his wife. That was
a random woman I'd never met before. And Alan never told
me what Jodie disclosed. If he had, I would've fired Leroy
and kicked him out. I can't believe how much goes on in this
place that I don't know about."

Eva thinks he's kidding himself. Part of him must've
known something.

"He's likely got a rap sheet for previous sexual assaults,"
says Dean. "You're not going to appreciate this but his body's
in Eva's bathroom. It probably smells pretty foul in there by
now. Make sure none of the employees find him."

"Who's going to clean that up?" asks Sandy.

"My team are on their way," says Eva. "They'll bring a
forensic team and the medical examiner. We'll take care of it."

Dean looks at her with a strange expression.

"It's a crime scene. Nothing should be touched until
they get here." She puts her hand on Sandy's. "You'll be
offered plenty of support. I know today has been devastating
for you, but please hang in there. You're not expected to cope
with this alone."

He nods.

Eva thought she was going to die in that basement. She
doesn't know how to process any of it: the conditions Travis
kept the girls in, the boy's face when he found out that monster was his brother, and seeing Garner shoot his son dead
before turning the gun on himself. She's still trembling and

she doesn't know how she'll explain all this to Sergeant Roberts when he arrives. Chief Carson needs to be investigated next. If any of what Garner said about Frank is true, then Carson must've known Garner killed him. Otherwise, he would've wanted a more thorough investigation into how he died.

As for Frank's involvement in the money laundering, she's numb to that for now. She's willing to give him the benefit of the doubt because of who the information came from, but she still doesn't want to think about it.

She takes a sip of coffee, which Laura filled with cream and sugar, and thinks of Alan Garner. What a terrible human being. How could he kill Frank, another police officer, just to avoid being exposed?

She'd felt a gun in Dean's coat pocket and immediately knew she would use it on Garner without hesitation for what he did to her husband. Now she's thinking rationally, she knows that would've been a terrible mistake.

If Dean hadn't emptied the weapon beforehand, she'd be arrested as soon as Roberts arrives. Killing another police officer is the very worst thing a cop can do.

Eva thinks of the detective from a small mountain town in southern Colorado who's been all over the news for months. Having killed a fellow officer, former detective Madison Harper is about to be released from prison. She's only served six years of her ten-year sentence for manslaughter. The outrage about her release, which is all over the media, shows the strength of feelings for cop killers.

Garner would've known that's what he was up against if word got out that he'd killed Frank. And he would've known that he and his son would be hated for the rest of their lives. In Eva's opinion, that's what made him take his own life. Not because he was sorry for his part in Travis' crimes.

It angers her to think Garner will never answer to a murder charge because he took the easy way out. He was too spineless to report his son's behavior and too spineless to face the consequences. And now she'll never get the satisfaction of seeing him convicted and sentenced to life in prison.

She takes a deep breath. She knows she'll have to let it go if she wants to be able to move on with her life. Besides, there are other things to focus on right now.

Dean told her Olivia is dead. That means there are now four dead people and one girl still missing. An internal investigation will be triggered and Eva will probably be suspended without pay while it's ongoing. Just what she needs, more money problems on top of everything else.

She realizes Dean's still staring at her. He probably thinks she's going to have some kind of breakdown. Maybe she will. It's been a tough month, to say the least. She wants to go home and speak to her foster dad. She needs him now. The thought of reliable, straight-talking George almost brings a tear to her eye, so she looks at Hannah as a distraction from her self-pity. Hannah's been through even more than she has, so she won't complain. Besides, she still has a job to do. She needs to get this girl taken care of at the hospital and reunited with her mother. And they still need to find Jodie Lawrence.

Dean comes over and gently rests his hand on her back. She owes him so much for the way he came to find her out there and then stuck by her when he could've walked away. He stopped her from killing Garner and he stopped Garner from killing her. She feels enormous gratitude but she doesn't know how to show it.

"Have some soup, it'll warm you up," he says.

Hannah's eating some too, really slowly. The first couple of mouthfuls came straight back up as she went too fast and her stomach has been starved of proper food for weeks. But she's managing to keep down smaller and slower portions. She looks like a skeleton; her eyes are sunken into their sockets and her cheekbones are protruding from under thin, pale skin. The soup is putting some color in her cheeks but she needs to get to a hospital as soon as possible. Eva doesn't think Hannah's condition is life-threatening but if she contracts pneumonia from the cold, or sepsis from her many wounds, things could quickly take a turn for the worse.

Eva leans forward and chooses a small bowl of soup and a spoon. The first mouthful tastes amazing. Her stomach growls greedily.

"I've finished all mine," says Dominic. "Can I have another bread roll?"

Dean smiles at him as Laura cuts open a roll to butter it.

Eva thinks about how resilient kids are. He takes the bread roll and asks if he can go and find his sisters in the restaurant next door.

"Of course," says Dean. "Don't leave the restaurant though."

Marshall is out there entertaining the kids with cheesy magic tricks.

Rocky's on the ground at Hannah's feet and Eva doesn't know whether that's to protect her or to catch any food she might drop. "Hannah? I hate to ask you so soon, but do you know what happened to Jodie?"

So far no one has mentioned her but if there's even a slim possibility she's still alive, they need to act fast.

Hannah puts her spoon down and pulls her new blanket tightly around her.

"She couldn't bear it any longer. She was convinced he was going to kill us next time he came, so she used a chainsaw." She stops and looks at Eva and Dean. Eva's heart sinks. They knew the foot had been cut off, but they hadn't known Jodie did it to herself.

"She cut through her own ankle." Hannah starts sobbing. "It was awful! She passed out almost immediately but it happened so quick. When she woke up her screams were unbearable but they were so loud I was sure someone would hear them and come to rescue us. But they didn't."

Dean exhales heavily. "I can't imagine how desperate she felt to have to go to those lengths. How did she get up after that?"

"I thought she would bleed to death within minutes but she strapped her belt around her leg to try to stem the blood flow," says Hannah. "Then she got straight up, to be on the move before she lost too much blood. It must've been adrenaline keeping her going. She even picked her foot up to take it with her, which is more disturbing than anything else. She said she wanted to leave it outside somewhere, like some kind of trail to find where she'd been if someone was looking for us. But we were disoriented after we were taken that night, so we didn't know where we were being kept. I think he drugged us. If I'd known we were so close to the lodge I probably would've done the same thing as her. She wouldn't have known where we were though. Before she left she kissed me goodbye and promised to bring help." Hannah looks down at her hands. "I told her I hated her for leaving me there. Those were my last words to her."

Dean moves to hug her. Eva feels depleted of everything: energy, motivation, and life. How can someone put a young woman in a position where she'd rather saw off her own foot than face the alternative?

"She'll know you didn't mean it," says Dean. "She wouldn't have taken it to heart. Olivia gave us your camera but it had some disturbing photos on it. Did Jodie have it with her?"

She nods. "She borrowed it on her date with Bryan. She must've kept it in her coat pocket because she used it while we were chained up. She wanted to see what damage Travis had done when he hit her over the head, so she took a photo of where he hit her. Just after she escaped, I saw some flashes. I assumed she was using it to light her way, because it was pitch-black outside when she escaped." She pauses. "Can I ask you something?"

They both nod.

"Do you think she's still alive?"

Eva looks at Dean, unsure how to respond.

"Did Travis ever say he caught up with her?" he asks.

"No. But he left us alone for long periods. It was only yesterday that he came back and discovered she'd gone. He ran straight out to look for her and I didn't see him again for hours. He came back with his dad close behind. And this time he brought Dominic with him. His dad was shocked when he saw me there. He left the building so angry he was yelling things about Travis. When he eventually came back, he had you with him." She looks at Eva.

"So Travis never found Jodie," says Eva. "That means she either collapsed and froze out there in the woods or she could've made it into a hiding place. She could still be in hiding, too scared to reveal herself." She takes a deep breath and softens her tone as she says, "But Hannah, I really don't think that's a possibility. I hope it is, but until we find her, we just don't know. She was badly injured. There's little hope of finding her alive. I'm sorry."

Hannah nods and pushes the rest of her soup away. Her appetite has vanished.

Laura's struggling to hold back tears. She puts her arms around Hannah.

"Are you able to look after them all?" asks Dean. "I have to go back out."

Laura nods.

Eva stands. "I'm going with you."

She picks up her service weapon from the table in front of Dean and he passes her the magazine he removed. She loads it. She doesn't have to ask where he's going. He wants to find Jodie. They both know she's out there somewhere, either frozen in the snow or hiding in an outbuilding. There may only be two of them but they can at least begin the search. Backup can take over when they arrive.

She's relieved Dean doesn't suggest she stays behind. He must know she needs to do this and he's just as exhausted as she is.

He looks down at Rocky. "Are you up for one final trip in the snow before we head home to Vegas?"

Rocky doesn't even bark. He turns around and runs ahead of them.

CHAPTER FORTY-ONE

They wrap up warm but the storm appears to have abated while they were inside. The sun is out, which is a relief to Eva. It's already melting the snow in places. The trees are dripping wet and Rocky's zig-zagging ahead of them, nose down and tail high.

When Dean mentioned Vegas, she was tempted to join him and get a flight out there instead of staying here to face the music. But she needs answers from Chief Carson as much as he'll want answers from her.

"I wish Roberts would hurry up and get here," Eva says as they head toward the woods, hopefully for the last time. "What's taking him so long? He could've walked here by now."

Dean stops dead in front of her like he's just remembered he left something back at the lodge. He turns around to face her, putting his hands on her shoulders.

"It wasn't the right time to tell you this earlier."

"What?" She's worried. She can't take any more bad news.

"Eva, I was talking to him on the phone before I came to find you."

He hesitates, which drives her mad. She shakes his hands off her. "And?"

"I think he's dead. I heard a loud gunshot from his end of the line and then Roberts wouldn't answer me. It was followed by breathing, as if someone was listening in to see who Roberts was talking to. But then the call ended."

Eva takes a step back. "*What?* But who would kill Roberts? And why? Just how many people are in on this?"

Dean moves toward her. "Maybe someone from your department followed him. Someone who stands to get dragged down in all this if exposed, or maybe one of the other casino partners. You know as well as I do what lengths people will go to in order to protect their money."

Eva's legs give way. She sits in the snow as she realizes no backup is coming. They're here alone and Roberts is dead. Kind, caring Nick Roberts was the only person in the department who was on her side. He could've helped her stand up to Chief Carson. He would've had her back when all this got out. He didn't deserve to die.

Dean crouches next to her. "Eva, think. Who could've been working with Garner? Because whoever shot Roberts is still out there and probably on their way here. I don't think they'd hurt the others inside, because that can't be pinned on Travis and they'd be exposing themselves. But they probably want us out of the picture."

She doesn't know what to say. Could it be Chief Carson? She can't think of anyone else as loyal to Garner, except Sheriff Bowerman. She feels completely despondent. Who is she supposed to contact for backup now? Her entire department could be in on it for all she knows, as well as the sheriff's office.

"I can't trust any of them," she says. "We need to call the FBI. This has gone too far."

"I agree," he says. "Head back to the lodge and call them. Tell them not to speak to your department until they've spoken to us face-to-face. I'm going to find Jodie."

She gets up. "I'm not leaving you alone out here. We'll phone them when we get back."

Frustrated, Dean says, "Eva, it's more important to get backup right now. I'll be fine, I have Rocky."

She walks ahead of him, ignoring what he says. He wouldn't leave her alone out here with a madman on the loose so she's not leaving him. "We're both armed and we can handle whatever's out here," she shouts behind her. "It's more important to find Jodie. She could still be alive."

CHAPTER FORTY-TWO

Dean has nothing but respect for Eva but that doesn't stop her from being infuriating. She's just found out her police department is corrupt, her husband wasn't who she thought he was, and he was murdered by another cop because of it. She should be inside, digesting that over a bottle of scotch instead of out here looking for Jodie. She looks like she's on the verge of passing out. There's only so much a person can take before they reach their breaking point and Eva must be near hers. Her pale skin and bloodshot eyes tell him she's not up to looking for Jodie right now. They could really do with the Feds here to take over.

He's hoping Jones has already called them but he knows he can't rely on that with Barbara being ill.

He catches up to Eva. Rocky has Jodie's scent from a scarf Hannah gave them and Dean just hopes the dog can work his magic again. He's running ahead of them with his nose to the ground. It's just a game to him.

They reach the location where they found Jodie's boot and slow down as they pass it. She could have collapsed at any point from here onward, so they need to be vigilant. As they look around, using sticks to search through the snow, Rocky runs in all directions. The scene around them would be beautiful if they weren't looking for a dead body. The melting snow falls as water drops from the branches, making relaxing dripping sounds, and the birds are out looking for food in the afternoon sunshine.

Rocky circles an area ahead of them before sitting down and looking back at them.

"What've you got, boy?" asks Eva.

Dean approaches them. It takes a minute but he finds a gold necklace with a butterfly pendant hanging from a low branch. From the way it's hanging, it's obviously been placed there on purpose, not just lost. They would never have spotted it themselves.

Eva lowers her eyes. "She was leaving a trail with anything she had on her."

Dean tries to ignore how sad that is. "Let's split up. You take the left side of the trail; I'll take the right. We need to find everything she left for us."

They carry on. Dean hears Eva trying to sniff back tears. He's not sure whether they're for Jodie or for the shattered memories of her husband. He doesn't attempt to comfort her because he knows she wouldn't want him to. He'll take her out for dinner when all this is over. They need to get drunk together and let off some steam. He just hopes she wants to stay in touch. It would be understandable if she didn't. She'll probably always associate him with the time she found out the truth about her husband.

It would be a shame though. He doesn't think he'll be able to forget her.

Dean stops for a second. His right shoe is rubbing against his heel and a blister is forming fast. They've reached a steep incline up to Wolf Peak. They stop at the wooden sign at the bottom and Dean can hear Eva panting. It's not surprising. They've walked a long way already and, although it's warm in the sun, it's still hard work after the day they've had.

They both look up.

"Surely she didn't make it up there?" says Eva.

Dean rests his hands on his hips. "I doubt it. Even in the dark she would've noticed the incline and realized upward wasn't the best direction."

He looks around and spots what appears to be a cave under the incline. The entrance is almost completely hidden by snow drifts.

Rocky spots something at the same time and runs over there. He starts barking and digging until he pulls something out of the snow with his teeth. He comes running over to them with a pink bootlace in his mouth. It matches the bootlace in the hiking boot they found.

Dean's heart sinks. He looks at Eva. "Stay here."

They don't both need to see whatever's over there. If he can spare her the sight of Jodie's body, he will. Not because he thinks she can't handle it, but because he doesn't want her to have to handle it. Not on top of everything else. Finding dead people is without a doubt the worst part of a police officer's job.

His feet feel heavy as he makes his way over to where Rocky's digging through the snow. Rocky makes it into the cave just as he gets there. Dean slowly raises his eyes to look into the hidden enclosure.

Someone's in there.

Before he enters, he braces himself. He doesn't want this to be the way Jodie's story ends, but he knows it's useless to delay the inevitable. Finally, he pushes his way in and with the snow drifts gone, the sun partially lights the cave.

There's a body on the ground.

It's Jodie. There's no doubt about it. She's missing a foot. He crouches next to her. She's in a fetal position, suggesting she was trying to keep warm. Her red hair is faded and tinged with blue ice, and her frozen eyelashes keep her eyes closed. Her skin is gray and lifeless. She covered herself in broken branches from the pine trees outside the cave, trying desperately to delay the inevitable.

Dean can't imagine what was going through her mind while she was out here all alone. Travis' death was easy in comparison, and the injustice angers him.

Although Jodie's probably been dead a long time, he touches her anyway. He places his hand on her face, knowing his body heat won't wake her but needing to provide some kind of comfort.

He lowers his head. "I'm so sorry, Jodie. I'm sorry we didn't find you in time."

Rocky sits close to Jodie and whines.

Dean hears Eva approach. He turns around to stop her. With a lump in his throat, he says, "Don't look. It's her."

She rushes forward and kneels next to Jodie. Tears of frustration and grief soon come pouring out of her unhindered.

Dean kneels beside Eva and pulls her to him.

CHAPTER FORTY-THREE

Rocky won't budge but Dean and Eva need to get back to the lodge to call the FBI. They reluctantly leave him there, next to Jodie. It's warming up outside the cave, thanks to the sunshine, and Dean knows Rocky will find his way back if they don't turn up with help soon. It's just something Rocky wants to do and there's nothing Dean can do about it.

Halfway back to the lodge, as the light from the day is beginning to fade, Eva collapses. "I need a quick break."

He thinks she's suffering from shock or exhaustion. Her body's trembling and she can't catch her breath. He looks up and faces the last of the sunshine in the hope of it recharging his energy levels. When all this is over, he needs a proper break. A vacation in the sun would be good. Maybe he and Rocky should move to Miami next. At least it's on the East Coast so it might not be as hot as Vegas is in the summer.

He hears footsteps crunching through the snow behind him. It must be Rocky. He spins around with a smile. It falters the minute he notices the gun.

A woman stands just ten feet away and she doesn't look happy. She's pointing a gun at Eva.

"You're the bitch, aren't you?" she says. "The one who falsely accused my husband of all sorts of crap. I recognize you from the news. Your husband was stabbed to death."

Eva doesn't respond and Dean quickly realizes this is Detective Garner's wife. Mother of Travis.

"Mrs. Garner?" he says. "I need you to put the gun down."

"Why should I?" she screams at him. "It was *her*, wasn't it? She killed my family! She's always had it in for us. Alan was always cursing her name at home."

She must've found her husband and son dead. But why is she even here and how did she know to go to that cabin? Did she know what Travis was up to or does she think he's the innocent victim in all this?

Dean moves closer to Eva, who's still sitting in the snow. She's being very quiet, which is unlike her. He can't risk looking back at her but he hopes she hasn't passed out. "Have you been up here the whole time?" he asks.

"I came to find my son." Her face is lined with anger. "Imagine my surprise when I met a cop on my way up here. He didn't know who I was. He told me he was worried something bad was going on up at the lodge and he needed to get there urgently. I knew then that something had gone wrong for Travis. I overheard him talking to someone on the phone about my husband. So I said I'd show him the way."

Dean realizes it was her who killed Sergeant Roberts. "Please, listen to me," he says. "We didn't shoot your husband."

"I don't care about him!" she yells. "You killed my son! He already had a hard life thanks to people like you and now you've killed him. How *dare* you?"

She waves the gun around like she doesn't even remember she's holding it. That could be good. It means she's easily distracted.

"No, you're wrong," says Dean. "Your husband shot Travis. Then he killed himself." He really wishes Rocky would turn up right about now and jump on her from behind. But there's no sign of him. He should've heard their raised voices.

Dean's heart skips a beat.

Garner's wife came from the direction they just left. Where they'd left Rocky, alone. Does that mean she's already killed him, in retaliation?

"Mrs. Garner, please. I understand you're upset but I need you to put the gun down." Dean can't reach for his own without it being obvious. "Your son was holding two teenage girls and a young boy against their will. He had them chained up and he was torturing them. We don't think this is the first time he's done it. I know this will come as a shock to you but I'm telling the truth. You have to listen to me." She doesn't acknowledge what he says so Dean continues. "We think your husband knew what Travis was capable of and may have been involved in covering up for him."

She scoffs. "Don't be so damned stupid! Alan didn't have the guts to help Travis. He might have overlooked a few things in order to keep his job but he was too chickenshit to help him. That was all me."

Eva gasps.

Dean's stunned. "Are you telling us you knew what your son was doing to those girls?"

She looks at him like he's the crazy one. "Of course I did! What mother doesn't know what her kids are up to? Travis picked his favorites and I sometimes had to help him. The feisty ones would need drugging and chaining. The younger ones were easier. I never stayed once he had them. I let him do whatever he needed to do." She must see the look of disgust on Dean's face because she pauses for a second. "You're judging me, aren't you? Who are you to judge me? Are you perfect? He's my son and if teasing others made him happy in his otherwise shitty existence, then so be it. If he didn't get it out of his system once in a while, he'd be unmanageable. It was the only way to keep him happy. I'm his *mother*. I need to see my son happy."

Incredulous, Dean says, "*Teasing*? You call what your son was doing *teasing*? Your son was so despicable to the two girls from this resort that one of them cut off her own foot to escape from him!" He's shouting, but he doesn't care. "Then she froze to death alone out here because she was so desperate to get away from Travis!"

Shirley Garner looks at him without shock or remorse. He realizes then that he's fighting a losing battle, because she's always known her son was a monster. She knew more than Garner did. But she never reported him. She's just as responsible for Jodie's death as Travis is.

She takes a step closer. "My Travis was a good boy. He only took those who deserved it."

"Really?" shouts Dean. "What did six-year-old Aaron Carlton do to deserve it?"

She smiles, convinced his abduction was justified. "Olivia's son? Oh, that was a good one. He was young and he squealed like a pig. It made Travis so happy. We picked him together, after I found out Olivia had been screwing my husband."

Dean's astounded at her rationale. "But Aaron was just a child. Why was that his fault?"

"It was his mother's fault. Aaron was collateral damage." She snorts. "Are you dumb or something? Can't you see Travis was just living out the pain of being rejected by his father? He felt mentally tormented so, in turn, he physically tormented kids who had it better than him. That was how he coped. His dad was always looking for a medical diagnosis for Travis, to find out what caused him to be that way. But *he* was the cause all along. And I think Alan knew that deep down. That's why he was never home. He never spent any time with his son, he never showed him any affection. So I had to protect Travis because I was all he had, and he was all I had. But you killed him. And now I have nothing left to live for."

Dean shakes his head. "You're wrong. Plenty of kids grow up rejected by their parents but they don't become serial killers. Your son was sick. Any doctor should've been able to see that. He should've been reported to the police the first time you realized what he was doing. Instead, you stood by and watched him get worse. You helped him kill *children*. You even encouraged him, in Aaron's case. How many were there all together, Shirley?"

She's mad now and he can see the physical resemblance to her son in her face. He wonders whether Travis did all this to please her. Could her twisted relationship with him be the real cause of his actions?

"There were more than you'll ever find," she says. "But you're wrong about Travis being a monster. He was just an innocent boy."

Dean can't believe she's still defending him. "You failed him as a mother and you're an accessory to murder. I'm going to make sure you pay for what you let him do."

She raises her gun before Dean can pull his out from under his coat. She shoots at him twice and the second bullet hits his stomach, tearing through his abdomen.

The pain is sudden, hot, and sharp, and it spreads quickly.

Just after he hears her gunshots, he hears another. She must have shot Eva too.

As he slowly sinks to the snow clutching his wounded stomach, Garner's wife drops to the ground in front of him. He notices the bullet hole in her throat before he loses consciousness.

CHAPTER FORTY-FOUR

McArthur, Colorado

Eva, Dean, and Hannah have all been treated in the same hospital. Eva came in at George's insistence. He came to stay with her the minute she told him what had happened. The hospital team fixed up her head wounds and the knife wound where Leroy had stabbed her arm, but they haven't been able to treat her depression.

It's not something she's ever suffered with before, but it hangs over her every minute of the day. She's been told it's part of the grieving process, so she's hopeful she'll get through it eventually.

Hannah Walker is doing well, thanks to youth being on her side and her mom joining her. She's being released from the hospital today. Her mom is taking her back to Vegas, where she'll be under the medical supervision of a doctor closer to her home.

Unfortunately, Dean isn't doing as well. He's been in ICU for a week now. He almost slipped away twice, during two major surgeries. The first surgery to remove the bullet didn't go well so they had to go in a second time a couple of days later. They got the bullet that time.

Eva doesn't know who his friends and family are as his phone was lost at the lodge. She hasn't had much time between giving statements to the FBI and trying to recuperate, but she needs to make it a priority today to find someone to come and visit Dean. Just in case the worst happens.

Special Agent Danielle Carter told her they were contacted by a detective in Dean's hometown which is why they eventually turned up at the resort, but Carter was reluctant to give Eva his name and number. She finally got that out of her after Dean's condition worsened, so Eva will start with him. Detective Harry Jones. She owes him a drink because the Feds arrived by helicopter within an hour of Dean being shot, while she was still out there with him, trying to stop his blood loss. She was convinced they were both going to die.

She visits Hannah first as she knows she and her mom will be flying out of here the minute she's released. As Eva enters the hospital room, Hannah's sitting on her bed, dressed and ready to go. She's gained weight and her bruising is a pale shade of yellow now, instead of black. The burns on her legs are no longer blistering and she has life in her eyes for the first time since she was discovered. She's made some attempt at wearing makeup, but it looks a little odd against her pale skin.

When Jackie sees Eva, she hugs her. "Thanks for coming to say goodbye. I still don't know how to thank you for finding her."

Eva repeats what she's already told her. "It wasn't just me. Be thankful you hired a good PI. I don't think I would've gotten the same results on my own out there."

She sits on the bed next to Hannah and touches her hand. "Are you ready to start college and get back to normal?"

Hannah smiles. "I'm ready to get out of Colorado and I don't ever intend to return. I just wish Jodie was coming with me."

Eva nods. Jodie's body was taken by the coroner and the Feds are trying to track down her family. Jodie's life story is sad from start to finish and Eva wishes it was a one-off, but she knows there are lots of kids living outside the warmth of a decent, loving family.

She regularly wonders whether, if they'd found her a few days earlier, she would've still been alive. But she knows in her heart that Jodie probably died the same night she escaped. It was a brave and daring thing she did but it didn't pay off, and that's the worst part.

A male doctor enters the room and smiles at them all. "Mrs. Valdez! My second favorite patient. I hope you've come to see me?"

She laughs. Dr. Casey is tall, dark, and just her type, and they've been pretending to flirt for days. She suspects he flirts with all his patients.

"Afraid not. I've come to see Hannah. We're just saying our goodbyes."

"Well, I'll add mine to those," he says. "You're officially free to go, Hannah. But you must take care of yourself. Don't push yourself too hard, and make sure you keep gaining weight. I don't want to see any selfies on social media with hashtag size zero."

Hannah laughs. "I'm going to eat my entire weight in chocolate as soon as I'm out of here so you don't need to worry about that."

"Good. And this is for Mom." He hands Jackie a sheet of paper and as he folds it in half, Eva notices it has the contact details for a psychotherapist in Vegas. "Make sure she goes regularly."

Jackie nods and slips the piece of paper into her purse.

Dr. Casey hugs Hannah. "Have a safe flight." Then he turns to Eva. "I'll see you in Dean's room."

Eva's heart sinks. She hopes it's not bad news.

She hugs both Jackie and Hannah. "I'm so glad we found you in time, Hannah. You've been given a second chance. You need to make sure you live life to the full now."

"This is my third chance," she says, referring to what happened with her best friend back in England. "I'll do it for both of them."

Eva nods. "You have my number. Call me if you need me."

"Please keep us updated on Mr. Matheson's condition," says Jackie.

"I will." She watches them leave. She feels her depression bearing down on her but knows she has to focus on what she and Dean *were* able to do, not what they weren't. Hannah's still alive. That's because of them.

She heads upstairs to Dean's floor. As she nears his room, she hears male voices.

She stops at his door and her mouth drops open.

Dean's sitting up in bed. He looks like crap but he's awake. He notices her approach and he smiles in that way that used to annoy her but now makes her smile back. He has serious bed hair, a jaw covered in stubble, and his face is crumpled from sleep, but he's finally awake.

Dr. Casey calls her in. "Are you just going to stare?"

"When did this happen?" she asks as she takes a few steps toward the bed.

"Great," the doctor says to Dean. "You've only been awake five minutes and she's already lost all interest in me."

Dean says, "Hey, Eva. How are you?"

He looks pathetic and sad and handsome all at the same time. She never expected to feel so relieved to see him awake. She rushes forward and hugs him. They've been through something together that no one else would understand.

"I'm so glad you're alive," she says into his neck.

He hugs her back.

CHAPTER FORTY-FIVE

Dean listens as Eva explains how the FBI swooped in and took charge of the situation, thanks to Detective Jones. The Feds have already found the remains of other bodies buried around the grounds of the resort and it's likely Aaron Carlton will be among them. It's going to be a long, complicated process to ID everyone and Dean's relieved he doesn't have to be involved in that, but all he can really think about right now is Rocky.

Eva hasn't mentioned him once and he obviously isn't here. To Dean, that can only mean that Shirley Garner was following them out there in the woods, after finding her son and husband dead. She must've killed Rocky before catching up with them. Dean can't bring himself to ask about him. After all, who else would be looking after him if not Eva?

His head's throbbing and he can barely move thanks to all the stitches in his stomach. Apparently, it was touch and go for a while and it's going to take time for him to heal properly. But if he has to add burying Rocky to the long list of crap to come out of this assignment, he doesn't think he could bear it.

"What's the matter with you, you're sweating," says Eva. "Do you need some water?"

He doesn't speak. His throat seizes.

She stands up and puts her hand on his. "Dean, what's wrong? Should I get the doctor?"

He shakes his head and manages one word. "Rocky?"

She frowns. "What about him?"

It takes a long, painful minute before she understands what he's asking. Her face relaxes into a smile. "He's fine, Dean. He's absolutely fine."

He looks up at the ceiling. "Thank God."

She takes his hand. "You sentimental douche!" She laughs. "Were you worrying about him the whole time I was babbling away about the Feds? He's at my house. My foster dad's taking care of him. He's finally got the grandchild he always wanted."

Dean laughs, but it makes pain tear through his stomach and he winces. "Bring him with you next time?"

"I'm not allowed, I tried. I had this Disney notion that because you're both so freakishly attached to each other, one lick from Rocky and you'd wake up. But the nurses wouldn't let me. They think dogs are unhygienic. And to tell you the truth, after seeing Rocky lick his own balls, I'd have to agree."

Dean laughs again but the pain returns. "Stop!"

She gets serious then. "He's pretty tired though. He won't even run over for a treat anymore; he just waits for me to bring it to him. He needs a rest, Dean. This adventure has worn him out. How old is he?"

Dean feels guilty. He knows she's right. "He's nearing old age. It kills me to say it but I think this might have to be his last case."

An unexpected visitor arrives.

Laura hesitantly walks in. "Am I interrupting? Hey, you're awake!"

Eva hugs her. "Thanks for coming."

Laura looks at Dean. "How are you?"

"I'm fine, now," he says. "Out of the woods in more ways than one. But what are you doing down here? You haven't lost your job, have you?"

She sighs. "Sandy's closed the place. He's finally given up and is selling it to one of the bigger resort companies. They've got big plans for the place, apparently, but not until the FBI has finished tearing up the grounds. They've made such a mess that Sandy couldn't have sold it for much."

Dean's not surprised. "Is he okay with selling it?"

Laura shrugs. "He said he couldn't go on living there now so many of his family members have died there. If you ask me, that resort is cursed. I'm sure that's what sent everyone crazy."

"I'm not so sure," says Eva. "I think it's more likely his family is cursed."

"Maybe. The new owners offered me Olivia's job for when it re-opens, but I couldn't do that. I've decided to go to college and study hospitality management. I'd like to run my own place one day. Just a small inn or a guest house. After all, there's never a dull moment in hospitality!"

"That's great," says Dean.

"Oh, I almost forgot," she says. "I found a cell phone in the restaurant. Is it yours?" She pulls it out of her purse and hands it to him.

He's relieved to have it back, but it won't switch on. "It is. Eva, could you plug it in?"

Eva goes to find a spare charger from one of the nurses.

"Do you know what happened to Olivia's children?" asks Dean.

Laura takes a deep breath. "Child Protective Services took them and I haven't seen them since. Olivia's funeral is next week and I'm going to go so, hopefully, I'll see them there."

Eva comes back with a phone charger and plugs it in next to his bed.

"I should go," says Laura. "I just wanted to drop your phone off and see if you were awake yet. I'm glad you both came to help Jodie and Hannah. It's reassuring to know not all cops are like Detective Garner."

They say their goodbyes and she leaves.

Dean switches his phone on and after a few seconds, it starts buzzing with notifications. He sees a text from Greg, the veterinarian, confirming Rocky has arthritis. He says it's common in older dogs and treatable, but he should be taking it easy now. That settles it. Rocky has to retire.

Dean doesn't want to think about that right now. Among the other notifications, he has eleven missed calls from Jones.

"Damn. I completely forgot about Barbara."

"You didn't forget anything, you've been unconscious," says Eva. "Who's Barbara?"

"She's Detective Jones' wife. They're like family to me. While we were in Lone Creek, he phoned to say Barbara was sick with flu."

"Flu's horrible but not life-threatening, right?"

"That's what I thought," he says, "but she was in the hospital last time we spoke. He wanted me to fly home ASAP but obviously I couldn't because of the storm. It was terrible timing."

Dean selects Jones' number with shaky hands. He hasn't been awake that long but he's exhausted already and can't wait to go back to sleep.

Jones answers on the fifth ring, which is longer than it usually takes him. "Dean." His voice is flat. "Where've you been?"

"Sorry I missed your calls. My phone's been missing. How's Barbara?"

Jones hesitates. "She's gone, Dean. She's gone."

He sits up straight and his stomach stings in protest. "*What?* What do you mean?"

With a sigh his friend says, "She died yesterday. We're all devastated. I wish you'd been here. You should've spoken to her one last time. You know what? I can't do this right now. I'm so disappointed." He hangs up.

Dean tries calling him back immediately but an automated voice tells him Jones has switched his cell phone off. He tries calling the home phone but there's no answer.

"What's wrong?" asks Eva.

Dean feels the blood drain from his face. "I can't believe it. She died, and now Jones won't take my calls. I have to go home." He pulls back the covers and tries to move his legs but the pain forces him back.

Eva notices his stitches bleeding through his gown. She pushes him backward. "Keep still, you're tearing your wound open!"

She presses the button for a nurse.

CHAPTER FORTY-SIX

Las Vegas, Nevada

Eva still isn't quite sure how Dean got her to agree to this road trip. He was adamant about going home to New Hampshire in time to make Barbara's funeral but he wasn't in any fit state to fly. Plus, there was the dog to consider.

Finally, she got so sick of him asking her that she checked with Special Agent Carter whether she was cleared to take a vacation. Agent Carter was pretty understanding, seeing as both Eva and Dean had now been interviewed a few times on camera about everything they did and witnessed at the Winter Pines Ski Resort.

Eva's still at their beck and call and they can tell her to return with a moment's notice, but she's been cleared of any wrongdoing in regards to Leroy's death. Her exemplary police record, together with what Agent Carter dug up on Leroy, meant they were satisfied she was acting in self-defense. The Feds believe that Leroy would have added murder to his record of sexual assaults against women if she hadn't shot him.

Eva wasn't surprised to learn he had a long list of allegations against him. Agent Carter said he hadn't actually been convicted of any assaults as they all occurred when he was in high school and none of his victims ever went as far as to give evidence against him, but the complaints were logged anyway. Eva wonders whether Detective Garner was involved in scaring his accusers into silence, to protect his family's reputation.

It doesn't bear thinking about.

Technically Dean isn't well enough to leave the hospital but he checked himself out anyway. He's made progress since then but it still hurts him to stand up and sit down, so he couldn't have driven himself.

She knows they both needed to get out of Colorado so she didn't put up much of a fight in the end. And she's never been to New Hampshire before. The way Dean talks about the place, it sounds too good to be true. He told her all about his old team at Maple Valley PD and how most of them had each other's backs.

Eva's nervous about her stay in Maple Valley because she had to admit to Dean that she's broke, mainly because of Frank's funeral expenses and going from a two-income household to just one. He immediately told her to stay with him at his house. Apparently, the woman who was renting it from him has moved in with her fiancé, so there are two spare bedrooms available. It's not that she's nervous about staying with him — after all, she shared a room with him in Lone Creek — but she doesn't like not paying her way. And she knows something went down before Dean moved away and he still hasn't opened up to her about it. All she knows is that his wife was murdered and he feels responsible.

They arrive in Vegas just as it gets dark. Dean needs to collect his belongings and say goodbye to his boss because he won't be living in Vegas any longer. Eva asked if that means he'll stay in New Hampshire after Barbara's funeral but he's adamant he won't. He keeps talking about Miami being the best of both worlds: East Coast but warm.

He gives her directions to drive through the strip to his apartment. The strip is illuminated, loud, and buzzing, even though it's only three days until Christmas. They're staying overnight and Eva intends to try to make some money in a casino.

"Is it true the house always wins?" she asks.

"I don't know," he says from the passenger seat. He's more awake now that he's almost home. "I haven't gambled once since I've been here." He turns to her and smiles.

"What?" she says.

"That could be your vice. Gambling."

She laughs. "Sorry to disappoint you but I just don't have an addictive personality."

"We'll see about that," he says. "Take a left here, I'm just across the street."

As she pulls into a parking space, she notices two women outside an empty store. They're waving at Dean. The small one is cute, like a mini-Dolly Parton.

Dean's out of the car before she even kills the engine and Rocky jumps out behind him. She watches Dean stumble over to them and accept their hugs. Rocky's tail is working overtime. She plans to give them all space and go for dinner somewhere on the strip, but the petite lady waves her over.

Eva locks up the car and crosses the road.

Happier than she's seen him for a long time, Dean says, "Eva, this is Marilyn and Martha. Let's go upstairs and catch up."

* * *

Marilyn is quite a character. She has them laughing so hard that Eva thinks Dean's stitches will tear open again. Marilyn brought two large bottles of vodka with her and Eva's already getting drunk on her oversized shots.

"Marilyn, if you keep drinking like this, you'll have another stroke," says Dean.

"I've already told her," says Martha.

"Stop ruining my fun," says Marilyn. "I'm retired, I can do what I want. Besides, we've all got to die of something, right?"

259

Their takeout pizzas arrive. Eva and Dean are starving. They eat theirs without talking, as Marilyn reminisces about Dean's arrival in town.

"You should've seen him when he first came here," she says. "He was like a little boy lost. You know those fish-out-of-water movies where a character stumbles around New York City like it's a different planet? Well, that was Dean in Vegas."

Martha interrupts, "You gave him two weeks."

She nods. "I did! I thought he'd drive home within two weeks. But credit where credit's due, he stayed. And he's a good PI. He goes above and beyond. But if you cut him in half, he'd have Maple Valley Police Department running through his core. He belongs there."

Martha raises her glass like a toast. "Amen to that."

Eva laughs. She can tell Dean's a little uncomfortable at being the subject of conversation but he's being a good sport. He's even keeping up with the shots, which she's surprised at because she's never seen him drink much.

"This isn't going to mix well with your painkillers," she says.

"I haven't taken any today," says Dean. "I knew there would be vodka involved with these two."

Martha and Marilyn laugh. They remind her of two drunk aunts who love talking about the good old days. She's genuinely enjoying herself and allows them to pour her another shot.

* * *

The next morning, Eva's head is pounding so hard she thinks her heart has moved into her brain. She doesn't remember how many shots she drank but she can feel every single one of them now. As they pack up the car with Dean's belongings, it looks like Dean's regretting the liquor too.

"You look like shit," she says.

"Thanks. It didn't help that I didn't take my meds yesterday. I definitely need them today."

She's worried about him. They have a long drive ahead. It's going to take two whole days to drive all the way to New Hampshire. She's glad she's flying home to Colorado after her stay and not driving both ways.

Marilyn and Martha arrive just as they're ready to leave. Marilyn's wearing thick black sunglasses. "You stay in touch now, do you hear me? Don't forget about us."

"As if I could." Dean kisses them both goodbye, and they hug Eva too.

"And Dean?" says Marilyn. "Follow your heart. You know where you belong. Stop punishing yourself for what happened."

Dean nods but doesn't say anything.

Eva wonders what Marilyn means. She'll google him at some point, if he doesn't open up soon.

He lets Rocky into the back of the car. The big dog struggles to get his back legs up onto the seat, but he eventually makes it.

Eva pulls away as Dean waves goodbye.

CHAPTER FORTY-SEVEN

Maple Valley, New Hampshire

It's two o'clock on Christmas morning when they finally arrive in Maple Valley. The road trip started out as fun, with cheesy driving games and even cheesier music, but Dean became more withdrawn the closer they got.

Eva knows Detective Jones is still avoiding his calls and Dean's too stubborn to explain the situation to one of their mutual friends so they could pass it on to him. She's told him a million times that if Jones knew he'd been shot and almost killed, he wouldn't be mad at him for not arriving in time to see Barbara before she passed away. But Dean has let his feelings of guilt get the better of him. He insists he needs to speak to Jones face-to-face, and so he hasn't told a single person he's coming home.

He found out from the local news online that Barbara's funeral is the day after Christmas — tomorrow afternoon — and Eva doesn't know if he's going to be up to going. Their road trip has been uncomfortable for him. His stomach is still painful and sitting for long periods hasn't helped. He hasn't complained once but he's needed lots of rest stops to get out and change position. As a result, her hire car is full of empty fast-food wrappers and disposable coffee cups.

As they pass the *Welcome to Maple Valley* sign, gentle snow starts falling, but not half as bad as it was in Lone Creek. The roads are slushy and the trees are all empty of their leaves. It's a shame she missed fall here; she's heard it's beautiful.

She drives slowly as they approach Dean's street. Rocky starts whining in the back and she wonders if he recognizes his old house. Dean sits up, alert. He stares at his neighbors' homes until he sees his.

"This is it. Pull onto the drive."

Rocky barks and Dean tells him to hush. He probably doesn't want to wake the neighbors.

He hesitates in the front seat for a few minutes so she stays where she is.

"It looks smaller than I remember," he says. "And it feels like someone else's house now."

Eventually, they all get out of the car and walk up the porch steps. It's a nice house, bigger than Eva's shitty apartment but not too big. She wonders how he can afford it on his own. Now he's unemployed he's going to struggle. But if he's serious about moving to Miami he could sell it. She wonders whether he'll make a complete break from Maple Valley this time and start over for real. After everything that's happened to her over the last month, she can see the appeal of a fresh start. Especially as Dean finally confided in her during the road trip. She knows now why he left in the first place and she can't say she blames him. Being fooled by a female serial killer has to be professionally embarrassing.

He tries to carry his bag but winces.

"I've got it," she says. "Get your ass inside and get the coffee machine on."

"Really? You want caffeine before bed? It'll keep you awake."

"Caffeine doesn't keep me awake; life keeps me awake. Go on."

He unlocks his front door and walks through the house, flipping switches and looking around. She follows him in. It's cold inside.

"It feels weird," he says. "Like it's changed somehow."

She looks at him. "Maybe it's you who's changed."

Whoever was living here while he was away left it clean and tidy. There's no milk though, as the fridge is switched off and empty, its door ajar to stop mold.

Dean makes her a black coffee. He looks exhausted. The harsh living room light highlights his dark circles and his skin's so transparent she can see his veins underneath. He needs a vacation somewhere hot.

"I'll show you upstairs," he says. "There are two spare bedrooms but only one has a bed."

He gives her a quick tour as Rocky follows them, sniffing everything loudly. He can tell other people have been here in his absence.

The room with the spare bed is empty apart from a dresser, but it has its own bathroom at least. She dumps her bags on the floor next to the bed.

"I'll find you some sheets," says Dean.

Eva touches his arm. "Dean? It's almost three o'clock on Christmas morning and we've all been awake for far too long. Go to bed. You need to be well for tomorrow. It's going to be a tough day."

He nods, looking defeated. "There should be some blankets in that dresser." He pauses before he leaves. "I just want to say thanks for driving me here. I couldn't have driven myself in this state and you could've said no."

She laughs. "I tried to, many times, but you wouldn't take no for an answer!"

He smiles. "Yeah, sorry about that. Now I'm here I don't know if I've done the right thing but I guess we'll find out tomorrow."

"Goodnight, Matheson. And you, Rocky."

"He's going to want to sleep on your bed, you know."

She scoffs. "No way José. I've just spent three days straight with you both. I need some alone time."

She ushers them out of her room and closes the door.

CHAPTER FORTY-EIGHT

Dean wakes up with a feeling of dread weighing heavy on his chest. It takes him a few minutes to remember he's in his own bed for the first time in a year. The dull ache in his abdomen reminds him of everything that happened in Colorado.

Both he and Eva slept through the whole of Christmas Day. He heard her moving around for coffee and bathroom breaks a few times, like him. But they mostly kept to their own rooms and just rested. He feels better for it and his wound is starting to look better now.

As he slowly shaves, showers, and dresses, he thinks about the best way to handle today. It's going to be tough, no doubt about it. Not just because of the situation with Jones and the fact they have Barbara's funeral, but he also has a big favor to ask Jones. He doesn't know how that's going to go. And he's worried about everyone's reaction to him being back in town.

He hears Eva talking to Rocky as he comes downstairs. She's trying to pull the remote control from Rocky's mouth and when she hears him enter the living room, she looks up at him.

"You still look terrible. You sure you don't want to sleep for longer?"

He smiles. "You're always telling me I look terrible. Can't you just lie?"

She shakes her head. "No can do. I don't come with a filter."

He takes the coffee she holds out for him.

"Want some breakfast?" she asks. "All I could find yesterday was some cereal in the cupboard but no milk. I'll go to the grocery store while you're at the funeral. We need everything."

Dean puts his cup down. "What do you mean? You're coming with me, aren't you?"

She gets off the floor. "I'll drop you wherever you need to go and pick you up again after, but I don't belong at a stranger's funeral, Dean. I don't want to upset anyone."

He thinks about it for a minute and realizes she's right. This is something he has to do alone. "I can't eat until I've spoken to Jones. Even though I'm hungry, I feel like being sick right now. Nerves, I guess."

She gives him a sympathetic look which just makes him feel worse. He looks out the window. The sun's coming up, which is good. The sky is clear. There's still some snow on the ground but at least it's not raining for Barbara's funeral.

He turns to look at her. "I'm ready to go."

She puts their cups in the kitchen sink and leads him out to the car in silence. He's grateful she's here and he knows he'll miss her when she leaves. He thinks of Miami again. That's what's keeping him going right now.

* * *

When they pull up outside Jones' house, Dean can see a light on inside. That's good. He suspected Jones might have gone to work this morning. He's old school and doesn't like to let things beat him, not even his wife's funeral. Dean feels like he's had five energy drinks, jittery and light-headed.

"Just tell him everything," says Eva. "He won't stay mad at you when he knows what we've been through."

Dean nods.

"Do you want Rocky to come with me? I'm sure I can find the local park while I'm out."

"No," he says. "Rocky needs to come with me."

Eva puts her hand on his. "Don't be so scared. You said this man was your friend."

"He is. But things will never be the same after today."

She looks confused but she lets them go. Dean waits for her to drive away before knocking on the front door.

When Jones opens it, he couldn't look more shocked. He also looks like he's aged a few years since their last Skype call. Jones hesitates for a few seconds and Dean thinks he's going to slam the door in his face, but instead, he pulls Dean forward by his coat and hugs him.

"I'm glad you came." He closes the door behind them and leads Dean to the couch. "But you look like shit."

Dean blinks hard, trying not to get overwhelmed. He missed everyone more than he was willing to admit. He looks around the house. All Barbara's things are still here, even her slippers.

Rocky's all over Jones, who's loving it.

"Have you been looking after him, boy?" Rocky barks an affirmative and rolls upside down for a belly rub. Jones is happy to oblige. "Still got your balls, I see."

"Jones, I'm so sorry." Dean tries to explain but he's struggling to hold it together. "I was stuck in Colorado, there was a storm and a dirty cop . . ."

"A dirty cop? I wondered where Detective Miller went. He told us he went fishing in Vermont."

Dean laughs. It relieves some tension. "Even worse than Miller, if you can believe it."

Jones sneezes. His voice is thick with a cold. "Listen," he says. "It doesn't matter, I don't need to hear any of it. You're here now. I'm pleased you made it for her funeral. She'll know you're here."

Dean wipes his face and winces as a bolt of pain shoots through his stomach.

"What's the matter with you?" asks Jones.

"That's what I'm trying to tell you. I was shot by a deranged woman. I was in the hospital for over a week."

Jones looks incredulous. "*What?* Why the hell didn't you call me? And, more importantly, why the hell do you attract so many deranged women?"

Dean laughs again. It feels good. "I'm fine now."

"The hell you are! You look like you're going to pass out. Here, lie down."

Jones plumps some cushions but Dean just leans back. "I'm okay, it was just a long road trip to get home and I've been so damn anxious."

"Don't tell me you drove yourself?"

"No, I had a friend drive me. She's staying at mine."

Jones looks at him with a twinkle in his eye and Dean immediately knows what he's thinking. "No, it's nothing like that. She's the detective I was working with. She killed the woman who shot me."

With raised eyebrows, Jones stands. "This sounds like something I need to hear. I'm sick of moping around the house and listening to everyone ask me in hushed tones whether I'm okay. I could do with the distraction. Let me fix you some breakfast and you can tell me everything. We've got five hours until Barb's party."

Dean smiles. *Barb's party.* That's a nice way of looking at it. He looks around the room and notices the Christmas tree is missing because Barbara's not here to put it up.

It finally sinks in that she's gone.

Jones returns with coffee and fresh pastries. As they eat, Dean tells him all about Eva, the Winter Pines Ski Resort, and the Garner family. He thanks him for calling the FBI and shows him his bullet wound, but only because Jones insists on seeing it. When he finishes, Dean senses Jones is keeping something from him. He looks nervous, like he has more bad news.

"What's going on?" he asks. "There's something you're not telling me. I can see it on your face." A feeling of dread settles in his stomach. He wonders what else can go wrong.

Jones lowers his eyes, as if he's considering keeping it to himself.

"Tell me," says Dean. "It can't be worse than Barbara passing."

Jones looks him in the eye and leans in. He puts his hand on Dean's back. "She's out, Dean."

He's confused. It takes him a few seconds before he realizes who Jones is talking about. The hairs on his arms stand on end. "What do you mean? Lizzie Glover's been released?"

Jones shakes his head. "No. She's escaped. Four days ago now. It's not on the news yet; we've been trying to contain it until we know what happened. She must've had inside help. An employee."

Dean goes dizzy. He's back in Maple Valley just as Lizzie Glover is on the loose. His timing couldn't be worse. "How could the hospital let this happen?"

Jones shakes his head. "I don't know. But we'll find her, Dean. Don't even worry about it. She wouldn't be stupid enough to come find you. She won't even know you're back from Vegas. She'll probably be halfway across the country by now. There's a BOLO out for her. It won't take long. It'll be all over the news eventually so someone will spot her."

Dean tries to pull himself together. Jones is right, she wouldn't come for him. It would be too obvious. She'd be caught immediately, and Lizzie values her freedom more than anything else.

Jones sits back and sneezes. He pulls out a tissue and coughs into it. Dean wonders whether it's the same virus Barbara had. He watches as his friend sips from a can of Max Life, an energy drink.

"What's with that?" he asks.

Jones looks at the green liquid. "Barb got me hooked. When she was volunteering at the secure unit a doctor told her it was good for a cold because the sugar and minerals give you a boost. I thought it couldn't do any harm because a doctor recommended it, right? It does get sickly after a while though. I always feel like I should brush my teeth after drinking it."

There's something about this drink that Dean heard in the news but he's struggling to remember what it is.

Without wanting to delay any longer, he knows it's time to ask Jones the favor he's been thinking about. He puts his cup down and clears his throat. "I need a big favor. You'll want to say no at first, but at least think about it."

Jones leans forward, intrigued. "Try me."

Rocky must know what's happening because he comes over and rests his head on Dean's lap. Dean can't bear it. He can't look at Rocky while he asks this. This might be the hardest thing he's ever had to do.

"Well, you see, the thing is . . ." he struggles to finish as his throat seizes. He feels stupid. But it's Rocky. He has this effect on him. "I've learned that Rocky isn't very young anymore. He's struggling with arthritis and the last investigation really took it out of him. He can't jump up like he used to." Dean rubs the dog's nose. It's surrounded by specs of graying fur. He looks at Jones who's staring at him open-mouthed.

"You're not going to ask me to shoot your damn dog, are you, Matheson? What kind of a man do you think I am?"

Dean knows he's joking. At least, he hopes he is. "Of course not. I just thought that, well, now you're all alone and about to retire, maybe you'd like to have some company? You'd be like a couple of senior bachelors, watching cop shows together and playing chess in the park. The older ladies would love you."

He's trying to make a joke of it but he's dying inside. It feels like a betrayal to give Rocky up. But if Dean wants to continue in law enforcement, whether that's back on the force or as a PI, he can't care for Rocky the way he deserves to be cared for in his final years. He can't leave him home alone all day. And what better way to spend his old age than with Jones? It would be good for Jones too. He'll go crazy on his own in this house, with reminders of Barbara everywhere. Cops already struggle when they retire. Perhaps he'd feel needed if he took Rocky in. They could care for each other. And it's not like Dean would never visit. Rocky might miss him at first, but he'd get used to it eventually.

Jones looks at Rocky, weighing it up. "You wouldn't miss him?" he asks.

Dean still can't look at Rocky. He's on the verge of losing it. "Are you kidding me? Of course I would. But he'd be in good hands. The alternative is that he's stuck at home all day while I'm out at work without him. A veterinarian told me he's probably only got a year, maybe two, left. He needs some home comforts in his old age." He clears the lump in his throat. "You'd need to take care of him properly though. At least two gentle walks a day and regular visits to Frankie's Diner."

Jones smiles and strokes Rocky's head.

"I'll still take care of his medical bills. He's fully insured," says Dean. "But only because I never declared he's an unofficial working dog who's been shot at in the past."

Jones nods. "Sounds like a good deal to me. What d'ya say, Rocky? Want to come live in my bachelor pad? A cute little poodle lives next door. I could introduce you to her."

Rocky puts his ears forward and then looks up at Dean with a confused expression.

Dean has to leave the house. He can't bear it. He knows Rocky won't live forever and this is the best option for him, but his emotions are all over the place.

Outside, he lets the tears fall. He can't hold them back. The dog means so damn much to him.

Jones gives him a few minutes before coming out to join him. "He'll be fine here, Dean. It's better that you don't watch him slowly fade. I think losing a pet can be worse than losing a family member. They're just so damn lovable."

Jones hugs him, which is good because Dean can't speak right now.

CHAPTER FORTY-NINE

The funeral is tougher than Dean could've imagined. He and Jones traveled to the church together, so Eva didn't need to give him a ride. They got there just after everyone else arrived so Dean walked into a packed church, with all eyes on him. People gasped as he walked to the front. He didn't make eye contact with anyone because he didn't want to cause a fuss. Today is about Barbara.

Jones stays strong throughout the service, but Dean hears others crying around them. During the ride over, Jones explained how quickly Barbara had deteriorated and it doesn't sit right with Dean. She'd been volunteering for a few weeks and suddenly came down with the flu. It wasn't the type of flu that's actually just a bad cold; it was the kind that had her bed-bound within a few days. But she was only sixty-eight and not exactly frail, so it should have passed easily. It didn't. It got steadily worse and she was admitted to hospital. Even there she continued to decline.

Jones said the doctors thought it was pneumonia but the drugs they gave her for that resulted in faster deterioration. She'd told them she felt like her insides were burning, and she kept being sick. It sounds like it was a horrific way to go.

Dean's no doctor, but even he could see this wasn't a virus. Jones declined an autopsy, saying he couldn't bear the thought of having her cut open, but Dean thinks he should've allowed it. Sheila could've run a toxicology report to see if it was caused by something Barbara ingested.

Worryingly, Jones coughs his way through the service until everyone trickles out to the graveside. This is where Dean thought his friend would lose his composure, but he manages to hold it together. He throws some dirt onto Barbara's casket and whispers a few words that no one can overhear. Dean follows his lead and is genuinely sad to say goodbye to her. He just wishes he could've told her how she made him feel. As someone who lost his parents too young, he felt like he was still part of a family thanks to her, and his mother would've loved Barbara for that.

As the funeral comes to an end, he's suddenly surrounded by his old friends and co-workers for the first time.

Sheila Didcott, Maple Valley's medical examiner, is the first one to hug him. "You could've told us you were coming back. It's a good job I cleaned your house after I moved out!"

"Hey, Sheila. It's very clean and tidy, thanks."

Steve Dalkin, Dean's old sergeant and Sheila's new fiancé, is next. "You don't look so good, buddy. The way Jones told it, I thought you'd been chilling out at a plush ski resort chatting up the hot ski instructors."

"I wish. Let's just say things got a little complicated out there."

Officer Marty Swan overhears him. "I wouldn't expect anything less from you, Matheson." He laughs as he claps Dean on the back. "Let me guess, there was a woman involved?"

Dean smiles. "There was, but not like you think. She'd kick your ass for even suggesting it."

"Maybe I'd like her to kick my ass," he jokes. "I have two questions; did you bring her with you, and is she hot?"

Sheila kicks Marty's leg. "Give it a rest, Marty."

Just then, Frankie from the diner comes bounding over, like he's going to give himself a heart attack, and launches his arms around Dean's torso.

"Deano! You're back! Here to rescue the profits of my ailing diner!"

Dean almost loses his footing. He feels his stomach wound ache. "Frankie, you'll be pleased to know that Rocky and I missed your food. There's nothing in Vegas that compares to it."

"Well, what did you expect? Nothing can compare to authentic Italian home-cooked food! Where is the big mutt? I'm catering the wake and there's bound to be plenty of left-over food for him."

"He's already at Jones' house. Make sure you put him in the backyard before you start preparing the buffet or he'll eat everything."

Dean spends some time catching up with everyone, but he's feeling worse by the minute. He excuses himself by saying he needs to use the restroom and goes to stand under a large maple tree. He leans against the trunk. Away from the group, he can see Jones is also struggling. He's sweaty and he looks tired. Dean needs to get him home for a break before the wake.

Watching Jones reminds him of what he'd heard on the news about that energy drink. Some guy had been slowly poisoning his wife's Max Life. She died from it and her husband got a big life insurance payout. Dean can't remember what he'd used, but the sugar and color of the energy drink had disguised the toxin.

He looks at Jones and dismisses the thought. Jones would never poison Barbara.

As his eyes scan the graveside gathering, he notices someone who looks out of place. A male. He's walking toward Dean's location and holding something up in front of him. He's pointing it at Dean.

It's so unexpected that it takes him a few seconds to realize it's a gun.

Dean straightens as he yells, "Everyone, get down!"

A gunshot fires but no one moves. They all turn to look at him.

Suddenly, Dean's on the ground and it feels like his whole body is on fire. He can't identify where the primary pain is coming from and hopes it's just his stomach wound.

He hears screaming from the crowd and then feet running toward him. His vision is too blurred to see anything now but someone stops next to his ear. They lean in close so that Dean can feel their breath on his face.

"Lizzie says welcome home."

It's the last thing Dean hears before he blacks out.

CHAPTER FIFTY

The stern female doctor lets Eva in to see Dean but only because Eva flashes her badge and pretends she'll start trouble otherwise. She'd seen a newsflash on TV about a guy getting shot at a funeral and immediately knew Dean would be involved somehow. She found the church and someone told her what had happened.

Eva's surprised to find she's genuinely upset at the thought Dean might die. She manages to hold it together as she enters his room.

An older man is sitting by Dean's bedside. He looks a little like Clint Eastwood.

He looks up at her. "Hi. Let me guess, you're Eva?"

"And you're Jones?" She smiles at him. He looks ill. "How did you know who I am?"

He nods to Dean. "He told me all about you. You sound like quite a detective."

"So do you." She takes a step closer to the bed. Dean's unconscious. "How's he doing?"

"They think he'll be fine," says Jones. "He was hit in the shoulder, but it's not life-threatening. He's been out cold since. To tell you the truth, his stomach wound is worrying them more." Jones starts coughing.

"Do we know who did this?" she asks.

"All we know is that it was a heavy-set white male of average height with brown hair. Someone saw him bend down and speak into Dean's ear, but in the confusion that followed, he managed to get away. My guys are out looking for him."

Eva looks at Dean. He doesn't have any tubes coming out of him apart from an IV drip. He has an oxygen mask on his face. She wonders if she's always going to have to visit him in hospitals. "Whoever did this didn't want him dead. If they spoke to him, they were close enough to finish him off. This was a warning from someone."

Jones raises his eyebrows. "My thoughts exactly."

She smiles.

Dean makes them jump by gasping for breath. His eyes fly open and he pulls the oxygen mask off his face. He looks at Jones and says, "Max Life!"

Jones looks around. "I don't have any. Let me see if they've got it in the cafeteria."

Dean grabs his arm. "No. Don't drink any more Max Life!"

Eva wonders if he's still dreaming. "Why not, Dean?"

He looks at her. "It's been poisoned. That's what killed Barbara. It was Lizzie Glover!"

Jones looks over at Eva and shakes his head, very slightly, as if to say don't pay any attention, he's delusional. "Alright, Dean. It's okay," he says. "Lizzie isn't here. You're just confused, that's all. It'll all come back to you eventually. Just take it easy."

Dean's so agitated that he tries to sit up. The hospital gown he's wearing immediately soaks through with blood. He's opened his stomach wound again.

"Dean, lie down!" Eva shouts.

Jones runs out for a nurse but his exhaustion causes him to trip on a chair and fall over. He lies still on the floor and Eva doesn't know what to do first.

"Nurse! Anyone!" she shouts, pushing Dean back onto the bed. "I need assistance in here!"

Two nurses quickly appear. They help Jones up and the doctor runs in. She's more concerned with Dean than with Jones.

"If you don't lie down and let us deal with your stomach wound, you're at risk of sepsis. You could die, Mr. Matheson."

Dean lies back, defeated. He grabs Eva's hand. "Listen to me, I'm not delusional. The person who shot me gave me a message from Lizzie Glover. She did this and she must've been poisoning Barbara and Jones."

Eva's so confused. As far as she knew, this Lizzie woman was locked up in a secure unit. But the look on his face convinces her he's onto something. "I'm on it, Dean. I'll take care of it. You just take it easy."

Dean sinks back and lets the doctor put his oxygen mask back on. Eva feels like all his hopes rest on her but she doesn't have a clue what's going on.

CHAPTER FIFTY-ONE

Eva has a busy week of dealing with the FBI over the phone, to tie up loose ends from the fallout of what happened in Colorado. She learns from Special Agent Carter that the investigation into Garner and the whole department is finding what Eva always suspected: that Garner was a crooked cop in every way imaginable.

Chief Carson isn't getting off lightly either. Special Agent Carter told her he was a regular at Garner's casino and even dabbled in the drugs they were buying and selling. So he knew some of what Garner was up to but there's no evidence yet to suggest that he knew Garner killed Frank, or that he knew what Garner's son was up to. Carson is no longer chief and it's unlikely he'll ever work in law enforcement again with several charges pending against him.

Eva was pleased to hear Sergeant Roberts wasn't involved in anything illegal. He was given a hero's funeral, which she couldn't attend, but George was happy to represent her.

Two dead cops and a crooked chief has left some vacancies at McArthur PD. Eva's added to that number by giving her notice to the interim chief. She couldn't stay there after everything that's happened.

Eva was surprised to learn that the Winter Pines Ski Resort burned to the ground on New Year's Eve. The new owners said it wasn't part of their demolition plans and there's evidence to suggest it was an arson attack. The FBI is currently looking for Sandy Garner. He's gone missing. She's sad he felt the need to torch the place, but she can understand why. She just hopes he hasn't done anything to himself.

Perhaps unsurprisingly, the media has chosen to focus more on Shirley Garner than her husband and son in their reports. Even though Alan was a cop and meant to be trustworthy, they're more interested in how a mother could help her son abduct and torture kids. It just proves that society is still more horrified by female offenders than male.

Now that chapter of her life is over it's time for Eva to follow through on her promise to Dean. He's still in the hospital. One day he's okay and the next he takes a turn for the worse. Taking two bullets in close succession will do that to you.

Frankie from the local diner has been only too happy to tell Eva the whole sorry story surrounding Dean and Lizzie Glover. Including the parts Dean left out in his retelling. From what she can piece together, Dean really messed up after his brother died and it's no wonder he ran away to Vegas to forget it all.

If she hadn't worked with him in Colorado, she would've thought he was incompetent for not seeing the warning signs before it was too late. But, on the other hand, she can understand how the grief of losing his brother in such horrific circumstances must've messed with his head. She was devastated after losing Frank. Nothing prepares you for it. And even after having Garner's claims confirmed by the FBI, she still has feelings for the Frank she knew. She just has to remind herself that that Frank never really existed.

Having seen Dean in action recently, she knows he belongs back in law enforcement. But, even after everything that's happened and even though he has such supportive friends here, he's insisting on moving away again and working alone as a PI.

He's still punishing himself.

When she heard he'd given Rocky to Jones to take care of, she was shocked. She asked whether that was wise, considering he might change his mind once he's feeling better, but Jones has really taken to Rocky. And once he stopped drinking Max Life he started recovering. Rocky has clearly helped with that and they're sweet to watch together.

At their hospital visit yesterday, Jones confirmed Dean was right about the energy drink being poisoned. The discarded bottles from his trash can were tested for toxins. They found pin prick marks in the bottles, suggesting someone had been injecting them, and tests found ethylene glycol, a deadly chemical found in antifreeze.

Intrigued, Eva researched it. It's a toxin that can slowly poison someone, giving them symptoms of a virus until they succumb to death. Loved ones and medical employees are usually none the wiser unless they know they're looking at a case of poisoning, because antifreeze is sweet-tasting and blends well with energy drinks. There was a high-profile case in the news about a husband doing something similar recently. Maybe that's where Lizzie got the idea.

Dean was devastated by the confirmation and Eva could tell he was coming to the realization that this Lizzie woman would stop at nothing to get to him. He'd asked them to leave soon after, saying he needed some sleep. Eva thought he wanted to be left alone with his guilt.

Even though Lizzie didn't pull the trigger that day at Barbara's funeral, and she couldn't have been the one to poison Barbara and Jones directly, she must've had help doing it. Someone helped her escape and someone was poisoning their drinks. Barbara was buying them from the hospital cafeteria and bringing them home to share with her husband. They must've already been injected when she bought them. So, if Eva were in charge of the investigation, she'd start with interviewing the cafeteria employees. Lizzie's obviously dangerous and good at manipulating people. She and her accomplice need to be found. And fast.

As Eva gets out of her rental car at the hospital, she feels excited for what's to come. Today, Dean's friends are gathering for a surprise because he needs to see he's not responsible for what's happened to Barbara, and that his friends are here to support him. Physically, he's well enough to get back on his feet and will be released soon, maybe even tomorrow.

Mentally, though, she can tell he's not himself. Her depression has shown signs of easing over the last few days but Dean's still suffering.

She joins his friends in the hospital lobby and they get in the elevator together.

CHAPTER FIFTY-TWO

Dean finishes his hospital breakfast of cereal and cold toast. He's hoping to be released today and will be glad when he's able to make his own breakfast again, or eat at the diner.

He's agitated at the thought of Lizzie Glover being out there somewhere and has had trouble relaxing. He doesn't think she'll come for him because she could've had him killed at the cemetery and didn't.

She wants to play with him instead.

Dean wants to leave for Miami as soon as he finds a new tenant for his house. He thinks about his plans. He has doubts about moving so far again if he's honest with himself, but he doesn't see a life here. There's just not enough petty crime in Maple Valley to keep a PI busy, so he'd never make a living at that.

He's been thinking about Eva and what she'll do next when she returns to Colorado. She told him yesterday her foster dad is driving her nuts. He wants to move in with her because she almost died up in Lone Creek, and apparently, she's the last person he has left, but Eva doesn't want to live with him. She values her privacy.

Whatever she does next, it has to involve law enforcement. She's made for the role.

He sighs as he puts his spoon down and sits back on the bed. He wonders whether *he's* made for the role. MVPD is obviously out of the question based on his history there. Besides, they've appointed Jones' replacement already; the hot shot from New Jersey Jones told him about a while ago.

He hears voices coming toward his room and before he can dress for guests his door is thrown open and a crowd enters. Jones comes in followed by Sheila, Steve, Captain Brown, and Marty. The sight of them all makes him nervous.

"What are you all doing here?" he says. "Did the doctor tell you something I don't know?"

They laugh.

"We have a surprise for you," says Marty. "You've been so miserable lately and, let's face it, no one loves a pity party more than you . . ."

"Marty!" says Sheila, shocked.

"What? It's true! We all know it. Anyway, you've been bringing us down so we thought we'd do something to cheer you up. You know, to make our lives easier."

Jones laughs.

Dean's surprised, and a little worried. This is Marty, after all. "Okay."

Eva appears. He's glad to see her but things feel a little awkward with an audience.

"Hey, Dean." She won't meet his eyes. He's never seen her nervous before and it makes him nervous. "I have some news I've been meaning to tell you and I hope you're okay with it."

He wonders why he wouldn't be.

"I've been offered a job at your old police department." She looks at him for his reaction. "I'm going to be their new homicide detective. You don't mind, do you?"

Dean's mouth drops open. He wasn't expecting *that*.

Captain Brown steps forward. "The hot shot from New Jersey didn't pan out. She didn't feel our small department was a good fit for her. The damn woman was just a glory hunter after her name in the press, but there's no glory to be had here. So, after talking to Jones about possible replacements, I interviewed Valdez and I liked her. I hired her on the spot."

He watches everyone smile but Dean's devastated. If there was a vacant detective role, why wasn't he considered for it? Do they have that little confidence in him?

He knows now that he has to leave for Miami. There's no choice anymore. He's happy for Eva, of course he is, but he feels rejected. He smiles at her. "That's awesome news, Eva. Congratulations."

"Jeez, say it with a little more conviction," says Marty.

"We haven't forgotten about you, though," says Steve. He has his arm around Sheila which feels weird to Dean as it's the first time he's seen them as a couple. So much has changed while he's been gone.

"What do you mean?" he says.

Captain Brown speaks. "There's the serious matter of Lizzie Glover to contend with. Tell me you're going to go after her and finish this once and for all?"

Dean's confused. Isn't that their job? "I can't. I'll have to leave her to Valdez because I won't be here."

Captain Brown passes something to Jones who holds it out to Dean. "Would this make you stay?"

It's a detective shield.

Dean doesn't touch it. He doesn't want to believe it in case he's misunderstanding the situation.

"What's going on?" he asks. "And what about Miller? I know you can't afford three detectives."

"Well," starts Brown. "Miller has decided, with the help of a surprise mandatory physical exam, that he'd rather work a desk job until he retires. Which leaves us in need of a second detective. We'd like that second detective to be you."

Dean looks at Eva who's beaming at him.

"Hey, partner," she says.

He can't believe what he's hearing. Is he even up to it?

His ambition comes back from wherever he's been hiding it these past two years. He realizes he wants it more than anything else. Nerves and adrenaline race through him.

He takes the badge from Jones, who says, "Go get that crazy bitch, Dean. For Barb."

Dean looks at the badge. He turns it over in his hand, not quite believing his luck.

Eventually, he looks up at Eva and smiles. "Let's do it."

THE END

ACKNOWLEDGMENTS

Thank you to the bloggers and readers who leave reviews for my books and inspire me with your enthusiasm about the series! I know many of you are crossing your fingers for more Dean Matheson books and have enjoyed my Madison Harper series too. Both series remain my priority right now, so keep an eye on my website and social media for updates!

Thanks also to my publisher and editor for allowing me to update this series, it was well overdue.

And thanks to my husband who has been on this journey with me. Our informal plot meetings make all the hard work worthwhile!

THANK YOU

Dear Reader,

Thank you for reading the second book in the Dean Matheson series. This was originally written in 2018 but I've updated it (along with the rest of the series) for its relaunch in 2023, and I've had so much fun returning to Maple Valley after all these years!

I know some readers like to dip in and out of a series, but this one is best read in order and, if you've read this book without reading book 1, I'd recommend reading that before moving on to book 3. You'll need the backstory book 1 provides. And you'll get to see how Dean and Rocky originally found each other!

I think it's safe to say Dean has matured somewhat since book 1, and I think he and Eva make a good team. He needs to prove to her now that he can equal her as a partner while learning from her experience. We'll find out in book 3 how he does. And don't worry, we haven't seen the last of Rocky yet! He's in the next book.

If you want to know more about the detective who served time in prison for killing another cop, you might enjoy the *Detective Madison Harper* books, which is my latest crime series. We follow Madison as she's released from prison, desperate to not only clear her name and get her job back, but also to find the son she lost to the care system while she was inside. Book 1 is called *Shadow Falls*.

If you enjoyed this book, please consider leaving a review or rating on Amazon, Goodreads, and/or Bookbub. Reviews will help it stand out against the many books that get published every day. If this series does well, it could continue beyond the current three books. Wouldn't that be exciting!

Happy reading.
Wendy

THE CHOC LIT STORY

Established in 2009, Choc Lit is an independent, award-winning publisher dedicated to creating a delicious selection of quality women's fiction.

We have won 18 awards, including Publisher of the Year and the Romantic Novel of the Year, and have been shortlisted for countless others.

All our novels are selected by genuine readers. We are proud to publish talented first-time authors, as well as established writers whose books we love introducing to a new generation of readers.

In 2023, we became a Joffe Books company. Best known for publishing a wide range of commercial fiction, Joffe Books has its roots in women's fiction. Today it is one of the largest independent publishers in the UK.

We love to hear from you, so please email us about absolutely anything bookish at choc-lit@joffebooks.com

If you want to hear about all our bargain new releases, join our mailing list: www.choc-lit.com

ALSO BY WENDY DRANFIELD

DEAN MATHESON
Book 1: WHO CARES IF THEY DIE
Book 2: WHERE THE SNOW BLEEDS